CATCH ME ON A BLUE DAY

CATCH ME ON A BLUE DAY
by M.E. Proctor

ADDITIONAL
PRAISE

"Declan Shaw is back, and this time he's investigating a friend's suicide—one that Declan finds too suspicious to leave alone. *Catch Me on a Blue Day* takes us to the quaint New England town of Old Mapleton, where secrets lie behind every door, and even the art galleries hide plots of violence, sex, and intrigue. In M.E. Proctor's capable hands, Declan shines as a determined champion of the truth, one whose struggles and complexities make him a worthy hero. Proctor's succulent dialogue makes the cast of characters spring to life as the plot moves from compelling mystery to imminent peril, and finally, to a conclusion that is both harrowing and satisfying. In the annals of mystery books, private investigators abound—but there can only be one Declan Shaw. This is the PI series you've been waiting for."

—C.W. Blackwell, author of *Hard Mountain Clay*

"Smart and sexy PI Declan Shaw travels from Texas to Connecticut to solve the mystery of a friend's death. Was it suicide? Or was the famous investigative reporter's death due to something much more sinister? *Catch Me On a Blue Day* is a propulsive and captivating read full of twists and turns you won't see coming, and it perfectly captures the claustrophobia of academia and small town New England. All skillfully and artfully told by M.E. Proctor."

—Barbara Byar, author of *Some Days are Better than Ours*

M.E. PROCTOR

CATCH ME ON A BLUE DAY

A DECLAN SHAW MYSTERY

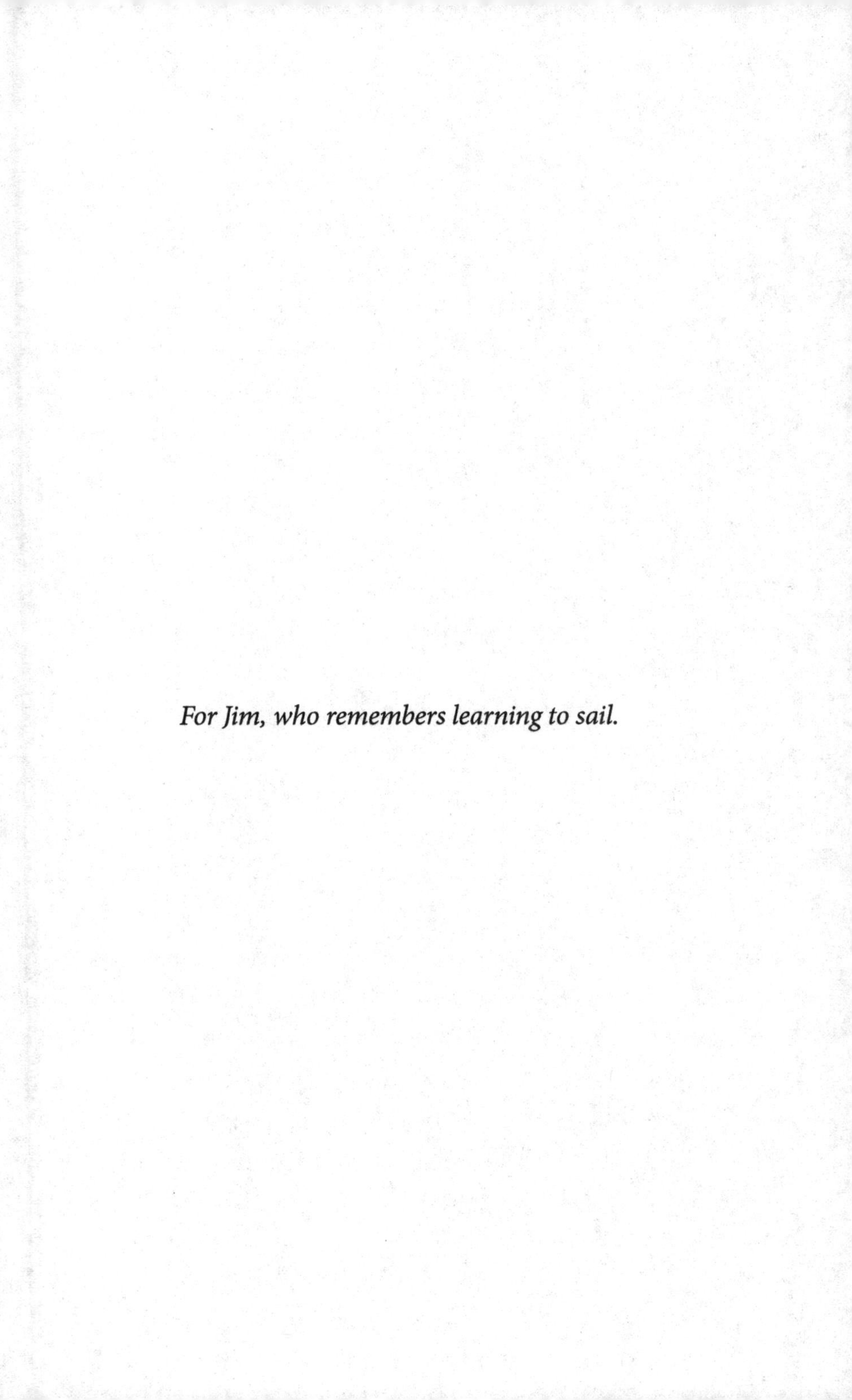

For Jim, who remembers learning to sail.

CATCH ME ON A BLUE DAY

ONE

DECLAN SHAW SHIFTED his weight to his good leg, the right one. After hours on the plane followed by hours in the car he had lost all the flexibility he'd worked so hard to regain over the past months. He should be soaking in a hot tub instead of standing there answering Chief Halston's questions.

He leaned on the windowsill. The view of the marina from the quaint Old Mapleton's police station was picture-perfect. A significant portion of the wealth of the small Connecticut town was out there, bobbing in the gentle swell of the sheltered harbor. Which explained the strategic position of the local law enforcement offices. Protecting private property was Burt Halston's main job.

"I think I'll stay for a bit," Declan said.

"We can do without troublemakers, Shaw."

"Is that a quote from the Tourist Bureau's welcome pack?"

"You're a private dick. You're the definition of trouble," Halston said.

Declan flashed him his most charming smile. "My roster of satisfied clients would disagree, Chief."

"Your current client is on a slab in the morgue."

Carlton Marsh was a friend, not a client.

By the time Declan boarded his flight in Houston, unaware of the events in Old Mapleton, Marsh's body was being prepped for autopsy, and the promise of a pleasant month of research and stimulating conversation lubricated with good whiskey had evaporated.

Questions remained.

• • •

The questions started with the trooper who intercepted Declan in front of Carlton Marsh's house. A house Declan had a hard time finding. Old Mapletonians didn't seem to believe in street signs and house numbers. It struck Declan as snooty, like: *The people who come to visit us know where we live. The mail person knows where to deliver.* In other words: if you're not in the know, we don't need your kind over here. It was a prelude to Chief Halston branding him a troublemaker at first sight.

After three loops of the town's seafront avenue and main street, Declan spotted a villa that matched the description Marsh gave him. A police cruiser was parked in front and masked the mailbox. The cop was dozing. Declan left his bags in the rental BMW and walked to the door.

"Hey, you!" The cop had not been asleep after all. "Where you think you're going?" He had his right hand on his holster.

"Going to ring the bell," Declan said.

"Nobody in there."

"Maybe I have the wrong house. Is this Carlton Marsh's residence?"

The cop grimaced. His fingers twitched near his gun. "You got an ID?"

They sure were welcoming in this New England burg. Declan knew better than asking why the trooper needed to know. He was a stranger in town and this kid—early twenties with the beginning of a potbelly and a fuzzy blondish excuse for a mustache—looked nervous, which made Declan nervous too.

"My wallet is in my back pocket." Declan turned on his heels and lifted his jacket to show the bulge in his jeans' pocket.

"Put the wallet on the hood of the cruiser and step back away from the car," the cop said.

Jeeze. What came next? Tar and feathers? Being carried out of town astride a rail?

"Texas, eh? You're far from home."

No shit.

"What you doing here?"

With all due respect, that ain't none of your business, pal. "Visiting a friend."

"Marsh's a friend of yours?"

Declan nodded. What the hell happened here? He wanted to pull out his cigar case and refrained. The expression on the young cop's face told him the less he moved the better.

"Get in the back of the cruiser. The chief will want to talk to you."

The cop opened the car door. Declan wondered how long he had been on the job. He hadn't developed street smarts yet, and the way he handled a potential suspect, he might not live long enough to acquire any.

"You should check me for a weapon," Declan said, against his better judgment.

The cop's eyes widened and the little mustache trembled. "What?"

Dear Lord. Declan sighed and assumed the position. Legs spread out, hands flat on the roof of the cruiser. "Pat me down, ki …, Officer. I'm not carrying, but you shouldn't take my word for it."

The frisking was rougher than it needed to be. A combination of heightened anxiety and humiliation. Giving a lesson in police procedure to a rookie wasn't the best way to make a friend, even if it might save the kid's life down the line.

The ride to the police station was short. They drove down the road that hugged the narrow beach. It was high tide. They went further north than Declan had gone earlier, past the fishing harbor, along the marina and its clutter of yachts, cabin cruisers, and sailboats. The police station was an odd Tudor structure that could have been a pub in another time. *Ye Olde Copper's Nest.* The young trooper was careful and diligent upon arrival. He motioned to Declan to go first and stayed five steps behind, out of reach in case his catch turned aggressive. The inside arrangement of the station, despite the plastic chairs and bullet-proof glass screening the counter, didn't dispel the impression that one had entered a tavern. The anachronism of dark beams and leaded windows made Declan smile. He pictured a crossbow-carrying sentry in scratchy wool hose standing guard in a corner.

"The chief is in?" the young cop said.

The officer behind the counter buzzed them in. "Anything for the blotter?" she said.

"Maybe later."

The cop kept his options open until he knew what kind of smelly roadkill he dragged in.

The chief's office was bright and modern. A large bay window faced the harbor, and an enormous stuffed fish glued to a varnished piece of wood hung in the middle of the back wall. With a large brass plaque underneath. Some kind of personal record for the Chief of Police. Declan's knowledge of fish beyond items on a menu was nonexistent. Various commendations and picture frames with men in suits and bemedaled uniforms documented a long career. A collection of trophies garnished the top of a filing cabinet.

The chief looked up from a stack of papers. He was a veteran in a starched uniform shirt. Wrinkles, coffee stains, and dried sweat rings must be frowned upon in Old Mapleton. He was brushing sixty, bald, with round wrestler shoulders and a hard gut that kept him at a respectable distance from the edge of his desk. He wouldn't be a fast runner but he could lift a cop the size of the young trooper with one hand tied behind his back. A chunk of tortured driftwood served as a desk name-plate: *Chief Burt Halston.*

"Who you got there, Craig?" The voice matched the body, pitched low and smoky. Small eyes, keen, deep-set, bored into Declan who towered a head above the trooper.

The cop, Craig, slid Declan's wallet across the desk. "Name's Shaw. Declan Shaw. From Texas. I picked him up in front of Marsh's house. He was on his way to the door. To ring the bell, he said. Friend of Marsh." Craig shot a quick sideways glance at Declan. "He's not packing."

"You checked, eh? Smart thinking, son."

The young cop blushed. Declan was more poker-faced than when he played high stakes Texas Hold'em. Chief Halston opened Declan's wallet and pulled out the driver's license. He grabbed a pair of half-moon glasses to study the document. The spectacles gave him a professorial air that was as incongruous as the façade of his police station.

"Declan Francis Philip Shaw. That's a mouthful. One middle name not enough for your mom and pop? Houston, Texas." Halston hummed. He gave Declan a quick up and down. "Six four. Yeah, I can see that. A tall customer you reeled in, Craig my boy." He riffled through the wallet compartments, examined the various cards, pulled one out, whistled. "Well, well, what do we have here now. You're a PI?"

"Correct."

"Not a friend of Carlton Marsh, then."

"I am. And a PI. Where's Carlton?"

"We'll get to that in a moment," Halston said. "Sit down, you make me dizzy. Are you just swinging by because you happen to be in this charming neighborhood?"

"Carlton invited me," Declan said. "I flew in today."

"Invited, uh? For the pleasure of your company?"

Truth might open the communication channels. "Carlton has a new book in the works and needs help with research. I'm good at that sort of thing."

"Not really an invitation then. He hired you. When?"

This looked more and more like a police interview. "He called me two months ago. I couldn't come right away. A medical thing."

An eyebrow went up and Halston's eyes veered toward Declan's legs. "You got shot?"

The man was observant. Declan's limp was slight. "Because I'm a PI from Texas? I took a nasty fall. Multiple fractures. On bad weather days, I wish I *was* shot. We decided I would come up after Labor Day weekend. I drove from Newark."

Halston cleared his throat. "Some coincidence. Go back to the Marsh house, Craig. Make sure nobody tries to go in."

The young cop gave Declan a curt nod and exited.

"Awfully green," Halston mumbled. "He behaved? They get cocky at that age."

"He was professional," Declan said.

The chief groaned. It looked like he had Officer Craig pinned down accurately. "How come you know Marsh?"

"I'll answer your questions, Chief, providing I don't break privacy, but before I do I want to know what's going on. Is Carlton okay?"

The chief linked his hands together on his paunch. "Mr. Marsh committed suicide last night."

The words took a few seconds to register. "That's impossible. I talked to him yesterday."

Chief Halston opened a drawer and grabbed a legal pad.

"Okay, this is getting interesting. I don't give a shit about privacy or the ethics of private dicks. What did you two talk about?"

"My trip. I confirmed the flight number and arrival time. I told Carlton I should be in Old Mapleton by cocktail time. He said he'd have the whiskey and the ice. We chatted. He said he looked forward to catching up. Last time we spent time together was maybe six years ago when he stopped in Houston on his way to Mexico." Declan watched Halston scribble. "He can't have killed himself. It doesn't make sense."

Halston held up his pen. "What time was that call?"

"Around eight. Nine for you. We talked for half an hour."

"How did he sound?"

Declan hiked his shoulders. "Upbeat about the book. Said it was a project he cared a lot about. We argued about my fee. He wanted to pay me and I didn't want his money. He provided room and board and that was enough for me. We agreed that he would cover my expenses, flight and car, and incidentals related to the research." He leaned forward to close the distance with Halston. "Are you sure it's suicide?"

Halston swiveled around to face the harbor. "It looks that way."

"But you're not sure. Why are you not sure?"

A grunt. "I was sure before you walked in." A sigh. "Sort of."

Declan stood up and went to the window. His leg muscles were seizing. He was in for a rough night. The physical therapist had warned him: gotta keep moving.

Then Halston said: "Pity you came all the way up from Houston for nothing."

And it awakened Declan's contrary nature.

• • •

"Take me to Carlton's house."

Declan stared at the marina. *Port de plaisance*, as they said in Cannes or Monte-Carlo. Pleasure cruises were in store for some people. Was Carlton Marsh an occasional passenger on these yachts? He was New England aristocracy. He must have known half the boat owners and all the bartenders at the yacht and country clubs.

"Why would I do that?" Halston said.

"You need a sounding board. Somebody to test your observations on. How well did you know Carlton Marsh?"

The chief tapped his pen on the pad. Impatient. Declan expected him to blow a fuse. You're asking *me* questions, boy? Well, he was getting impatient too and the pain in his leg had a lot to do with it.

"I had a drink with him at the country club a couple of times. They have these soirées. I'm always invited. Courtesy. Occasionally I accept. Makes everybody feel better. Like they tamed the bear. How well did *you* know him, Shaw? He was a few months short of seventy. Could have been your father."

"I knew him from college. He gave a series of lectures. Geopolitics. Central America. He witnessed a lot of political turmoil. He was as close as you can get to living history. I was in awe. I almost changed my pre-law secondary to journalism. I joined his writing group. We kept in touch over the years."

Halston relaxed in his chair. "You know he was gay."

Declan's leg twitched, reminding him of the pills, inaccessible, deep in his bag in the trunk of the rental car. He should have pocketed a couple. "Unless I'm on a case and paid to poke, I don't give a damn who people sleep with."

"He had a boyfriend," the chief insisted.

Lovers quarrel, heartbreak? Declan couldn't square it with world-wise Carlton Marsh. His dry wit, his cynicism, his fierce independence. "A live-in boyfriend?"

"He's a resident at an artist colony outside of town. A painter. Successful, apparently. Jack Corvill's the name. He's in Canada right now, left a week ago. Some kind of art exhibition. We haven't contacted him yet." The chief folded his glasses and beat a finger tattoo on the desk. "Makes me wonder what Corvill would have said about you moving in."

"We might have hit it off." Declan pointed at the stuffed fish. "What is that?"

"Albacore. I caught it right off the point out there. Biggest thing I ever brought in."

"It's good looking. You still need my wallet?" Halston pushed it over the glossy surface of the desk, and Declan pocketed it. "I would like to see the house, Chief."

Halston jumped to his feet. He was quick for his bulk. "All right. Fresh eyes. Might be useful."

TWO

BEFORE TURNING THE KEY in the lock, Halston handed Declan a pair of latex gloves.

They stood on the threshold, looking down the entrance hallway.

"It's as we found it this morning, after the housekeeper called nine-one-one."

Declan stepped to the side to avoid treading on the carpet runner. He went down on one knee, ran a gloved hand on the carpet. He could feel the cold wetness through the latex.

"It rained last night?"

"All day yesterday and all night," Halston said. "It cleared up around ten this morning. Impossible to say if Marsh went in and out or if other people came in and out. The identifiable footprints belong to the housekeeper."

The woman's heels had left indents in the carpet.

The hallway led to a large sitting room. Curtains were closed and lights were on. A baby grand piano occupied the right corner, with loose sheets on the music shelf. A fireplace with bookshelves on both sides took the entire left wall. A heavy desk covered with books and documents loomed in the left corner. A couch, armchairs, and side tables were spread around. It didn't look cluttered because the room was wide.

Halston pointed at the carpet between the fireplace and the couch. "Blood spatter and body position tell the story. He stood here. Blew his head off. Fell to his knees, here, then keeled over with his head toward the fireplace."

"No mirror," Declan said.

Halston frowned. "Why the fuck should there be a mirror? You think he'd want to watch himself put a bullet in his brain?"

"Why did he do it standing?" Declan said. "It's theatrical. Or military. There are plenty of chairs, armchairs, sofas, even the piano bench. Why would he stand? What was he looking at?"

Halston pointed. "The windows."

"But the curtains were closed," Declan said. "What kind of gun?"

"Colt .38. Numbers filed off. A street gun. It's pretty clear cut. Marsh's fingerprints are on the gun, nobody else's. Gunshot residue on his right hand, and it was a contact shot. We have the gun and the slug. And he was right-handed, of course."

"A single shot fired?"

"Right."

Declan sat on the piano bench. The music was *Rhapsody in Blue*. Halston perched on the arm of the sofa. They kept silent, taking in the room, trying to see what might have happened and what might still be there.

"How familiar was he with guns?" Halston said.

"He reported from every war zone on the planet for forty years," Declan said. "He was embedded with troops; he was shot at multiple times. I assume he knew his way around guns."

"Anything else you want in here?"

Declan ached for a smoke. "You mind if I look at the stuff on the desk?"

Halston motioned. "Knock yourself out. There was no suicide note."

There were typed notes, printouts from websites, scribbled quotations, index cards with names and dates, handwritten fragments, and pencil-marked references. A writer's work in progress.

"If I get Carlton's publisher's approval, will you let me take all this?" Declan said. "There might be family members I'd need to clear it with. I have the contract he signed for my services."

"There's no direct family that I know of. The boyfriend might know if Marsh had a will or a lawyer."

"We can ask Carlton's publisher. I know him. We met, years ago. I have his number."

"That'll be handy. We'll box all this. Keep it safe at the office."

"I don't see a computer," Declan said. "You took it. Did you manage to get in?"

Halston snorted. "I hope the boyfriend can. If not, I'll have to send the laptop to New Haven."

"I know somebody who can hack it."

Halston smiled. "I'm sure you do. I can't afford to pay for specialized services. It'll have to go through regular channels."

Which meant it would take forever. If it happened at all. Cops don't bust their balls for a suicide. There would be no quick answers to Declan's questions. Carlton Marsh's possessions would be disposed of through the succession process. The computer and work product were covered by whatever arrangement he had with his publisher.

They left and Halston locked the front door. Trooper Craig was outside, leaning on his cruiser. Declan lit a thin cigar. He inhaled and the pleasure was borderline painful. He felt lightheaded. He hadn't eaten anything since breakfast.

"What kind of book was Marsh writing?" Halston pulled off his gloves and took Declan's. Both pairs went into his pants' front pocket.

"A follow up to his articles. He published a compendium of his frontline reports a few years ago and wanted to bring them all together in a narrative. His beat was Central America. He wrote at length about the Iran-Contra scandal and he wanted to do the same for El Salvador in the eighties. It's a hot-button issue. Many of the current immigration problems can be traced back to the violence of those years. He told me he wanted to remind people that history doesn't exist in a vacuum."

"And what research were you supposed to carry out?"

"Track down witnesses, survivors."

"In the U.S.?" Halston said.

"Immigrants, legal and undocumented, regime cronies that were given citizenship because of CIA ties, Mara Salvatrucha, MS-13, you heard about them, right? They have links to El Salvador."

"Dangerous people to mess with," Halston said.

"That's why Carlton needed me." Declan puffed on the cheroot with relish. "His alley cat days were long gone. He wanted to do the tracking himself and I talked some sense into him."

"You call that research? It's more like walking in front of a firing squad."

"I know how far I can go, Chief. And now, I'm not going anywhere. The book is stillborn. It will never be written."

They stood by Declan's rental car.

"I can't close the case," Halston said.

"What do you mean?"

"Fingerprints. Missing." Halston let out a long, deep breath. "Fingerprints that should be there and aren't."

Declan crushed the remains of his cigarillo on a fence post and lit another one. He presented the open case to Chief Halston. "They're mild. I can't smoke these fat phallic symbols. They make me sick."

Halston took one in his big fingers. "Cheroots, eh? What's wrong with plain old cigarettes?"

"They give you ashtray breath. You never know when you might want to kiss somebody." Declan offered him a light. "What missing fingerprints?"

"You know how to load a gun without leaving partials on the casings? A suicide won't worry about wearing gloves."

"That's why you wanted to know if Carlton knew how to handle a gun. In case somebody loaded it for him. It's a hot gun. He could have bought it fully loaded."

"If he wasn't an amateur he would have removed the slugs to check they weren't duds before reloading the thing."

Declan agreed. Carlton wasn't an inept amateur. "What are you going to do?"

"I'll hold on the suicide ruling. See if the autopsy delivers anything unexpected. Look at Marsh's phone calls. Talk to the neighbors again. Sit down with the boyfriend. What's that publisher's phone number?"

Declan scrolled down his contact list. "Andrew Hulten, in New York. You're not running me out of town, I gather."

"You're tolerable. For a troublemaker."

• • •

Chief Halston gave Declan a couple of B&B addresses. He struck out on his first try. The place couldn't accommodate him for the next two nights. He was luckier further down the road. Jean and Bill Heyzer rented cabins to budget-conscious vacationers. The kitchen and bathroom were up-to-date, the king-size bed was pure heaven, and the internet connection was slow but acceptable. Declan booked a one-week stay. Jean told him that extending wouldn't be a problem. The season was over, kids were back in school.

Declan dropped his bags in the cabin and went shopping for basics. Groceries, a bag of ice, and a bottle of scotch. By the time he closed his door for the night, he limped low. While the bathtub filled up, he poured a large whisky. He stripped and took his drink to the bathroom. The small space filled with steam and the mirror turned opaque. The skin under his eyes was warm and tight, like a fever. He tested the water and it was a little hotter than he could bear. He eased in, letting the good leg do all the work. Relief didn't come right away. Maybe the metal rods, the plates, and the pins in there needed to reach the right temperature. He glanced at the long thin scar that ran from ankle to groin. It puckered and remained pale in the scalding water. Surgeons had done a masterful job cobbling his bones back together. They had made a lot of headway on the mechanics. In matters of the mind, progress was less clear. Declan drained half his glass and rested his head on the rim of the tub. He let himself sink lower. He felt drowsy. Maybe the soaking would be enough and he wouldn't need the chemical magic tonight. He didn't hunger for it. There was nothing good there, nothing that moved the puck toward the goal post. He thought of Carlton Marsh who might have decided he would never manage to reach the end of the field for a score. It was disturbing. If Carlton, after the most accomplished career, despaired of his life achievements, committing suicide, what hope was there for everybody else?

"He didn't shoot himself," Declan muttered, and swallowed hot water. He had slipped below the flotation line.

He pushed himself up and finished his drink. He had to do something about Carlton Marsh's death. He couldn't rely on Chief Halston, however good intentioned he might be. In a community like Old Mapleton, suicide was way more acceptable than murder. Halston might manage to delay for a few days but he would soon be pressured to wrap up the case. The news of Marsh's death would spread fast. He was a top-tier reporter, a best-selling author. There would be calls from journalists, enquiries from editors who worked with Carlton. Declan wondered if he should get in front of it. He didn't want to upset

Halston and make his stay in Old Mapleton problematic. Better to sit back and observe. For now.

He could call Carlton's publisher in the morning. There had to be a way to get to the computer. He closed his eyes and let the heat envelop him.

He got out when the tub started losing its cocoon feel. The bad leg cooperated long enough for a tooth brushing and a shave, then it started hurting again. The physical therapist had warned that there would be no short cuts. It would take months to rebuild the muscles and tendons, to rewire the nerve endings, and if he was lax with the exercises, he would slide back and delay recovery with possible long-term damage. It irritated Declan that a single day of travel was enough to throw him off course.

There were furtive animal sounds on the roof and the porch of the cabin. Raccoons and possums going about their nocturnal business. Declan lay on the bed and listened to them run and jump. He envied their nimble freedom.

He turned off the light, and hoped that the alcohol would lull him to sleep.

It almost did, before a lancing pain speared him and left him gasping. He resisted for a while. He didn't want to give in but the torture was relentless.

The orange pill bottle was in the travel kit. It looked innocuous. It was lethal. And so seductive.

Declan contemplated the pill in his open palm, hoping against hope that just looking at the little bastard would be enough to quiet the stabbing hurt that made it hard to stand straight in front of the bathroom sink. He grabbed the counter to steady himself. He looked at his reflection in the mirror and didn't recognize much. The eyes weren't the usual green-hazel, they were as muddy as a Louisiana swamp, sunk and lifeless. His light tan had turned gray, and the dark hair was lank and unkempt. He looked like a bum.

"Won't get me in spitting distance of the yacht club," he mumbled, thick-tongued from the whisky. "Trooper Craig would give me a one-way ticket to the drunk tank. *I am* a troublemaker, Chief Halston." That made him smile and he snapped his mouth shut because the look on his face scared him. He swallowed the pill with a trickle of tepid water from the faucet and the whisky fumes left on the bottom of his glass.

Relief took its sweet time. It had to be coaxed, wooed. It was the pill's payback for being denied, and intended as a lesson. You think you can do without the dope, boy? I'm gonna show you how helpless you are behind the swagger, the arrogance, the pride of the smart and wily. You're putty, you're a knot of raw pain, you're a scream in the night, you're a baby at the teat. You are *need*. That's all you are.

All that Declan didn't want to be.

His anger was directed at his own weakness. He had given in to the pill too many times. He had to claw his way back.

When sleep came it was a tumble down a canyon. The kind that leaves skin and blood on rocks as sharp as monsters' teeth.

THREE

DECLAN HAULED HIMSELF out of bed around ten the next morning. He would have slept later if Jean Heyzer hadn't knocked on the cabin door to ask if he needed anything. She brought a handful of pods for the coffee machine. It gave her access to the sanctuary.

Declan had wrapped himself in the bulky comforter. "I crashed." He shot her the kind of grin that never failed to improve his batting average in the bar pick-up game.

She smiled. "Why don't you say you had a drink too many. We're aware of the ways of the world in this backwater, you know."

She collected the empty bottle of scotch with a flourish and dropped it in the waste basket. Declan felt the heat spread from his neck to his face. All the skin that was visible. Maybe the rest of him blushed too.

"Gossip is like wildfire in a small town. You're a friend of Carlton Marsh. We knew him. He was a good man. Don't feel bad because you got a hangover. Would you care for breakfast at the lodge, Mr. Shaw? It's more like brunch, actually."

"Call me Declan, please."

"And I'm Jean. See you down in half an hour?"

"I should manage to be presentable by then."

"It won't take much. A little dusting."

• • •

The food was excellent and plentiful. Declan didn't think he would be hungry after his nocturnal dive in junkie neverland but he inhaled the eggs, salmon, and muffins. Jean Heyzer kept refilling his coffee cup.

"They don't feed you wherever you come from?" Her smile erased whatever judgment the words suggested. "Oh, don't stop, please. I'm glad you enjoy it. Bill has a stomach ulcer and he doesn't eat with his old appetite anymore, he nibbles. Like a squirrel. Or a picky cat."

"It's delicious, Jean." He let out a satisfied sigh. "I'm sorry for Bill. Is he all right?"

"Oh yes. He's in New Haven haggling with contractors. Two of the cabins need refurbishing. There's always something to do around here and we try to complete indoors work during the winter." She refilled her big coffee mug. It said *Have a Whale of a Time—New Bedford* with a drawing of a breaching humpback.

"How long have you had this place?"

"Twelve years now. We left Chicago when Bill retired. We thought of opening a B&B somewhere on the coast, something small that we could manage with minimal help. Look what we ended up with. A lodge and twelve cabins!"

There was a story and Declan wanted to hear it. Jean Heyzer was fun to listen to. He had to smile when he looked at her. She was round top to bottom. A round face above a round body. When she laughed you couldn't help joining in.

"You got snookered into buying this place?" Declan said.

"We hesitated. For about five minutes. The price was

ridiculous because nobody knew what to do with it. There were historical restrictions. Let me show you."

She went to a roll-top desk pushed against the back wall and extracted a magazine. It was a *Sunday New York Times* supplement. She pushed away Declan's plate and silverware to make room. She leafed to the article.

"The property belonged to a New York industrialist, a minor robber baron. This was his summer camp. Lavish parties and fishing trips. He took a big hit on Black Tuesday. The Great Depression, then the war. It all went to seed. A developer tried to revive it in the fifties, turned it into a motor court, but he ran afoul of the local authorities. The cabins rotted. Somebody had slapped a historical preservation label on the property at some point and that froze everything, except the rot and the forest encroachment. We got a bargain with strings attached."

Declan looked at the pictures and scanned the captions and call boxes. "You had to restore it to its twenties look." He shook his head. "You guys are brave."

"Labor of love," Jean said. "We only had to preserve the outside. Nobody cared about period-correct plumbing or electricity."

"Or bedding. Thank you. It's most comfortable." Declan pointed at a picture. "That's Carlton Marsh, with you." He looked at the date of publication. It was a year old.

"Carlton arranged the article with his contacts at the *Times*. Big boost for us. We were fully booked after it came out. He was a dear friend, Declan. How close were you?"

"Emails, a call here and there. He asked me to help with his new book but we hadn't met face-to-face in a while. You saw him more than I did. Was he distressed?"

Jean took the plates and dishes to the kitchen. "I'll make a fresh pot of coffee."

When she came back, Declan had scanned the *Times* article. It was a double feature. One part covered the history of Bill and

Jean Heyzer's camp, the other was picture-heavy and included profiles of the artists working at the Old Mapleton art colony. For a reporter interested in societal trends, it was the ideal combo. Nostalgia and golden age vibes in the Heyzer camp, side by side with a crop of upcoming artists. There was something for everyone. And that didn't include the people that came for the fishing.

"Jack Corvill," Declan said. "Dark abstract, if that's a category."

"I like paintings that represent something. That moody stuff is depressing. He's selling, from what I hear."

"He was close to Carlton."

She shot him a piercing glance. As piercing as her kind face allowed. "Who are you, Declan?"

He wanted to give her the round-the-bend answer, the philosophical brush-off that would be adjacent to the truth, the existential dread that oozed out of the oxycodone that skulked in its bland container tucked in his kit.

"Didn't the town gossip answer that question?"

"Oh, hush," Jean said. "You don't want to know the town gossip. It's bad for you and bad for Carlton, and I won't have any of it." Her round cheeks had lost their cheerful color.

"I'm a private detective. Carlton hired me to do research for his new book. Find people. That's my specialty." Declan raised his hand. "Now, if any of this ever makes it to the gossip grapevine, I will be very angry with you, Jean."

"Why?"

"I'd rather have people believe I was competing with Jack Corvill for pillow space."

She made a face. "That's crude. Why?"

"Because I don't believe Carlton shot himself."

She didn't have an opportunity to answer because the front door opened and Bill Heyzer walked in. He was a medium-size guy who looked tall because he was so stringy. His jeans flapped around his legs and the plaid shirt had room to spare. A long, thin neck with a knobby Adam's apple led to a long, narrow head topped by an improbable thatch of gray hair that matched bushy eyebrows. Amazingly, the general impression wasn't evocative of a Halloween mask. Bill Heyzer came across as a down to earth straw-chewing farmer out of an Andrew Wyeth painting. The contrast with his wife was cartoon funny.

"Ah, our guest. I'm Bill." Heyzer held out his hand. "Sorry I missed you last night."

"It's better this way," Declan said. "I wasn't at my best."

"A little shook up, eh?" He grabbed the coffee carafe and a mug that wasn't as colorful as his wife's.

"Chief Halston suggested I get on the next plane back to Texas."

Bill Heyzer chuckled. "Not gonna happen, right?"

"Right."

"Care to explain why?"

Declan was in a place he didn't know, with complete strangers, in circumstances he hadn't had time to process. These people wanted him to commit before he was ready.

"I'm compulsive," he said. "Obsessive. I chew on things until I understand them. And there's too much I don't understand right now. I talked to Carlton two days ago and we discussed the research he wanted me to do for the book. He was enthusiastic and rearing to go. And now he's gone. It's like I opened a door and there's nothing beyond the threshold. I'm on the edge. If that makes sense."

"Not everything can be explained. How can we know what goes on in people's heads?" Bill Heyzer said.

"Carlton wasn't a hermit living in a cave. He was engaged, with people, with the world. He communicated. Even if he kept important things private, there will be clues."

"And that's your job," Jean said. "Run the clues to ground."

Declan smiled. "You make me feel like a truffle-sniffing dog."

"He's a private detective, Bill. Like in the movies." Jean had refilled her big coffee mug and the liquid was steaming. "You should wear a hat. You'd look good with a hat."

"Hair's too long. I need a haircut."

"Rosie's Studio, in town. She does a good job, and it's gossip central."

"You're showing dispositions for my disreputable trade," Declan said. "Why don't you fill me in on Carlton Marsh? I understand his family's from here."

"He was the end of the line." Bill pulled out a pipe and tobacco pouch. He ignored his wife's frown. "I'm a history buff. Had to dig into that when we bought the camp. I've looked at stacks of old photographs and documents. After a while you notice the same names coming back all the time. Marsh, Cavendish, Morton, Anderson. The local elite. Mayors, lawyers, doctors. You have good ole boys in Texas, Old Mapleton has its own version of the connected set."

"The country club membership roster," Declan said.

"Problem is that the fertility rate didn't keep up. They had to admit new members to the party. Money, like everywhere, gives you access. The aristocracy is still hanging on, exsanguinated and doddering." Bill puffed on the pipe. "I don't regret the demise of the stuck-up spinsters, but some of the recent additions are even less palatable."

"How did Carlton fare in these troubled waters?"

"Until a couple of years ago, he didn't spend much time here. A few weeks in the spring, a few more in the fall," Bill said. "He traveled. Then he had a nasty bout of pneumonia that forced him to slow down. The family home needed work and I helped him. I have a reliable list of contractors from when we restored the camp. We became friends. Jean and I are retired professors, we like intelligent conversation and Carlton was great company. We'll miss him."

"Did he talk about the book project?"

"In general terms," Jean said. "It was very close to his heart and I believe he didn't want to jinx it."

"He was preoccupied lately," Bill added. "Excited one day and irritated the next. He was deep into research."

"He told me he might change the focus of the book." Jean refilled her husband's coffee mug. "He said it needed work. He acted all mysterious. Did he tell you who he wanted you to find?"

"I wish he had, but he was cagey with me too. He said he would explain everything once I got here. I hope he confided in somebody. What about Jack Corvill?"

Bill Heyzer snickered. "Insufferable little pissant. Artist with a capital A. A like asshole. If he'd been a girl, I'd say he found a sugar daddy. Maybe he has a wisp of talent, but he sure has a mass of attitude."

"He made Carlton happy, Bill," Jean said.

"For a price."

"What's the deal with that artist colony?"

"It was here before we moved in," Jean said. "Gabriel Schulman founded it. He made a fortune in real estate and decided to use his money to help artists. He owns art galleries. There's one in town—Isthmus Gallery. On Main."

"Profitable?" Declan said. "Old Mapleton isn't a big tourist hub."

"He has galleries in New York and L.A., it's in that *Times* article," Jean said.

Bill puffed harder. Talk of art and artists got his hackles up, it seemed. "I bet Schulman makes more money in charity tax deductions, unless it's a money laundering scheme."

Jean gathered the brunch leftovers. There wasn't much, Declan cleaned the spread.

"You're turning into a typical New England curmudgeon, Bill. Don't listen to him, Declan. He must have fought with the contractors again. Who was it this time? The plumber?"

"The electrician," Bill mumbled. "Blooming idiot."

The back and forth amused Declan. It was well-rehearsed and both actors knew their lines. "How's the hiking around here?" If he didn't get moving, he risked another disastrous night.

"There are two well-marked trails starting near the camp entrance," Jean said. "Four- and five-miles round trip in the woods. If you prefer the sea views, there's a path along the coast. You'll need the car to get to the other trails. I wouldn't advise walking on the road. The locals all believe they're grand prix material."

She plucked a map from a drawer and gave him directions. He accepted the loan of a refillable water bottle but passed on a sandwich. He wanted to walk off the big breakfast.

• • •

The hike was strenuous and took Declan to the top of a hill with a sprawling view of the town. He located Carlton Marsh's villa and the police station. The day was clear with a light breeze, and both the commercial fishing harbor and the marina showed signs of activity. It reminded him of Chief Halston's albacore.

He was on his way back when his phone rang. It was Andrew Hulten, Carlton Marsh's publisher. Halston had called him.

"It's unbelievable. Carlton sent me three fantastic chapters last week-end. He was confident he could deliver the book by year-end. I don't understand what happened."

Declan sat on a tree trunk. "It stinks, Andy."

Silence on the line. "Is that police chief spinning a tale? A convenient suicide? These small towns always try to bury scandals. All they see is tourist revenue. They freak out when something threatens their pristine reputation. I imagine what police investigations must be like in that place."

"Halston seems competent," Declan said. "He doesn't want to bury the case but he doesn't have much to work with." He gave Hulten a run-down of the evidence, or lack thereof. "The chief is as puzzled as I am. I told him I talked to Carlton the evening before, and didn't catch any toxic vibes."

"What about that boyfriend of his?"

"You know him?"

"I met him," Hulten said. "I didn't know what to make of him. One moment puppy soft, the next feral cur, fangs showing. At times, he acted the tormented artist, prickly, arrogant, and then he did a one-eighty with his tail between his legs as if he'd been beaten senseless. He was on something, I swear."

"How did Carlton react to the mood swings?"

"He ignored them. You know how he could be. Self-centered."

"He's always been a cool customer," Declan said. "Jack Corvill left for Montreal a week ago. The police will check him out. I met people who think Corvill's a conman who was fleecing Carlton."

"Not a chance. Carlton was a tightwad. If he spent money on Corvill, it didn't make a dent in his bank account."

"How do you know?"

"Because Carlton's lawyer gave me a financial status. She's been handling his affairs for years. There's a will. Everything goes to a foundation that supports academic programs in journalism and the families of reporters killed in the line of duty. There isn't a cent going to Jack Corvill or anybody else Carlton might have been close to."

"What about the material for the new book?"

"Contractually, it belongs to us," Hulten said. "Carlton got a substantial advance."

"I want access to the notes and the computer files, Andy, but they won't be released until the case is closed."

A longer silence on the line. "Can you clarify your thoughts, Declan?"

"It would be better if his death was ruled a suicide. Two reasons. We get the notes that may shed some light on Carlton's state of mind, and, more importantly, if this was *not* a suicide, we let the killer believe they're off the hook."

"And why would you stay in Old Mapleton after the cops close the case?"

"It isn't the worst place for a vacation. Just push Chief Halston in the right direction, Andy. Not too hard. Try to be subtle."

"And how do I muzzle the pesky newshounds that will swarm that pastoral corner of Connecticut as soon as the news of Carlton's death gets out?"

"You'll find a way."

* * *

Declan felt good after the hike. The bad leg had loosened. He hoped the night would be quiet. He had to stay on his feet, though. Sitting down with a book was not an option. After another tub soak and a change of clothes, he went to have a peek at the town.

He drove from the Heyzer camp to the port, and left the rental BMW in a convenient parking spot, midway between the commercial fishing harbor and the marina. Carlton Marsh's house was a stone's throw away but he didn't go that way. He walked along the seawall, turned into a quiet residential street, and emerged on Main. He wandered into a couple of antique stores that carried upscale merchandise and curios. The prices seemed inflated, targeting weekenders from New York. Still, it was fun to imagine where some pieces could go in his Houston loft. He had a double espresso in a coffee shop and decided he would buy a box of macarons for Jean Heyzer on his way back. He could see how humdrum life in Old Mapleton would get. No wonder Carlton Marsh kept traveling well after his risky foreign correspondent days were over. Unless you had a book to write, monotony would turn your mind to mush.

FOUR

ISABEL SANDERS LOOKED UP from her computer when the bell tinkled. The man who walked into the art gallery was tall and lean. The high-heeled cowboy boots gave him an extra and unnecessary lift. This guy was swagger top to bottom. The dark hair was a little too long and messy for corporate respectability, the leather jacket—a classic brown number with significant mileage on it—hugged the broad shoulders just right, and the black jeans were a perfect fit. She wished the door didn't close by itself, so he would have to turn and she could have a good look at his ass. She bet it was also perfect. She sighed. It had been a dull and dispiriting day. An elderly couple had walked in, looked around, and walked out when they realized the gallery didn't sell posters—"for our granddaughter's bedroom, something with unicorns, she's very much into unicorns." Hell, who wasn't? This guy, who folded his sunglasses—aviators, what else—and hooked them in his shirt's open collar, was Isabel's version of a unicorn. Mythical or extinct, choose your poison. He took a right—most right-handed people tended to turn right, Isabel remembered reading somewhere—and she had a glimpse of his face. Damn, he was a knock-out. People would kill for those cheekbones. The mouth was good too. Thin. Hard. None of that slobbering, slug-like sensuality that made her want to puke. Okay Isabel, gather yourself. He's either married (to a goddess!) with a brood of cute kids, or he bats for the other team. Nothing like *that* could ever walk unfettered into her gin joint.

The guy ignored the seascapes displayed near the entrance for the walk-in tourist trade. He paused by the disemboweled raven, a metal sculpture that gave Isabel a jolt each time she caught a glimpse of it from the corner of her eye. He smiled and patted the gruesome bird on the head. Isabel sighed. He had a quirky sense of humor. Too good to be true. Ten to one he was gay.

He turned the corner and, predictably, froze.

Isabel couldn't see the large canvas from where she sat but she knew what the dude was looking at. Xandra Mohr's *Sea Rhapsody*. The unsaleable megalodon of the Isthmus Gallery. The thing was as wide and a foot taller than *Guernica* and way more colorful. It took the entire back wall of the gallery. It knocked everybody's socks off. Considering that most people did not have the wall space, it was impossible to offload.

Isabel noticed that, contrary to almost all potential customers drawn to the painting, this man did not walk toward it. He stood at the appropriate distance to appreciate the intricate composition. Isabel walked toward him. The pinch in her stomach was not unpleasant.

"You could drown in it," the man said.

Isabel stopped in her tracks. She hadn't made any noise. "It's a powerful piece."

"I'd say."

He walked a few steps to the right to study the painting from a different angle, then a few steps to the left. He went down on a knee, frowning. He hadn't looked at Isabel but she was certain he could describe her with his eyes closed. She felt awkward. He was younger than she'd initially thought. Early thirties. Exactly in her range. He looked fit but she noticed a little hitch in his step. He favored the left leg.

"Xandra Mohr is the artist. She grew up close to the ocean, in Maine." Isabel was eager to break the silence that made her uncomfortable. "She incorporates water in all her compositions."

"Is she an art colony resident?"

"Ah, you know about our project. All the artists we feature at Isthmus are or have been residents."

"Like a loyalty program," he said.

It was, but Isabel wasn't paid to admit it. "Many of our artists have gained worldwide recognition. They still entrust us with some of their pieces."

"I apologize if I upset you, Ms.?"

"Sanders. Isabel Sanders. I'm not upset." She was aware she blinked too much. He unnerved her. "Most of Xandra's pieces have been sold, but I still have two beautiful drawings, preparatory studies for this composition. It's called *Sea Rhapsody*."

"This is the one I want." He sighed. "Shipping won't come cheap."

She almost blurted, *oh, we can arrange that!* and caught herself. "Where would it have to be shipped?"

"Texas. Houston."

She had detected a slight drawl, a touch of southern, but there was something else too that she could not place. "You realize it takes a lot of space."

"I live on top of an old warehouse. There's room. I'll have to move a few things around but it won't be a problem."

"It's not just the wall," Isabel said and felt foolish. What was he going to think, that she didn't want to sell, that she was some Yankee bitch who refused to sell to *him*? "This piece has raised a lot of interest since we unveiled it last year. People want it, then they go home and take measurements, and they realize it won't work. I have a simulation on my computer that shows the effect, if you want to check ..."

"*Il faut du recul,*" he said, with a half-smile. "You need distance *and* clearance. Let's play your simulation."

He preceded her to the desk. Great ass, indeed. He never looked in her direction but he had known all the time that she was there, that she watched him. This was more than unnerving. She was being seduced and he didn't *do* anything.

She sat in front of the laptop and clicked on the graphics program. He took the visitor's chair.

"Do you know the dimensions of the room, approximately?"

"I'll enter them." He turned the laptop around.

He ran the thing as if he'd done it all his life. The rendition appeared, perfect. He raised a hand as if to say *Voila*! There was no wedding band, no ring on any of his fingers. Of course that didn't prove anything.

"That is a large open space," Isabel said. "It can't have been easy to furnish properly."

"It's my office and apartment. I believe in less is more. Talking about more. How much do you want for the piece?"

Direct. Isabel liked that. Now they would see. She was still convinced the sale would crater. "Twelve thousand."

He leaned back in the chair, looked at the ceiling, wistful. "A bargain. Because you can't get rid of it. What does Xandra Mohr think of the price tag?"

Xandra was pissed off, but *Rhapsody* had turned into an albatross for her too. She avoided coming to the gallery because she couldn't stand looking at it anymore.

"She wants it to find a good home," Isabel said. It was a direct quote. Xandra said that. She didn't say it in that tone, however. When Xandra was in a foul mood, she bit everybody's head off.

"I'd like to meet her."

Where did he learn to smile like that? It should be illegal.

Isabel felt catlike. She wanted to flop on her back to have her tummy scratched. "I can arrange it, uh, Mr.?"

"Shaw. Declan. Would you like my credit card? I'd prefer to know about shipping before we close the sale."

That was it. What she couldn't place. A touch of Irish that peeked through the drawl like music playing in another room. "I can check right away."

"No hurry. Tomorrow is fine, but I want to make a down payment. I would be livid if somebody walked in here later and snatched it from me."

There was very little risk of that happening. The canvas had been exhibited, not for one year but two. Truth didn't always get you the sale. Little white lies helped. Isabel took his address and phone numbers, cell and office.

"Are you passing through, Mr. Shaw?"

"I have a cabin at the Heyzer camp until the end of the week."

"A place with a lot of history. What brings you to Old Mapleton? It's off the beaten path."

"I came to see a friend. Unfortunately, it fell through. I didn't feel like going back home right away." He looked at her. "Doesn't this call for some kind of celebration, Ms. Sanders? You just dumped your white elephant on an unsuspecting traveler."

It was a pass and Isabel could pretend to be offended, but his choice of words made it acceptable. It was very deftly done. "Nice sleight of hand, Mr. Shaw. What do you do for a living?"

"Any bubbly left from some vernissage before I answer that question?"

Isabel could use a drink. There was a bottle of Laurent Perrier in the kitchen fridge. Shaw was right. Selling Xandra's *Rhapsody* deserved a toast. She would enjoy clinking glasses with him. She wondered if he was any good in bed. Handsome men, in her experience, were often disappointing. Too preoccupied with themselves.

She brought back the bottle—icy, it had been in the fridge

for months—and two stubby glasses. "We get the champagne glasses from the caterer. I don't have any here."

"I can't stand the flutes," he said. "Too narrow for my nose."

They toasted.

"To you, Declan Shaw, unsuspecting traveler."

"To you, Isabel Sanders, wily art dealer. What are you doing in Old Mapleton? Do you commute from a more exciting locale? I detect a slight Boston accent."

Like her, he had an ear for regional quirks. "I've been with Isthmus for four years now. I move with the seasons. L.A. next, then Miami in the winter. New York after that and the cycle starts again."

"Hamster in the wheel."

Isabel bristled. "You're a wealthy guy. You buy art. What do you know about making a living as an art historian? My dad warned me it was a dead end."

"Bless his heart," he said with just the right amount of fake condescension.

It acted like a cattle prod. Champagne on an empty stomach scrambled Isabel's senses, including her common sense. "Declan Shaw, you're a prick!"

"I'll take you out to dinner. Anything good around town?"

God, he was skillful. And she was such a patsy. "Give me one reason why I would agree to go on a date with you."

"Because you're intrigued." He gave her an aw-shucks grin. "And you radiate *ennui*. You sit in your little box flogging decorative crap. Not Xandra Mohr. She has talent. Whoever made the exploded raven has balls too. The rest is derivative and you know it. Now I'm stroking your ego and telling you what you want to hear, that you know your art. Dinner at eight? I'll pick you up, just tell me where."

Isabel was intrigued. And a little scared. She hadn't been a little scared in a long time. "Seven thirty, here. There's a good restaurant outside of town. I'll make a reservation."

He was gracious. He didn't smile at her unconditional surrender.

• • •

"Gabe?" Isabel said, on the phone. "I sold the big Mohr today." It didn't sound as triumphant as she hoped to make it, but it didn't matter, Gabriel Schulman had no ear for vocal nuances. He was a crude individual for all his bespoke suits and expensive shoes.

"That's wonderful, Isabel." A pause. "Is this another case of potential buyer remorse? We've had a few."

"I ran the computer simulation. He has the space. And the money. He put fifty percent down to guarantee the transaction."

A long whistle. "No haggling, eh? Did he have a referral?"

"Just walked in. He looked at a few things and then went straight to the Mohr."

"They all do. Who is he?"

"Up from Houston. Declan Shaw. I have no idea what he does for a living. Young, in his thirties. I've asked for a shipping quote, then we'll finalize the transaction. He'd like to meet Xandra, but it's not a condition for the sale. You know how she is, when she's in one of her moods."

"Yes, pain in the ass. If only we didn't have to deal with the artists." He laughed. "Congratulations. What if we put a bit of that cash aside for your gambling habit?"

He said it with a twinkle of humor but it still hurt. *I'm not gambling, you pompous jerk,* she wanted to scream. She made informed artistic decisions. Her art buying was more thoughtful than his ever was.

"That would be great, Gabe."

"I'd like to meet this Mr. Shaw. I'm out of town right now. I won't be back for a couple of days. How long will he be in the area?"

"Until the end of the week, he said."

"We'll make it work. Treat yourself to a nice dinner, Isabel. On expense."

She had been happy with her good news and now she was fuming. She hung up before saying something she might regret. Schulman always made these perks sound like charity. She should go to New York, visit that gallery owner in Brooklyn who had been intrigued by her *gambling* choices and had suggested Isthmus didn't use her talent properly.

• • •

The blue BMW pulled up in front of the gallery at seven-thirty on the dot. Shaw came around to hold the door open for her. No irony. Isabel was glad she chose the dark green silk dress she hadn't worn since that horrible cocktail party in Miami last winter. It had been too subdued for Florida. She had been lost among the long legs and generous décolletés. Not a bad thing considering how touchy-feely the males had gotten after a couple of drinks. Shaw—should she call him her client? It sounded kinky—had made a few sartorial adjustments. He replaced the leather jacket with a black blazer and the cowboy boots with black oxfords. The dress shirt was dark blue and the black jeans were belted. He had run a comb through his floppy hair.

"Do you always wear black?" Isabel said.

"It makes decisions simple. Where are we going?"

"North on Main, I'll give you directions. It's a French restaurant. A young chef. Imaginative. And the wine selection is excellent."

The car radio played jazz at a low volume.

"I told Gabriel Schulman, the gallery owner, that you bought *Rhapsody*. He would like to meet you. He should be in town in a few days."

"Sure. Did he give you a raise for your good deed?"

Isabel chuckled. "He promised me a bonus and told me to go get a nice dinner, on his dime."

"Not tonight. I don't want his ghost hovering over our table."

"Take the next right. It's a narrow, winding road. Deer jump at you."

Dinner was exquisite. She was pleased when Shaw chatted in French with the chef. It was different from her other visits, with residents of the art colony. They were a lot of fun, but not sophisticated.

"You're fluent," she said. "Just a little bit of an accent. Where did you learn?"

"My mother. She was old New Orleans. She spoke French to me. I've tried to keep it up." He smiled. "I don't have as many opportunities to practice as I'd like."

"Declan is Irish, isn't it?"

"My dad was Irish."

"What do you do when you're not visiting art galleries?"

"You didn't google me? That's imprudent, Isabel. I could be on the FBI most wanted list. I looked you up. I wanted to know what the omniscient internet said about Isabel Sanders."

"Why did you do that for?" It was borderline offensive. She never had a date tell her they did a web search.

"Professional habit. I'm a private investigator. I was relieved to see you had no moldy skeletons in your cupboards."

"A detective? Really? Wow." She stared at him. "You're not how I imagine a detective, in real life I mean, not in the movies."

He refilled her wine glass. "We're not all thick-necked, hob-nailed pavement beaters. One of my friends runs an agency in Florida. She has a master's in biology. Another one used to be a journalist. We come in many flavors."

She tried to square his occupation with his interest in art, fluency in French, and knowledge of wine vintages. "You know about art. You disregarded the minor talents at the gallery."

"My first big case was recovering a collector's misplaced masterpieces. I learned a lot."

"Art theft."

"I specialize in finding lost things and lost people. The paintings were lost and those who took them were lost even more. In my business, you learn that things are rarely what they seem."

Isabel enjoyed the light buzz. The champagne cocktails, the good wine and most of all his voice, warm, low, promising. She noticed his hands resting on the tablecloth. He had beautiful hands. He used them to emphasize a word or a turn of phrase. He was relaxed, loose-limbed, and focused on her. She had found his attitude disconcerting at the gallery, but in these surroundings, it was soothing.

"Are things rarely what they seem in love too?" she said.

He looked away and she felt a chill. There had been warmth in these eyes—green, brown, changing—as long as they were set on her. Cold seeped in now that she wasn't in the beam anymore. He soon focused on her again and relief flooded back in.

"Catch me on a blue day and I'll say yes. Love is often not what it seems."

"And on a non-blue day?"

"There are accommodations. Coffee? I'm not much for dessert unless you want to split something."

They approached that point in the evening where awkwardness would creep in. Isabel wondered how he would negotiate the challenge. He had been impeccable so far, polite without being stuffy, amusing without trying too hard, tender without insinuation. And he hadn't touched her at all. These beautiful hands had not brushed hers. Maybe he was gay after all. Oh well, it had been a wonderful evening. She couldn't remember one that nice in at least a year.

He excused himself to go to the restroom and when he came back Isabel had finished her coffee.

"I'd like a smoke," he said. "The maître d' recommended the

garden in back." He looked under the table. "He said it was a sandy path. You could take your shoes off."

"You have a foot fetish?"

"We'll find out."

They went out the back to a balcony. A few steps led down to the garden. It was a clear night, with the moon bright enough to dim the light of the solar-powered lanterns that lined the path. Shaw pulled out a flat silver cigar case and lit a cigarillo. To Isabel's relief he didn't smoke the kind of fat, stinky rods Gabe Schulman puffed on during business meetings.

She followed his suggestion and unstrapped her sandals. He offered her an arm to lean on. It was their first physical contact and it felt natural.

"I've never been here," Isabel said. "I had no idea this even existed."

"They grow herbs for the kitchen in the raised gardens."

"We should come back for lunch, when we can see what's around us."

"Definitely," he said.

He seemed content to smoke quietly and adjusted his long stride to her shorter one. The silence could have been embarrassing and was anything but. They completed their tour of the garden. Isabel slipped her shoes back on. She leaned a little heavier on him this time, and he led her through a side gate back to the parking lot. Isabel appreciated his delicate touch. He had used his trip to the restroom to settle the bill.

He opened the door of the BMW for her. Without fuss, as if this was the most natural thing in the world to do. Some of Isabel's friends would sneer at the old-fashioned gestures of gallantry. Male dominance, the moldering debris of the patriarchy. Before tonight, she would have agreed. She realized it depended on who did it and how it was done. Shaw didn't treat her like a fragile hothouse flower. His courtesy was practical as much as well practiced. He was self-confident and he didn't have to prove anything. Isabel didn't know many men who could pull that off without appearing conceited. Or manipulative.

Wait a minute! He was manipulative. And arrogant. The way he had taken control at the gallery. When he commandeered her laptop.

She looked at him. His driving was focused. She had no idea what he might be thinking. Maybe he wondered how to get rid of her with the appropriate level of politeness before prowling the streets of New Haven for some rented love. He said things were rarely what they seemed.

On a blue night.

They were out of the woods, on the road to town.

"I need directions," he said.

She caught a hint of a smile and her heart fluttered. She kicked herself mentally. How old was she? Sixteen and hormones boiling?

"You remember the white church at the edge of town? Take a left after it, then the first right. It's a dead end." How appropriate. "My apartment building is the last one on the left."

He pulled into the driveway, turned off the engine, and did a little jog around the car to open her door. This time she beat him to it. He smiled and closed the car door behind her. It made a subdued *thunk*. The doors of luxury cars had a sound all their own.

Isabel was irritated now. She reached her front door, keys in hand, in a few quick steps. Would he wish her goodnight with a little bow? Or grab her shoulders, turn her around and slam her against the door? She felt a thrill of anticipation.

"Isabel."

He was behind her, at a distance calculated to be non-threatening. She turned around. The key was in the unlocked door.

"I have a proposal."

There was no harm in listening. She was one step from the safety of her home.

"One kiss. If you decide it's blah, I'll see you at the gallery tomorrow."

Nobody had ever tried that line on her. "And if it's not?" She couldn't believe he would just drive away.

He hiked his shoulders, head tilted. The kid who pointed at the cat and the broken vase, *Mom, I didn't do it.* She couldn't repress a chuckle. "You have some nerve."

"That's all I got."

It was the unexpected sadness in his voice that did it.

• • •

They were well beyond the offer of a nightcap by the time they tumbled sideways on the bed. There had been a short attempt on the couch but he nixed it.

"I have a bad leg." His voice was hoarse. "I need a wider playground."

Isabel suspected he had passed on the cowboy boots tonight because they would get in the way. He was hard and big, and she was ready. She grabbed his waist to pull him on top of her. Then he threw her for a spin.

"Not yet."

There was that doubt again, in the middle of her need, that he was not what he pretended to be, that he was a freak who would slice and dice her while she kept pleading for more.

"Get inside, damn you." She brought her fists down on his shoulders, as hard as she could. There was a solid layer of muscle there and her efforts didn't lead anywhere.

"You're so impatient," he muttered.

Impatient? Isabel wanted to scream, and soon after, she did. He went down on her and sent her all the way up a tall pole.

"You're killing me." Her hands grabbed the top of the headboard.

He raised his head, giving her a brief respite. He was grinning ear to ear and she wanted to punch his smile, out of frustration because he kept her on the insufferable edge of completion.

"I'm fucking your brains out." In the same voice he used to order wine.

"I hate you." She exhaled as her back lost contact with the bed. "I'm going to come."

"Uh, uh. Hold it."

His fingers took over from his mouth, tongue and what-ever else he used on her. Tonsils? She let out a deep lowing that belonged in a dewy meadow. It was so outrageous that she laughed. And couldn't stop. Big bursts that made tears run down her cheeks.

She never had a fit of laughter during sex. Wouldn't that turn him off? Or make him angry. He would think she mocked him. But she couldn't stop. This was so much fun.

"Oh God! I'm sorry. I'm sorry!" It was a desperate plea and she was still laughing.

He entered her in one smooth thrust.

• • •

"You said pretty silly things."

"Did I?" Isabel remembered the way her entire body did what she could only describe as a somersault. She stretched. His body was against the entire length of hers. It fit snuggly.

"You apologized before coming." He chuckled.

She tried to turn to face him but his arms were wrapped tight around her waist. "I had an attack of the giggles."

"I love that sound." He kissed her neck. "It means I'm doing the right thing."

"You're weird."

He blew air into her ear and ran a hand down her side. "You think sex is a serious thing. It isn't, sweetie. It's an opportunity to get out of ourselves."

"You have knobby knees, Declan."

He moved a little sideways. "I apologize for my sharp bones."

Isabel buried her face in the pillow to stifle the laughter that surged again. She expected him to respond in kind but his arms fastened around her middle, hard and squeezing, painful. She tried to pry his fingers loose. They dug deeper. Then the pressure stopped and she jumped out of bed.

"What the hell do you think you're doing?" She switched on the light on the nightstand. Her heart beat like crazy.

He was on his back, shivering. Then the screams started. Low moans at first, rising to loud shouts of pain. He turned to muffle them in the pillow.

"You're having a seizure?" Isabel stood by the bed. She didn't know what to do. "I'm calling nine-one-one."

"No. No." Haltingly, reedy.

"Declan, what can I do? Tell me. Please."

"Cigar case."

He needed a smoke? Isabel went through his jeans and jacket pockets and retrieved the silver box. "What do you want me to do with it?"

He shook so hard she feared he might fall off the bed. She tucked in the bedsheets.

"Pill," he mumbled through clenched jaws.

There was a single white pill under the cigars. Isabel gave it to him and ran to the bathroom to get a glass of water. She tried to make him drink and the glass clanked against his teeth. She managed to get a few drops in.

The pill didn't take effect immediately. The seizure continued, and the sounds of pain. Isabel sat on the bed. It took all her strength to keep him from falling off. When the crisis abated, her arms hurt.

"I'm thirsty," he said.

She handed him the glass of water. His voice was normal, controlled, low.

"What happened, Declan?"

"My leg injury. It's a major annoyance. I'm sorry. I should go."

"You're in no condition to drive. What did I give you?" She knew these pinpoint pupils. He wasn't high yet but he would be soon.

She slipped back into bed, pulled up the bedsheet and the duvet, lay alongside him, and held him tight.

"Now, you close your eyes and ride it, lover boy. Tomorrow we talk about this."

• • •

Isabel woke around eight. Shaw was still asleep. She raised on an elbow and looked at him. He seemed younger in sleep. There was a blue shadow under his eyes that she didn't care much for. His breathing was normal and that reassured her. She lifted the comforter and studied him. He was built nice. Long, flat muscles. He worked out. She ran a finger along his cock and was delighted to see it react. She was tempted to test how far her teasing would take it. It wouldn't be right. You didn't take advantage of a sleeping person. The leg injury was at the same time discreet and overwhelming. A long cut, scalpel-straight that had sliced through flesh and muscle to reach the bone. She replaced the sheets, and padded to the bathroom to take a shower. Then she went to the kitchen to brew a pot of coffee.

When she walked back into the bedroom with a big mug of steaming coffee, he was stirring. She sat on the side of the bed and set the mug on the nightstand.

"Hi." He rubbed his eyes with the heels of his hands. "Good morning."

"I brought you a cup of coffee. You took it black yesterday."

He sat up and leaned on the headboard. "Thanks."

"How do you feel?"

"Great." He shot her a lopsided smile. "There's a lesson here."

"Yeah?"

"Don't try to go cold turkey on a first date."

Not funny. "That injury is a corker. What happened?"

"I fell off a staircase. Long fall, bad landing."

"If I'd had the bottle instead of a single pill, I would have given you the entire load. You were in terrible pain. It freaked me out."

"I can see the headline: *She Killed him with Kindness.*" He sipped the coffee. "I thought I had beaten it. That I would have a good night. It isn't wishful thinking. There have been some."

"Can't the doctors do anything about it?"

"Pain is a strange thing, Isabel. Some people can't feel any. They tend to die young. Their alarm system doesn't work."

"What does that have to do with anything?"

He tapped the side of his head. "In there. My leg is fine. I limp when I'm tired or when the weather changes. The pain is an illusion. A mental misfire."

"The fuck it is."

He took her hand and caressed the underside of her wrist. "My resident demon craves the high. He's a smart little bugger. He knows that the way to get satisfaction is to stage a freak show. These past few nights I've been unable to wrestle him to the mat. That's bad because he's gaining confidence."

"I don't believe what you say, about the pain not being real. You hurt so much."

"Why did it happen after we were done? Because we were *occupied.* There was no room for mind games."

Isabel smiled. "The solution is simple then. We just have to keep doing it."

"I might need to switch to a different kind of chemical. I need a shower. Do you have a spare toothbrush?"

"In the drawer under the sink."

He got out of bed and went to the bathroom. Isabel couldn't see the leg scar at all.

FIVE

DECLAN HAD WALKED into the Isthmus Gallery because the place warranted a visit, after Bill Heyzer's acid comments about Gabriel Schulman who made a fortune in real estate and became a patron of the arts. Men like Schulman didn't sink money in losing ventures without an ulterior motive.

The rest was pure happenstance. Xandra Mohr's amazing piece bowled him over, and Isabel amused him. She was bored out of her mind and too smart for her tedious job. What satisfaction could she find in Old Mapleton? He asked her out on impulse. As he watched her sip her wine and relish the seduction game, he thought she might be just the excuse he needed for staying in town. An end of summer romance. They would be seen together. Restaurants, cafés, strolling on the seawall. The gossipers' tongues would wag and it wouldn't be about him and Carlton Marsh.

A relationship with Isabel had other benefits. Through her, Declan had access to the art colony. He would start with Xandra Mohr and work his way to Jack Corvill, artists were even more gossipy than small town denizens.

Declan stepped out of the shower and wrapped a towel around his waist. He caught Isabel's reflection in the bathroom mirror. She was on the bed, her robe arranged for another round of lovemaking. He didn't mind. He could show her a few more things that were guaranteed to make her laugh again. That was by far his favorite sound in a bedroom.

"Won't you be late for work?"

"We open at noon."

He untied her robe and kissed her tummy. "Now I understand why you stay in the job. I'll swing by the gallery later and write you a check. I'll cook for you tonight, if you want."

"Do you know how strange that sounds," Isabel said.

"I can cook."

"Not that. The check."

"I'm not buying you, sweetie, I'm buying Xandra Mohr."

"I need to call her," she said.

●　●　●

Back at the cabin, Declan considered his actions of the past hours. If Isabel had said good night and thanks for dinner, he would have driven back home and popped the oxy in private. In the woods, the only living things his screams would have disturbed were the raccoons. He might have been better off. Ah, fuck it, no regrets.

Like his decision to buy the painting.

Sea Rhapsody would look fantastic in the loft and it was a smart purchase. Xandra Mohr was talented. She would soon be snatched by an agent and set sail for brighter exhibition locales than Old Mapleton. Declan looked forward to meeting her. Preferably without Isabel, to get the scuttlebutt on Schulman and Jack Corvill.

He checked his messages. There was a note from Andy Hulten. He dialed the publisher's number and his call went to voice mail. He changed clothes, filled his water bottle, and pocketed a handful of energy bars. A couple of hours on the trail would do him good. Doctor's orders.

• • •

Before meeting Isabel at the gallery, Declan had a look at the harbor. Chief Halston's stuffed albacore beckoned. If the weather remained clear, he should plan a day at sea.

He parked the BMW in the same spot as before, ignored the marina and its luxury yachts, and walked to the commercial fishing harbor. The smells were vigorous—tar, algae, and fish guts. He leaned on the dock railing and took in the sights. The boats had weathered a lifetime of storms. They were sturdy, patched-up, not pretty but reliable, and their owners' main asset. It was a tough life.

There was movement on one of the boats and he watched a tall, dark-haired woman carry a bucket to one of the fish cleaning stations. Her sharp-edged face demanded attention. Declan lit a cigar and indulged in one of his favorite pastimes. Where does she live. What does she dream of. She was a little older than Isabel, more physically competent, harder in bone and muscle. Less sensuous. She wouldn't giggle but she could bite. There was a sophistication in her, a natural elegance that Isabel lacked. Maybe it was the environment these two women had grown up in. Isabel was urban, arty, adaptable. This woman looked like she had been tested by harsh winds and seas, and maybe a few harsh men too.

Watching her work was a pleasure.

She cleaned the fish. The knife was precise and firm, the cuts practiced and economical. Declan focused on her hands. The ballet of her hands. Hypnotic. Meditative. Till the acute shrieks of the seagulls attracted by the shreds she threw in the harbor broke the spell. He thought that if he could watch her clean fish tonight, he might not need a pill.

"I bet you could clean them with your eyes closed." Declan raised his voice above the shrillness of the birds.

She didn't respond. The knife stopped cutting for a fraction of a second then resumed its capable task.

"Would you take me out fishing, one fine clear day?"

She seemed to gather herself. The straightening started at the waist and ended in the neck. She kept her back to him. "Does my boat look like a charter to you, Mister?"

The accent was so New England it came with barnacles. It was a caricature. It reminded Declan of the drawl that he calibrated to fit the circumstances, or the Irish he injected in his *one fine clear day*. She threw his con back at him.

"Maybe you can point me in the right direction. Not the marina. Not my scene." Declan didn't intend to give up without a fight. This woman would despise him for it. Somehow it mattered.

"You can lay a few bills on it?" She turned around to look at him.

There was that blink he was familiar with. She was sizing him up. Was he a lightweight, a non-entity to be shoved aside with a shrug? Declan resisted standing taller. He had a few puffs left in his cigar and he made the best use of them. Her dark stare told him she was not fooled.

"I'm not interested in a miracle catch. I just want to go out there."

"You said you wanted to go fishing."

"How would you have reacted if I'd said I wanted to go on a cruise?"

A hint of a smile. "Mike might take you. Mike Hannigan, on the *Sea Robin*. She's further down the dock."

Declan crushed the butt of his cigar under his boot heel.

"Much obliged." He should have tipped his non-existent Stetson at that point. "Can I say who referred me? For legitimacy."

She pinched her lips to repress a smile. "Kate Redmont. Who are you?"

"Declan Shaw."

She turned her back to him, and resumed working on her catch.

Declan walked the length of the seawall, identified the *Sea Robin*, and went back to his car. Kate Redmont. Mike Hannigan. Maybe Jean Heyzer knew them.

• • •

"Xandra can see you tomorrow morning, after ten," Isabel said, as soon as he walked into the gallery. "I negotiated a good deal on shipping. But you'll have to find a way to get the painting to your rooftop loft."

"An artist friend of mine lives on the ground floor. He knows everything about moving big things. His sculptures wouldn't fit in your gallery." Declan signed the credit card slip. He was now the proud owner of *Sea Rhapsody*.

"It'll ship in a couple of days. You'll get an email with the expected delivery date."

It wasn't the best time to tell her about his decision to blow off their dinner date, but Declan didn't want to string her along. "About tonight …"

"You want a rain check?"

She looked disappointed. It was flattering. "I won't subject you to another meltdown. I plan to stay away from the dope tonight. I have to do it alone."

"Because I would get the pills at the first alert."

He came to her side of the desk and leaned down to kiss her. It was a tender kiss but it wasn't what she wanted. She threw her arms around his neck and kissed him back, hard.

Her warm hands were under his jacket, pulling at his shirt, fingers inside his waistband. He grabbed her wrists and she resisted, not to be denied.

"The door," he said.

In a couple of seconds, she was at the door, locked it, and turned the little board to show *Closed*. She also switched off the lights.

He took her right there, on the desk, with the laptop pushed to the side and the documents all over the floor. The violence of their coupling, the suddenness of his release, made him dizzy.

He pulled up his jeans with trembling hands and leaned on the desk, eyes closed for what seemed longer than the sex act.

"Are you all right?" Isabel reached for his shoulder and he shivered as if she'd touched an open wound.

"Nerves are raw." His voice too was raw. He was spitting needles.

Isabel fixed her dress and went down on her knees to gather the leaflets and catalogs scattered around the desk as if a gust of wind had blown in.

"Let me help you," he said.

"It's done already."

She was angry at him. Maybe angry at herself too. She set the events in motion and wasn't satisfied with the result. Welcome to the wonderful world of sex between thinking adults, he wanted to tell her. The mechanics are as natural as breathing and everything else is not.

"I should go," Declan said. "Will you come with me to see Xandra tomorrow?"

"She hates it when I sit in on interviews. She thinks I'm there to monitor her. She doesn't realize that if she puts her foot in her mouth, *her* career suffers, not mine."

"I'll call you later."

He was near the door pulling his cigar case out, when she called after him.

"Declan? I … I don't know why …"

"Hey, I didn't run away blushing." He smiled. "We can't always do the slow burn."

She rearranged a stack of papers that didn't need rearranging. "It wasn't very good for you. I used you."

He sighed. "An equal opportunity offense. It wasn't the best fuck and it wasn't the worst. In two minutes it will be a distant memory. We have a benchmark now. In our next quiet post-coital moment, we'll ponder: plus or minus versus the desk?"

She stared at him, dumbfounded. Then she smiled and the planets were properly aligned again.

• • •

Declan stopped at the grocery store and the liquor store to get salad stuff, energy bars for his hikes, a bottle of wine, and a good whiskey. He seldom got drunk on expensive booze. It was a waste when you couldn't taste anything anymore after two drinks. At the cabin, he took his fourth shower of the day. He was a one-man water conservation disaster.

The salad was tasty and the wine cold. He ate with the TV on a news channel. It was hard not to think about the looming overnight ordeal. He was running an online search on Kate Redmont, Mike Hannigan, and Gabriel Schulman when his phone rang. It was Carlton Marsh's publisher, Andy Hulten.

"Can you come to New York?" Hulten said. "I want you to meet Jennie Watts, Carlton's lawyer, and we should discuss next steps."

"Any news?"

"Jen had a long conversation with Chief Halston. She agrees with you. She said Halston was solid and straightforward. Which in this case might not help much."

"Now I'm intrigued," Declan said.

"I'll let Jen explain face-to-face. The cops got in touch with

Jack Corvill. He has an ironclad alibi. He was at a Montreal shindig the night Carlton died. The cops have photos and video footage. Anyway, he'll be back at that artist retreat some time tomorrow. Don't rush to go see him. Chief Halston gets first dibs. When can you be here?"

"Day after tomorrow. I have an appointment at the art colony tomorrow for a heart-to-heart with one of the artists."

"How did you swing that?"

"I bought a painting."

"Ah, so simple. If we come to an agreement with Jen, you might be able to expense it."

Something was brewing. The publisher wouldn't dangle that carrot if it was just small talk.

"Without knowing how much I paid for it, Andy? I'll take the commuter train from New Haven."

Declan got on his tablet and started a file. He recorded names and addresses, connections, and all the pieces of information he had gathered so far, and emailed the document to Moira Perkins, his agency partner, with a short memo for background. It was a habit born of painful mistakes. He had misplaced notes, lost phones and computer files. He was a firm believer in back-ups.

Moira must have been online because she called immediately. "I thought you were rehabbing in cool climes."

"And doing research for a friend. He allegedly committed suicide."

"And because he's a friend, you think he didn't," Moira said. "If you decided to retire to a monastery, you would manage to find monks hanky-pankying."

"People misbehave, it's what makes them human."

"I'll have that printed on our business cards. Anything you want me to do?"

He was tempted to give her the web searches but he needed something to do to keep him busy tonight. Dope and boredom were a hellish combo. "I want to gather more info before I ask you to jump in. How's the business going?"

"You've been gone three days. We haven't filed for bankruptcy yet."

"You're a rock, Moira. Talk to you later."

• • •

Kate Redmont wasn't a salty fisherman's daughter. She was a Columbia sociology professor. Born in Old Mapleton, daughter of Royce Cavendish and Amelia Linder.

Cavendish. Declan knew that name from somewhere. Ah, yes, Bill Heyzer mentioned it when he talked about the old families. There was Marsh, Anderson, Cavendish. And another one. Morton. Declan's memory was a reliable instrument. He wrote down the names.

Kate Redmont's Columbia page listed her publications. Her specialty was social theory. She studied in Melbourne, Australia, then transferred to Yale for her postgraduate. A deeper search revealed that she was thirty years old and divorced. She must be on good terms with her ex or she would have ditched his name.

What was she doing in Old Mapleton? School had started. Did she commute to New York? Declan scribbled questions. Melbourne. Underlined.

There wasn't much on Mike Hannigan. An obituary for Brigid Doyle Hannigan who died five years ago *after a long illness*, code for cancer. She was thirty-two. She was survived by her husband, Michael, and their daughter Bernadette. The captain of the *Sea Robin* was a single dad. Unless he remarried, but nothing showed he did.

The online search on Gabriel Schulman returned a shower of information. Press releases about the art colony, exhibitions at the galleries. He owned four. New York, L.A., Miami and the odd duck, Old Mapleton. He got wealthy making real estate deals in Florida but the data was sketchy, as was his biography. Apparently, he was born in Miami, no date provided. The oldest article mentioning him was about a mall project in the mid-nineties in the suburbs of Fort Lauderdale. The gallery addresses were unusual. The New York shop was in Queens, in a middle-class area. Decent but too off-center to draw the moneyed elite. It was the same in L.A., and the Miami gallery was in a suburban strip mall. Was the mall a Schulman development? Moira could sink her teeth in the guy. None of these galleries could possibly be making a fat profit. It smelled of money laundering, Bill Heyzer's hunch.

It was a little after eleven. A decent time to turn in for the night.

• • •

Declan had been asleep for a couple hours when the pain jerked him awake. It was a repeat of the night with Isabel. The sweating, the shakes, muscles seizing, difficulty breathing, heart beating like a steel drum. He didn't muffle the screams. The cabin was near the top of the hill, far from the lodge and the other cottages. Jean put him in the remotest cabin because he didn't mind the steep walk up from the parking lot.

He fell off the bed twice. The second time he was in too much pain to climb back in and remained on the floor. He couldn't cover the distance to the bathroom to get the pills. Solitary detox wasn't such a brilliant idea. He thought his heart would give up.

When the torture ended, hours later, he had lost his voice, his knuckles were raw from banging on the floor, and his knees were bruised from knocking against the bed frame. He tasted blood, from his nose that he had punched somehow. He didn't try to get in bed. He wrapped himself in the comforter, shivering with fever and exhaustion.

• • •

Jean Heyzer found him in the morning. She said she knew he was in because she had seen him park the BMW. She got worried when he didn't answer the knock at the door and the ring of the phone. Her cool hand on his forehead was soothing.

"Dear God, what happened?" She helped him get on the bed.

"The doc prescribed painkillers for my leg and I want to stop taking them. It's difficult."

"I'll make coffee. Go take a shower. You look like shit."

She did more than make coffee. She toasted bread and scrambled eggs, and sat at the little table waiting for him to emerge. "Do you need the medicine?"

"The leg is healed but I have to keep moving. The pills have a life of their own, Jean. I had a shaky hold on them when I left Houston, and my first two nights here have been a nightmare. Yesterday, I decided to stop taking the medication. I'm a wreck but it has to be done."

The eggs were fantastic. What did they feed their chickens in this town?

"You should sleep at the lodge when you're doing this withdrawal thing. It's not safe to be alone. You could have knocked yourself out." Jean pointed at his swollen nose. "It looks like you tried."

"I'm loud," he said.

"You haven't heard Bill snore. Stay at the lodge tonight, Declan. Unless you have a better offer. She sure is a cutie."

Gossip ran at Olympic record speeds around Old Mapleton. "Who squealed?"

"Small towns. We're more effective than these cameras that track people."

"I might stay another week," Declan said.

"I reckon."

SIX

JUNO OR QUEEN BOADICEA. Declan shook hands with Xandra Mohr. A firm handshake to match a strong personality. He understood why the tall, handsome, Black woman did not want Isabel hovering near when she talked to visitors.

"You're younger than I expected." She jammed her hands down the pockets of her paint-splattered jumpsuit. "What possessed you to buy my piece?"

"It's the ocean I feel when I dream of an ocean. Disquiet on top, cavernous enticement below. I didn't think I'd be able to afford it but the price was absurdly low."

Seeing how her fists balled in her pockets, it was clear she didn't set the price tag.

"I painted it three years ago. I've moved on. Are you scouring local art galleries looking for deals? To find the next Basquiat in the woods?"

"I came to see Carlton Marsh. You know him?"

She stiffened. "Let me show you what I'm working on. That's why you're here, right?"

A door in the back led to her large work space. The studio

was bright, and the view of the sea was unexpected. The winding road through the forest had scrambled Declan's sense of direction. Three paintings were propped on easels giving the impression she worked on all three at the same time. The pieces differed in subtle details and were meant to be displayed together. She said she was still painting a water universe. It wasn't a turbulent ocean that inspired her this time, more the gentle, oily swells of a deep lake traversed by conflicting currents. The silky surface was sensual with a transparency that made Declan want to touch the canvas. The progression of the three pieces was toward increasing turmoil, in color and texture.

"I wish I had more walls," Declan said. "You play with my heartstrings, Ms. Mohr."

"Call me Alex. Xandra is for the catalogs."

"Don't show this at Isthmus. It deserves better."

She perched on a stepladder and pointed at a stool for him. "What's your relationship with Carlton Marsh?"

"He was an old friend. He asked me to help with research for his book. How did you come in contact with him?"

"Like you, he admired *Rhapsody*." She smiled. "He didn't go as far as buying it."

"There isn't enough room at the villa."

"He agreed with you, he didn't want my trilogy to gather dust at Isthmus. He said he'd help me … Can I offer you something? Carlton left a bottle of cava in the fridge. I'd rather drink it with a friend of his."

They toasted the memory of Carlton Marsh. Xandra-Alex said Carlton planned to get her an interview and photo session with a *Times* reporter to raise her profile with agents and galleries.

"Are you under some sort of contract with Isthmus?" Declan said.

"Schulman gets fifty percent of what I produce while I'm here. It's the same for all colony residents."

"It's steep."

She swirled the wine in her glass. "We live rent free. No water bill, no electricity bill. The problem is that the sales don't bring enough. I can afford supplies. I just can't save enough to move out and get my own studio." She had a sip of wine.

"With the work you do, I'd think an agent would be eager to snatch you."

She chuckled. "It's a closed world. Referrals, buddies, art schools. I'm self-taught. I can't get a foot in the door. I was at the end of my rope when Schulman rescued me. I keep reminding myself of that."

Declan didn't doubt Schulman laid on the gratitude shtick pretty heavy. Bill Heyzer had to be right. Why would Schulman sink money in low-tier galleries and an art colony that might not even cover the utilities? It reeked of a scam.

"Are your fellow residents in the same situation?"

"Have you seen their work?"

"I saw what's at the gallery. I was not impressed," Declan said.

"Cass Holborn is good. She's a sculptor. Metal."

"The exploded raven. Cute bird."

She shot him a glance. "You need to have your head examined."

"How did you run into Schulman?"

While doing the rounds of New York galleries to try to get a spot on a wall. One afternoon, she walked into Isthmus. "Schulman was there. He liked what I brought and displayed it right away. He looked at my book and told me about the colony."

"You didn't think it was fishy?"

"And how! I thought it was human trafficking, or a cult. He gave me money for the trip, told me to come have a look, and call him if I was interested."

Declan refilled her glass.

"And here I am with a bunch of other misfits."

"You're not a misfit, Alex. What about Carlton's boyfriend, Jack Corvill, is he any good?"

"All he knows about art is that Picasso was a stud. Jack knows how to do some things with a brush but none of them includes slapping paint on a canvas in a meaningful way."

"Ouch. Carlton must have liked something in him."

"The something hanging between his legs. Jack is good looking, in a sleazy way that some people find attractive." It was clear she didn't. "Jack knows how to play the anguished artist. There's a lot of flash and hot air in the art world. Jack will find himself a wealthy patron, and retire to a location with a view."

"Some kind of artistry," Declan said. "I might be able to help you, Alex. I don't have Carlton's connections, but I did some work for a collector. A real one, not a cash-strapped amateur like me. He's always eager for new talent. His name is Bernie Mellon, look him up. I'll ask Bernie to get in touch. If he's interested he'll pay a fair price for your trilogy, or whatever else you may want to show him. Do you have to sell through the gallery?"

"I sell from the studio sometimes. Schulman doesn't care, he gets his fifty percent anyway. You don't have to do this."

Declan could see she itched to ask questions. Her foot tapped the stepladder while she pondered.

"What kind of work did you do for that guy, Mellon?"

"I'm a private detective. I recovered paintings for him."

"Detective. Yeah. You have a way of asking questions. Did Carlton really kill himself?"

"It looks like it. Schulman wants to meet me. What should I expect?"

"I need a cigarette," she said. "Can't smoke in here. There's a small porch in the back."

Two plastic chairs and an ashtray on a wooden crate furnished the deck. Declan lit her cigarette and got one of his cigarillos. Old Mapleton was not visible, only the sea, hundred and eighty degrees of sea. Fishing boats were out. He wondered if Kate Redmont's was among them.

"Didn't Isabel tell you about Schulman?" Alex said. "Aren't you fucking her?"

Declan puffed on his cigar.

"Old-fashioned discretion, I see. I don't live in town but I know that the steamy romance *Isabel and the Stranger* is top of the best-sellers' list."

"Old Mapleton is amazing," Declan said. "What baffles me is that in a place where people know everything about everybody, nobody has anything worth a damn to say about Carlton's suicide."

"Killing yourself is a very private event."

So was making love to Isabel. "Who's Gabriel Schulman?"

"Gimme time to gather my feeble brains, Sam Spade," she croaked.

"Come on, Alex. You don't like the guy, and it chafes because you can't drop him. I think he's running some kind of con."

"You think it has something to do with Carlton Marsh?" she said.

"He was one hell of an investigative reporter. If I can smell something rotten, Carlton must have gagged on it."

"I came here five years ago and the colony had been going on for a while. Schulman seems to be in his sixties. He hasn't gone to seed. He's a big success at the country club. Rich and into the arts, what's not to like."

"You went to parties with him?"

She made a face, crushed her cigarette, and lit another. All in one smooth move and too fast for Declan to do the gentleman thing with the lighter. "Once. That was interesting. You know, the *Elephant Man* movie, with the people paying to see the freak? They didn't throw peanuts at me but it was close."

"They weren't going to throw the olives soaking in their martinis. It would have been a waste."

"You tend to run at the mouth, don't you? Ever been smacked because of it?"

"Ayuh, as they say in New England."

"It's a stuffy town, full of stuffy hypocrites. They tried to reel Carlton in. They invited him to parties, cocktails, dances. He showed up with the most outrageous partner he could find. Eventually, they gave up. He hated every single one of them. Of course, they fawn over Schulman. They *adore* him. I think he's playing them. Or he enjoys the attention."

"They give him status in the community. It must be worth something to him." Maybe not financially. Alex was right, it could be an ego trip. Self-made man craves acceptance. "He might have something to prove."

"In Old Mapleton? Not shooting too high, is he?"

She had a point. What gratification could anybody get from the admiration of blue-haired country club matrons? They smoked in silence, looking at the sea. This ocean wasn't like Xandra Mohr's paintings.

Then she hurled an unexpected spear at him. "Don't trust Isabel. She isn't true."

"If you mean she's a clever opportunist, I agree with you," Declan said.

"We're tainted by the company we keep."

That hit home. He pictured Kate Redmont on the fishing harbor dock, her hard, angular face, an uncompromising etching. He remembered how Kate handled the sharp knife.

How he took Isabel on the metal desk.

"Wouldn't it be nice if we always knew without a doubt where we're going," he said. "I'll call Bernie Mellon."

SEVEN

DECLAN DROVE BACK to town and had a couple of crab cakes at an outdoor café near the commercial harbor. The boats were in. He went to seek out Mike Hannigan and the *Sea Robin*. Maybe he would catch another glimpse of Kate Redmont. He knew enough about her now to have a conversation that didn't revolve around fish guts.

Kate's boat, the *Yarra Moon*, looked deserted. A girl, ten or twelve, was busy with brush and bucket on the deck of the *Sea Robin*. It was after three, school was done for the day.

"Hey there," Declan said. "Do you know where I can find Mike Hannigan?"

"What's it about?"

"Kate Redmont sent me. You know her?"

The girl leaned inside the cabin door. "Da! There's a guy to see you. Kate sent him."

The smell of fish was pervasive. No amount of scrubbing and scraping could ever get rid of it. It had permeated every plank of the old boat.

Hannigan emerged from the cabin. He wiped his hands on

a dirty rag. Curly auburn hair, a field of freckles, and washed out blue eyes. Forty something. Like Kate Redmont his features were angular, carved by wind and sea. A nylon rope held his cotton pants up. They hung loose on his bony frame. He gave Declan a long look. His wide mouth pinched in distaste.

Declan thought: *This guy dislikes me.* And he knew why right away.

"Kate, uh? What's the deal?"

"None yet but there might be one. Mind if I come aboard?"

"Aye."

The natives were not friendly.

Hannigan stepped onto the dock. His sulky attitude reeked of mistrust. He did that little head to the side shift that Declan associated with rogue dogs and knife-wielding juvenile delinquents. In response, Declan pulled out his cigar case. He lit up, careful not to meet Hannigan's eyes. There would be a challenge in them, he knew the type. The captain of the *Sea Robin* was older than the punks he too often had the misfortune of dealing with but this was New England. Maybe they blossomed later. A cooler climate thing.

"I asked Kate who would agree to take me on a jaunt out there and she suggested I talk to you." Omitting her last name did the trick. Hannigan paled. The dude pined for the woman. Was she interested in him? Declan twisted the knife. "She implied you could use the dough." Color flushed into Hannigan's face. The freckles popped out. There was a dangerous light in the pale eyes. "I'm Declan Shaw. Donegal roots. You?"

It took Hannigan by surprise. "Cork," he blurted. The color faded from his cheeks. He shook his head, as if he needed to clear it from drunken cobwebs. "What's that got to do with anything?"

"I figured, if I have to spend some coin, might as well do it with another potato eater. Except you're more into fish than chips."

Hannigan moved his weight from one leg to the other. He loosened up, boxer-style. "You have a mouth on you. What's the idea?"

Declan told him that he was in town for a few days and it seemed stupid to stay on land when there was all that water everywhere he looked. Kate Redmont didn't want to take him out—that pleased Hannigan—but she suggested Mike.

"I'm not geared for sport," Hannigan said. "I don't have swivel chairs and rods and lines and all that. I catch fish for a living, if it can be called a living."

"I don't give a fuck about catching the kind of fish you stick on a wall. I just want to see the land from afar for a few hours. I'd ask you to take me on a work day but I might be in the way. You go out every day of the week?"

"I try to keep Sunday off. Unless the weather's good. The tough season will be on us mighty fast." Hannigan stared at Declan again. Straight on this time. The feral tilt was gone. It made him a lot more pleasant. "We could try Sunday. If we run into a good one, I might get some business done. How much you're laying down?"

"Five hundred," Declan said.

"Eight."

Declan knew hard knocks but that was too much. "Six."

They haggled and cut a deal at six fifty. All-day trip.

"I won't shake hands because they're not presentable," Hannigan said, "but we're square. Sunday at five. You're staying in town? I gotta check the radar before we leave."

"At the Heyzer camp."

"I'll call you at four thirty to confirm. Your number?"

All set. Declan was surprised Hannigan didn't ask him how he knew Kate Redmont. Maybe he didn't want to know.

• • •

An elderly couple was at the gallery when Declan walked in. Isabel gave him a quick warning glance. The clients were in the tourist section where multiple versions of harbor views competed with forest paths and quaint small-town streets. It looked like the potential buyers were close to a decision.

The woman pointed at a canvas. "I like this one best, Harry. That spot of color on the dock is a perfect match for the dining room drapes. It will go well with our other picture, the one we bought in Italy. They're the same size."

Declan turned to hide the smile that threatened to turn into a chuckle and studied a vivid abstract composition. The green circle in the middle was the same color as the lamp on Moira's desk. Maybe he should get it.

"We always buy something for the house on our trips," Harry, the husband, said.

"It's a great idea," Isabel said. "Taking photographs is all right, but how often do you look at them again, while an object is part of your daily life. It brings back all the memories."

The Boston accent that she didn't bother to hide when she talked to Declan had vanished. She also slowed down her speech tempo to match the clients'. It was a superb performance. She was an instinctive mimic, a key talent when success depends on your ability to read others. Salespeople, interrogators, crooks.

"It's a road trip this time," the woman said. "We always buy more on road trips."

"Load the good ole chariot," Harry said.

"Where are you coming from?" Isabel said. "I'm always interested in knowing who visits our community. I had a traveler from Texas a few days ago."

"That cowboy wandered far from the ranch," Harry said. "We came from Fairfax, Virginia. We might drive as far up as Maine."

"I told Harry, we're a little early for the foliage."

"It's starting to change," Isabel said. "It will be beautiful in the woods, as you go north."

"But we're taking all your time, dear," the woman said. "Shouldn't you attend to this handsome young man? He seems very interested in the modern pictures." She giggled. "Not my thing. We've decided, haven't we, Harry?"

"Pack the goods, girl."

Isabel plucked the harbor scene from the wall and walked over to Declan.

"I will be with you in a few minutes, sir."

Declan smiled at the elderly couple. They looked like kind grandparents at a dance watching awkward young couples try new steps.

"I'll be right back." Isabel took the canvas to the storage room in the back.

Declan noticed she walked straight and kept her hips from swaying. She knew she had three pairs of eyes staring at her backside. He broke his contemplation and focused on the label affixed next to a loud and busy piece. Ironically, it was a still life.

"This is horrible," the woman said. "Why do they show such things? What is it?"

"It looks like a gutted bird," Harry said. "I've seen prettier roadkill."

Declan knew they stood by the raven. He thought the sculpture was hilarious. Not everybody shared his sense of humor.

"It reminds me of what Lisa did with the pumpkin, at the carving party, with all the kids," the woman said. "It was like the insides had exploded. And Lisa and her friends laughed their heads off. I can't look at this thing anymore."

"Let's sit a minute. You've been on your feet all day."

From the corner of his eye, Declan saw Harry take his wife's arm to lead her toward the desk and the visitor chair. Good people with bad taste. Well, that was subjective, wasn't it? *Tous les goûts sont dans la nature.* He was a snobbish jerk. Harry and his wife acquired an original from a local artist to decorate their house. They could have driven to the nearest big box store and bought some mass-produced shlock. But they didn't. They wanted something real, made by a painter who signed it.

Isabel came back with the canvas as carefully wrapped as if it had to go in a plane cargo hold.

"The certificate of authenticity is in a sealed pocket attached to the back. I recommend that you leave it there, otherwise it might get lost."

"It comes with a certificate?" the woman said.

"Oh yes, we insist on it. We also keep track of all the pieces we sell." Isabel smiled. "In case there is an exhibition or a retrospective of the artist's work. It's useful to know who owns what where. Your name doesn't appear, of course, for privacy reasons, the reference just says the artwork is part of a private collection."

Damn, she was good. Declan should put her on retainer. In case he decided to run a confidence scheme.

Harry paid for their purchase and Isabel insisted on carrying the package to their car. They were parked in front.

● ● ●

"I would have bought the other harbor scene, or even better, both," Declan said.

"They're identical."

"There are noticeable differences even if the subject matter is the same, and together they make a statement."

Isabel sneered. "What statement?"

"That life is a study in repetition."

"You should have told that to the buyers." Her smile mocked him.

"You did a fantastic job, by the way. They will tell their friends about the pretty blond girl at the gallery who was so friendly, not at all snooty like others in these kinds of establishments."

"Like I'm some glorified shop girl."

He'd sensed she was prepared for a fight from the moment he

walked in. He wasn't going to humor her. A fit of anger would lead to tears, and a sack romp he couldn't afford. He needed another solitary night to fight the omnipotent pill.

"Don't you want to know how my visit with Xandra Mohr went?"

"I'm sure she made a big impression." Isabel sat behind her desk and hit the laptop keys as if they belonged to an antique typewriter. Appropriate clanking sounds would have helped.

"She's too good to be stuck in Old Mapleton."

Isabel sniffled. "She can go anytime. Nobody's stopping her."

"Why doesn't Schulman organize a show for her? He could hire a PR firm, do an advertising blast, and recoup his investment tenfold. I don't understand his strategy for running this place."

"Ask him. He should be in town this weekend." Isabel stopped hammering the keyboard. She pulled a sheet from the printer and dropped the document in a drawer. "What do you want, Declan? You didn't call this morning. I worried about you all day, then you saunter in, as if nothing happened, and you want to talk about stupid paintings. Are you tired of me already?"

She had grounds for complaint.

"The night was as nasty as I expected it to be. I'm glad you weren't there. I'll do it again tonight. Jean Heyzer asked me to stay at the lodge. For safety reasons. I gave her a bad scare this morning."

He saw her entire body relax. "We could have dinner, nothing as fancy as last time. There's a seafood restaurant at the marina that's quite good. We can walk to it. Cocktails at my place."

He had no good reason to decline. "You mean I don't have to buy a piece this time?" She looked for something to throw at him. "Actually, I want to buy your raven. Bundle it with the other shipment."

"Seriously?"

"It turns people off. The woman commented on it while you

were wrapping their purchase. It's one of the first things prospects see when they walk in. If it was Halloween week, it would make folks smile. This time of year, it's creepy."

"But you want it."

"It's a good fit for my office. My *Maltese Falcon*, you know?" But she didn't know. The allusion drifted miles above her head. Declan didn't feel like explaining. "What do you want for it?"

The price tag was fifteen hundred. Gabriel Schulman might be a savvy real estate developer but his art radar was way off.

"I close at five," Isabel said. "We can make it an early evening. That would be on the safe side for you. You never have a crisis in daylight, do you?"

"Cross fingers. I'd like to pay for the bird now. And I will need the certificate of authenticity."

"You're an asshole."

The Boston accent was back.

EIGHT

THE BMW PULLED in around nine. Jean Heyzer had almost given up on Declan heeding her advice. She couldn't compete with the gallery girl. Jean didn't believe *all* the gossip, but the girl had been seen with different men over the summer. Evening pick-ups and morning drop-offs. Expensive cars. None of the men lived in Old Mapleton. At least the girl was discreet that way. Don't shit where you eat, as Bill would say. With New Haven nearby and the college life, there wasn't a shortage of eligible males to choose from. Jean believed the girl was after money.

If that was the case, Declan was the wrong choice. He wasn't rich and he wasn't in a business that would make him rich. And he didn't strike Jean as the marrying kind. What her mother would have called, with a sour mouth, a *womanizer*. The word conjured a thin mustache, slicked-back hair, tight suits, and a big wallop of sleaze. None of that fit Declan. She thought he was a man who loved women; loved to hop in bed with them. She doubted his infatuations lasted very long. He seemed impatient. It was the way he asked questions. He sorted through data, was quick to dismiss what was irrelevant, and in a hurry to move on.

He did it for a living. Work a case. Close a case. Next case. Pity the woman who falls in love with him. He was a moving target.

Jean didn't pity the gallery girl. She was a hard little bitch.

She lit a match under the kettle on the stove. She had no experience with addicts and withdrawal but she had an unshakable belief in herbal tea. She treasured her collection of infusions and with the forest nearby she collected her own herb supply. Bill often joked that he married a healer. Or a witch. Unfortunately, she hadn't yet found the miracle cure for his cataclysmic snoring.

She was about to trudge up the path to the cabin to inquire about Declan's intentions when he came in. He carried a backpack.

"I decided to accept your offer." He handed her a pill bottle. "To use only in the most dire circumstances. And then, only one."

"Your room is on top of the stairs, right in front. There's a communication door with the room I'll use tonight."

"Deserting Bill?" he said, with a smile.

"I told him what you were going through. He doesn't have the stomach for pain. Bill is a softie. He fainted when I delivered our first son. For the next two he waited in the hallway."

"I don't know what to expect tonight, Jean. Why am I fine during the day? It's not logical. If I craved the dope, I should crave it all the time, not just after sunset."

A shrug twisted his body sideways, in a sort of what-the-hell question mark that made Jean smile. He was a kid under that grown-up street-wise cleverness. She could see what he must have looked like at fifteen or sixteen, all gangly, with a mop of dark hair and these green eyes, and a smile that said I dare you. She swallowed and bit her lower lip to keep the tears from welling up, damn it.

"Maybe you're a vampire in reverse," she said, "or a werewolf going through the change. I'll keep a spike and hammer in reach. Drop your stuff upstairs and join us in the lounge. We'll play a board game, or cards, have a nightcap, and lively conversation. Sounds good?"

"I warn you, I'm a damn good poker player. I'll take you for everything you got."

"We play for beans."

· · ·

He wasn't boasting. He was an excellent poker player. He soon had enough beans in front of him to feed a family.

"Where did you learn to play like that?" Bill had a few legumes left.

"In New Orleans, years ago. And I have a photographic memory," Declan said.

"Flagged in casinos?"

"I don't play in casinos. I prefer the private games, where I know the people. They won't slap me around afterwards because they think I can't possibly be that good and I pulled a fast one."

Jean didn't tell him that she didn't like smoking in the house. She didn't mind the smell of his cigar and she liked the way he squinted when the smoke enveloped him. It was exciting to watch him shuffle the cards—he had long-fingered hands—and deal almost in slow motion, with the cheroot stuck in the corner of his mouth. The warm feeling in her tummy was at once enjoyable and bothersome.

These errant thoughts didn't help her focus on the game and she gave her beans to Bill. She fixed fresh drinks for the men. Scotch drinkers both. Watered down for Bill. He had his serious face on. He was overmatched but he wouldn't go down without a fight. She loved him for that. She also loved him when he folded his cards and conceded.

"You convinced me to stick to the minor leagues, son," Bill

said. "It takes a special kind of mind to play like you do. There's very little luck involved."

"A little. Nothing that can't be overcome." Declan smiled that sad-sweet smile that went all the way to his eyes and made Jean swallow dry.

Out of nowhere, Bill said: "You've had a hard life."

"Nothing that can't be overcome," Declan said again. There was no smile this time. His eyes had lost their amused twinkle and for a brief moment he seemed to have withdrawn so deep inside himself that he was no longer there for Jean to see. Then, as suddenly, he was back. He gathered the beans and returned them to the cloth bag. "Do these go to the game room or the pantry?"

"They'll go in a slow cooker," Jean said. "We're a thrifty lot. It's almost eleven. What do you think, Bill, time to call it a day?"

"I didn't realize it was that late." Bill sounded uncertain.

Jean knew he had questions. They had raised three boys, their youngest was about Declan's age, and Bill had always managed to bond with them, even during the confused teenage years. He wanted to slip into the dad role and feared he would be rebuked.

"I'll go up with you," Jean said. "Is it too early for you, Declan?"

"I need to check email. I'm supposed to meet Carlton's publisher and his lawyer tomorrow."

"Are they coming here?"

"I'll catch the train to New York."

Really? He expected a repeat of the ordeal of the past night and planned a trip to New York? It was foolish. "You might have to cancel," she said.

"I was fine all day."

Jean recognized that frown and the way he thrust his chin forward. Just like her sons, or Bill for that matter, when their minds were set and no amount of arguing would convince them otherwise.

"Well, you know where I'll be if you need anything," she said.

She went to the master bathroom to brush her teeth and take her pills. Bill was in there doing the same.

"He didn't like what I said. I didn't mean anything bad."

"We're complete strangers," Jean said. "Why would he tell us private things? He isn't the kind that gushes out at the slightest prompt."

"He told you about his drug problem. That's damn private, don't you think?"

"He didn't have a choice. I was about to call nine-one-one."

She doubted she would sleep much but put on a pair of pajamas anyway and a flannel robe that used to belong to Bill. He had discarded it saying it turned him into a geezer. She also took her phone, a book, and her clothes.

"You can come back here to get dressed in the morning, you know," Bill said, amused.

"I don't want to wake you if I have to leave during the night. I mean, if I have to take him to the hospital, or get something from the pharmacy. I don't know, Bill. I just like to be prepared." She got on tiptoes to kiss him. "Maybe I just worry silly and nothing will happen."

• • •

And for a couple of hours nothing happened.

Jean read for a while but couldn't keep her eyes open. The communication door between the two rooms was ajar—Declan had opened it and wished her good night when he came up a half hour after she did—and she couldn't hear anything. It was so quiet without the deep rumble of Bill's snoring that it troubled her. Still, she fell asleep.

When Bill asked her what happened and Jean tried to recall the sequence of events, she couldn't tell what woke her. It wasn't a scream. Maybe it wasn't a noise at all but a sense of imminent danger, an old instinct tucked away in the remnants of the primitive brain. The sense that there was something with teeth lurking in the dark depth of that cavern. Whatever it was, it jerked her awake in alarm.

She ran to Declan's bed and switched on the lamp on the bedside table. He moaned. The sheets and the comforter were on the floor. One of the pillows was a good distance from the bed where his flailing arm had sent it. His T-shirt was soaked with sweat; his face and arms were coated with it; his hair dripped with it. He looked like a nightmare, a mask carved in wood, sunken cheeks that made his cheekbones look so sharp Jean expected to see blood where they pierced the skin. The eyes were pools of tar. Then he screamed.

The pill bottle was next door, in her room, in the first drawer of the dresser, and she went to get it. His heart would give, she was certain of it. These were the extreme circumstances he talked about. Let him have relief. He could check into a clinic later, with proper medical supervision, cared for by people who knew what they were doing and how far they could let the crisis go.

All this went through her head like lightning. She was halfway to the door when he started retching. He hung his head over the side of the bed and his body's wild jerks made him fall to the floor. His head barely missed the corner of the night table.

Jean went back to the bed. The pill would have to wait. He could hurt himself, knock against the furniture. There was no way she could lift him or carry him. She grabbed his ankles, not an easy thing to do, he bucked like a wild animal, and a kicking foot glanced off her hip bone. She winced. A bruise would bloom there soon. She dragged him away from the furniture, helped by the small rug by the side of the bed. She was glad she had not yet bought the anti-slip strips that Bill kept bugging her about.

As soon as she let go of his ankles, Declan curled in a fetal position. He howled and banged his head against the floor, and now she had to take care of that. She got a pillow, grabbed his head by the slick wet hair, and slipped the cushion underneath. He retched again. There wasn't much. The puke was whisky-infused. Jean went to the bathroom and brought back a wet towel to wipe off his face. He struck a fist at her but she was cautious now and avoided the blow.

"I should get a rope and tie you up. Jesus. Settle down. I'm trying to help, you idiot."

The cool wet towel seemed to pacify him some and she went to get another one. He burned with fever, she could feel the unnatural heat through the towel. He was also dehydrating. When she told Bill she could see his heart beating through the sticky T-shirt, he stared at her in disbelief. But it was true. His heart beat much too fast and his raspy breath sounded like a boat dragged over gravel. His teeth clacked and the shivers made Jean cringe.

Then it got worse.

His bowels and bladder emptied.

Jean's first thought was that it was lucky he wasn't in bed anymore. No funky mattress to deal with. She cringed, ashamed of her reaction. Bedding didn't matter when a man's life hung in the balance. She was convinced Declan was dying. And she was angry at him. Why did he have to kick the habit, right here, right now, in her lodge. He didn't seem to be impaired by the pills. But he had to understand the danger better than she did; he was *using*. If you could get out from under that cloud, you should, right? Jean was confused. Action always helped her get her bearings. The mess had to be cleaned. She fetched a bucket and rags.

When she came back, she found Declan calmer. He had gone limp and the screams had stopped. The frantic energy was expended. Even his breathing, still reedy, had lost its rocky edge.

"I'm sorry, Jean," he muttered, and she almost jumped out of her slippers. "I made a mess."

"I was born on a farm. Have you ever cleaned a barn, Declan?"

"I haven't had the privilege but I decided not to join the circus when I found out how much elephants pooped."

You wouldn't guess he was howling at the moon a few minutes ago. "We have to get you in the shower. I can't lift you but I can give you a solid shoulder."

It was a long, protracted effort. He got on his knees and she brought a chair for him to hold on to. He rested on it for the longest time, catching his breath.

"I'm strong," Jean said, "built square. Lean on me."

"I'm filthy."

"We have running water in Connecticut. On good days, it's even warm. Can't stop progress." Prattling steadied her and it helped her steady him.

They stumbled to the bathroom. She sat him on the toilet to remove his T-shirt. He didn't want her in there when he took off his soiled shorts but he lost his balance and crumpled to the tiled floor.

"Dear God," he mumbled.

"I gave birth to three boys, Declan, and I happen to be married to a guy. I've seen a few peckers in my life."

"You haven't seen mine."

She was relieved to see his sense of humor was back. The crisis was behind them. She helped him get in the shower. He sat on the built-in bench and she unhooked the wand. She kept it away from him until the hot water kicked in. She gave him the wand with a washcloth and a bar of soap.

"You can handle it from here. Call me when you're ready."

She collected his soiled underwear, took stock of the room, and set to work. She rolled the small rug, mopped the floor, stripped the bed, bundled the sweat-soaked sheets with the comforter and pillows, and carried everything outside. She opened a window to get rid of the smell. Maybe the stench would keep the mosquitoes out.

She went to her bathroom to clean up before going downstairs to fetch her trusted herbal remedies. Declan called when she was back in the room putting fresh sheets on the bed. He leaned against the side of the shower. The wand at his feet sprayed in every direction.

"I can't turn it off." He was irritated at his own incompetence.

Jean helped him out of the shower. He was shivering. She wrapped him in a towel and led him to the clean bed.

"I leak like a sieve," he said. "You don't want me in there."

"Don't be silly. You're pumped dry." She fixed a giant mug of herbal tea and added two big glops of honey. "You're going to drink this and another one just as big. You're dehydrated."

"I can't control my plumbing, Jean."

"Nothing that a beach towel can't fix. I'll get you diapers in the morning. I'm an old lady, nobody will bat an eye."

"You're not old." Declan drank the tea. Color was coming back in his face.

"You scared me worse than I've ever been. I was *that* close to giving you the pill."

"I'm grateful you didn't. The longer I delay the reckoning, the worse it'll get."

"Why do doctors give that stuff to people? Is it because it's easy, less complaints from patients?" She filled another mug and watched him drink. She tucked him in like she used to do with the boys when they were struck down by the multiple ailments of childhood.

"It wasn't like that for me. They inserted rods and pins down there. They worked hard on me. There was nothing easy in any of it. I needed the pills to heal. And I'm healed. Nothing wrong with the leg anymore. I made a bad decision. I was working a case, hours of surveillance, day and night. I took the pills in anticipation of a problem and I created a bigger problem in the process. I chose the easy solution, not the doctors. And I made the same mistake again, when I got here."

Jean was beat. Sitting there on the bed, with the pine smells and muted sounds of the forest at night coming through the window, she knew her age. It had been many years since she had spent a sleepless night. The last time was when Bill was in the hospital after he fell off the roof of the lodge. He was lucky. He could have died.

She stood, knees cracking, with a dull pain in the hip where Declan's foot had struck her. She would be useless all day. Well, she volunteered, didn't she? Nobody else to blame. And she believed this man was worth it. Carlton Marsh was worthy of her affection too and now he was gone. Complicated people both. Oh, God, don't let harm befall this one.

"I'll go get a towel for your leakage," she said. "I doubt it will be needed but we'll both sleep easier."

NINE

THERE WAS the disorientation of waking in a strange room compounded by the fact he was naked under the sheets, with a beach towel wrapped around his hips. He'd survived another night of mindless terror. And Jean had witnessed it all.

Declan raised on one elbow and looked at the communication door. It was closed. The room didn't look the least disturbed. One of the windows was open and he didn't remember opening it. The air was cool and crisp. His phone was on the night table and he checked the time. Ten after nine. He should be on the train to New York. He tried to stand and plonked down again, the room was twirling.

He sat on the side of the bed, hands on his knees, head down, aware of his breathing and the uneven rush of his heartbeat. The bedside rug was missing. He would forever be unable to describe what happened that night. All he knew was that it was much worse than the night before, which didn't make any sense. He endured this torture to get rid of the damn addiction. The body rebelled, shouldn't it concede at some point?

"I licked you two nights in a row, motherfucker," he muttered. "You're down. Give up."

Of course this was not the way it worked. He was fighting with the kind of freak that came back after the credits to tease a sequel. The freak also flourished unheeded in idleness.

Declan called Andrew Hulten.

"You're on the train?" the publisher said. "I'll send a car to Penn Station to pick you up."

"I came down with a bug overnight. Can we do it Monday? Sorry for the late notice."

"That's unfortunate. We can't wait, Declan."

This was not how Hulten sounded the other day. "What happened?"

"It's complicated. And fucking important."

"Can't we meet remote?"

Silence stretched on the line. "If Jen agrees … you'll have to find a place that's private and secure."

"Not a problem."

"I'll call you back."

Jean Heyzer walked out of the kitchen when Declan entered the lodge's breakfast area. Two tables were occupied, guests that had checked in the evening before. Declan remembered seeing cars in the parking lot. They must not have stayed at the lodge; his screams would have scared away a flock of banshees.

She beamed. "Good to see you."

"I slept well after you tucked me in, Mom."

She giggled. "Hush. These people don't know about us. How do you want your eggs?"

"Fried, on toast, with your biggest pot of coffee."

"Help yourself to the buffet. I recommend the banana bread."

He was famished. He was finishing the eggs when Hulten called.

"Jen was reluctant but I convinced her. I'll send you a

conference link for eleven this morning. Find a desert island, Declan, I'm not kidding."

"What bit you, Andy?"

"If you have the opportunity between now and our call, do a web search on Ella Cavendish."

Cavendish. Kate Redmont's maiden name. It reminded him of something else, that he couldn't place. *Ella* Cavendish. Why did it sound familiar? "What is it about?"

"You'll see." Hulten cut the call.

Declan finished his breakfast. This must be what a recharged battery felt when the light turned green. The other guests had gone about their touristy business and he was alone. The lodge restaurant wasn't the appropriate location for the call with Hulten. He could hear Jean talk to somebody in the kitchen and a cleaning crew walked through the reception area. A phone rang somewhere.

Jean came by with a tray to bus the tables. "You should take it easy today. You got the stuffing knocked out of you. I hope you're not thinking of going to New York."

"I'll go for a hike. I'll take plenty of water."

"Take nut bars too. There's a stack on the buffet. Call me if you feel woozy."

He promised.

"And you stay here tonight. No debate. I want to keep an eye on you."

After the paranoid conversation with Hulten, that sounded borderline threatening. "I don't plan a repeat performance, Jean."

"As if that was under your control," she said.

Declan went back to his cabin and changed for the hike. He packed his tablet and chose the trail he took on the first day. It led to an overlook that would give him a good signal and clear views of whoever might be approaching.

• • •

Declan reached his destination with time to spare. The wi-fi signal was strong and he went online to do a search on Ella Cavendish.

When the Wikipedia entry popped up, he understood why the name rang familiar. He was too young at the time to have any memory of the events, but the case had gained the popular culture celebrity status of the Black Dahlia and JonBenét Ramsey, and generated a similar media frenzy.

July 24, 1992, the decapitated body of seven-year-old Ella Cavendish was found in a culvert two miles away from her home in Old Mapleton. The head hung by the hair from the lowest branch of a maple tree. There was no apparent motive. The parents, Royce and Amelia, were questioned at length. Amelia—everybody called her Amy—had reported the child missing four days before the horrific discovery. Royce was in New York at the time. The investigators excluded him as a potential suspect. No so with Amy.

Declan pulled up archived articles. Ella was Kate Redmont's sister. Kate was a two-year old toddler at the time and she played a role in the drama. Her mother was taking care of her in the nursery. Ella was outside with a friend. The girl vanished from the house's backyard. The friend didn't see or hear a thing. Not a cry. Nothing. The investigation focused on Amy. Wouldn't the child have resisted being taken by a stranger?

Declan's tablet flashed a warning. His conference call was coming up. He tore himself away from Ella's case and tested the Zoom link. He wasn't thinking about his nocturnal trip to hell anymore. Why was Hulten interested in a cold case and what the hell did it have to do with Carlton Marsh?

Mindful of the publisher's warning, he checked his surroundings. There wasn't a soul in shouting distance.

Hulten came online. His first words: "Where are you?"

"A clearing in the woods." Declan turned the tablet around to show him the sights. "The ocean in front, the forest way back there. I'm sitting on a piece of rock that will dig into my ass before long. I may go lie down in the grass to relieve the ache. How are *you* doing, Andy?"

"Being a stuffed shirt in an office on a Saturday. Jen is with me. Say hello to Jennie Watts."

She had a long face, with hair pulled back and intense black eyes that cut through the fuzziness of the screen image. A strong personality. More explosive than Hulten. They might balance each other.

"Ms. Watts," Declan said.

"Did you look up the Ella Cavendish case?" she said.

No small talk. Declan liked that. "I haven't had time to read everything yet. How does it connect with Carlton?"

In typical lawyer fashion, she didn't answer the question. Declan liked that too. He tended to do the same. "Do you know what Carlton was working on?" she said.

"An exposé on the civil war in El Salvador in the eighties, and how the U.S. foreign policy of the times still impacts government decisions today, in relationship with immigration and crime issues." He was aware he sounded like a book blurb, and what did Carlton's book have to do with little Ella? Or Carlton's suicide?

"Very well put, Mr. Shaw," Jennie said. "And do you know who he wanted you to search for?"

"He was vague. Survivors, immigrants, witnesses of the Salvadoran civil war who'd gone to ground in the U.S. He wasn't planning to send me to Central America. I asked for more details but he said he would fill me in when I got here."

"Did he sound worried?"

"Not a bit. He was excited. Don't leave me hanging, Ms. Watts, what is it all about?"

"We believe Carlton flushed out a war criminal. We believe he was going to ask you to find him."

Declan looked away from the screen at the peaceful blue

expanse of the Atlantic and imagined all the turmoil down there he couldn't see from his vantage point. Like a Xandra Mohr painting. "And he conveniently committed suicide."

"Exactly."

"What makes you think this was what Carlton was up to?"

"Hints in the chapters he sent to me and conversations he had with Jen, but the clincher is what happened to Marcia," Hulten said.

"Who the fuck is Marcia? No. Wait. Let's do this in order. Walk me through it. What did Carlton share with you, Ms. Watts?"

"He was concerned about the information he had gathered, in case something happened to him. He told me he was onto something big. And he mentioned Wiesenthal."

Hulten jumped in the conversation. "We believe he planned to go after a war criminal the way Wiesenthal went after Nazis. Paramilitary groups and death squads were notorious in El Salvador during the civil war. Carlton reported on them extensively."

"Did he mention a name?"

"No, but the name must have been in his manuscript. Marcia Cartwright died two days ago. It cannot be a coincidence."

"Slow down, Andy. You're losing me," Declan said.

A sigh. "Marcia was Carlton's beta reader. He always sent his work to her before anybody else had a chance to look at it. I believe the book was finished and she died because of what was in it. The identity of a war criminal."

Quite a deductive jump and a ton of assumptions packed in a couple of sentences. Declan felt an urge to hit rewind. Hulten was a serious publisher. Jennie Watts seemed like a rational person. Without missing a beat, they threw a multiple murder plot at him. On a Saturday, in bright sunlight, by the sea. Life is full of coincidences. And so is death. You can draw correlations between anything and everything, and connect dots that have no business being connected. Declan knew how investigators could be led so deep into a maze they never found the way out.

"How did Marcia Cartwright die?"

"Her house went up in flames with everything inside including her," Hulten said.

Okay, it didn't smell right. Accident or arson. What did the investigation reveal? It was worth checking. "You have an address for Marcia?"

Jennie must have sensed his skepticism. "Jefferson, North Carolina. We think Carlton sent her the manuscript, but there's no way to know for sure."

"We need Carlton's computer. Will Chief Halston give it to you?"

"I talked to him," Jennie said. "Carlton's death will be ruled a suicide. The police released the body. I arranged to have it sent to a funeral home in New Haven. There will be a private ceremony sometime next week. The journalism community will want to pay their respects, but I believe we should delay until we know what we're dealing with."

"Agreed. Can I help with the arrangements in New Haven?"

"I might call you."

"The police said we could retrieve Carlton's documents and laptop on Monday," Hulten said, "and we can visit the house."

"We'll come to Old Mapleton together," Jennie added.

Declan grunted. "You should let me handle it. It could be dangerous."

"If there was anything incriminating on that laptop, wouldn't the killer have taken it?" Jennie said.

A valid question that didn't resist examination. "Couldn't. A missing laptop raises suspicion, and the suicide theory crumbles. Leaving everything in place is the smart move. The cops have no reason to hack into the machine if Carlton killed himself, and the murderer will have opportunities to destroy it once it's out of police custody. How much of the manuscript have you seen, Andy?"

"Dedication, acknowledgments, and three chapters. I thought about it after we talked. Nobody writes acknowledgments for a partial. Carlton must have completed the book. And then we learned of Marcia's death. The answer has to be in the manuscript."

If it was, why did Marsh need Declan's help? What kind of research could he have done for a book that was finished? Then it came to him. The reference to Simon Wiesenthal. Marsh wanted more than naming the guy. He wanted to nail him, bring him to justice. The ultimate feather in a reporter's cap. Because he couldn't go hunting himself, he hired Declan. And the hunt would take place in country, not in Central America. Carlton Marsh knew that his quarry was in the U.S., close enough to strike, it turned out.

"What do we do now?" Hulten said.

"Get the laptop from the cops and give it to me."

"Then you'll be in danger," Jennie said.

"I'm already in the crosshairs. I didn't fly back to Houston when I should have. There must be eyes on me. If I identify the snoops, we'll have something to work with. What's the connection with the Ella Cavendish case?"

"The book's dedication," Hulten said. "*For Ella and all the innocents slain by soulless men.* I asked Carlton about it. I assumed she was a Salvadoran victim, but he told me she was a kid from Old Mapleton. It dawned on me that she was the Cavendish girl, from that horrible murder. When I asked him why he chose her, he gave me that annoying author's response: You'll have to read the book."

"Violence is borderless and can happen next door," Jennie chimed in. "Horror isn't miles away."

That didn't sound like Carlton Marsh. He wasn't inclined to preachy blandness. What he shared with priests and ministers was the pulpit fire. He didn't thunder in church, he spat brimstone on paper. "You don't think he had something more precise in mind? He always chose his words carefully."

"Yeah, he did," Hulten said. "I have the first three chapters in front of me. The first one describes a massacre in a remote village. It claimed 128 victims. Among them were thirty-six children. Fourteen were decapitated, all girls. Their heads were displayed, hanging by the hair from clotheslines. Carlton went to that village. He was at the scene and wrote about it for AP. He drove in with the regular army when they moved into the area. The FMLN was blamed for the violence."

Decapitated girls. Heads hanging by their hair. Like little Ella. Who was murdered years after the massacre in El Salvador. In Marsh's home town. The similarities must have hit him like a rocket.

"Declan?" Hulten said.

"Just a minute."

Declan had re-read Carlton's books and articles in preparation for his trip. The FMLN was the Farabundo Martí National Liberation Front—in Spanish, *Frente Farabundo Martí para la Liberación Nacional*. He read the report from the U.N. Truth Commission. Frontists were responsible for five percent of the civilian deaths during the twelve-year-long conflict. 75,000 people died and the majority of them were civilians. 95% of the casualties were the responsibility of the government and the army.

"In his articles, Carlton accused the military. I remember reading about a village that was burned to the ground, a couple of kids escaped and lived to tell the story. I didn't see anything about decapitated girls and clotheslines."

"His dispatches were sanitized for publication," Hulten said. "The circumstances of Ella's murder must have rattled him."

Declan knew, from listening to the reporter's lectures and reading his work, that he was a deliberate man, punctilious about expressing his thoughts in a manner that wouldn't leave any uncertainty. He was an old-school journalist intent on laying out the facts. When he injected a personal opinion, he did it in clear delineated paragraphs. Ella Cavendish deserved a closer look. She was more than a dedication.

"Did Carlton know the Cavendish family?"

"He was born and grew up in Old Mapleton," Hulten said. "The Cavendishes were natives too. He must have known them, by name at least."

"Email me the three chapters, Andy. Ella Cavendish mattered to Carlton. He had plenty of victims to choose from, and he chose her." As expected, the chunk of rock was digging painfully in Declan's backside. "Let me know when you plan to get here and I'll meet you at the police station. How did you learn about Marcia Cartwright's death?"

"She was on the list of Carlton's contacts," Jennie said. "I called all of them to let them know Carlton had passed. When I called Marcia, a police officer picked up."

"I sent you the three chapters," Hulten said. "I don't need to tell you not to share this with anybody …"

"Andy."

"I mean … I know you're in the discretion business, but I have to say it, right?"

Declan sighed. "See you Monday."

He closed the app and read the brilliant, haunting, first three chapters of Carlton Marsh's book, propped on his elbows, in the grass, with the sea a glossy topaz blue in front of him. A cool breeze ruffled his hair.

It wasn't the right setting at all.

Horror should be a thing of night.

TEN

"YOU LOOK MUCH BETTER. How do you feel?"

Jean was pruning a bush that spread toward the porch. Judging from the pile of cuttings, she must have been at it for a while.

"I think I'll go have a bite in town. Anything I can get you while I'm over there?"

She smiled. "A sweet treat maybe? The chocolate cheesecakes at Grandin are to die for."

"Consider it done."

"And please join us for dinner. Nothing fancy, we'll have sandwiches."

Declan didn't intend to go to the gallery to see Isabel on the vague, and unfounded, suspicion that sex might be connected to his night horrors. It couldn't do any harm to vary his pattern of behavior. And he was supposed to go out with Mike Hannigan the next morning and that meant a very short night. If the dope fiend allowed him to shut an eye.

He was finishing his late lunch at the café when Isabel called. He was tempted to let her message go to voicemail.

"Hi there," he said.

"Mr. Shaw."

He almost dropped the phone in surprise

"Mr. Schulman is here. He wants to know if you would have time for him today."

The boss must be standing right next to her.

Declan planned to read more about the Ella Cavendish murder and didn't feel like chumming with the gallery owner. He would have to make it quick.

"Does Mr. Schulman have a time preference?"

"He has business to attend to at the art colony, but he can see you before or after."

"Would five o'clock at the gallery be convenient?" Declan said.

The phone went silent. Isabel must be checking with the boss.

"It's perfect. We will see you then. Thank you."

That took care of it. There would be no fucking around. Not with her employer in the vicinity. Declan ordered another carafe of wine and moved to a small table in the back of the café where he wouldn't be in anyone's way.

• • •

Declan went deep down the internet rabbit hole and its multiple bifurcations. The Ella Cavendish case had been covered ad nauseam. Articles, conference papers, true crime blogs and, recently, podcasts. He took extensive notes. Names and places. Suspects and cops. The forensics data were scant. If the police had more, they didn't share with the media. The news coverage from 1992 was overheated and prurient, with reporters taking sides and rushing to assign guilt. It was the printed version of Old Mapleton's gossip. The private lives of the parents, Royce and Amy Cavendish, were exposed with no consideration for their grief. They had an apartment in New York where Royce stayed when he had to work late and that became juicy fodder for rumors. He was a successful investment banker, a man about town. There was talk of wild parties, call girls, booze cruises on the Hudson, all uncorroborated. Amy was dissected. Unscrupulous newshounds got their hands on her medical records. Her diagnosis of post-partum depression after Kate's birth became fodder for pseudo-scientific pontification. The unconscionable reporting infected the investigation. The cops were swamped with so-called revelations, witness testimonies that were recanted, then affirmed again with even more fervor.

After hours of slogging through the muck, Declan was beyond disgusted. Xandra Mohr said the town was full of hypocrites. She was putting it mildly. These people were out for blood. Ella's murder case turned into a modern-day witch trial.

What did the Cavendish family do to these people? Was it envy? A young handsome couple, well-off and well-bred. They were privileged, but so were thousands like them in old Connecticut towns. Their house wasn't a mansion, they didn't have domestic help beyond a babysitter and a cleaning lady who came once a week, they didn't have a yacht berthed at the marina.

Declan read pious statements pretending to empathize with the family while stabbing them in the back with whiffs of old scores being settled. "It had to happen. Sad that the poor girl had to pay for the sins of others." What responsible paper would print that kind of trash? All of them did. In that poisonous atmosphere, the cops couldn't do their job. The FBI was called in to work the kidnapping case. It calmed things down for a few weeks until madness took hold of the town again, more rabid for having been forced to hit the pause button. The hacks' focus shifted to Old Mapleton's seedy underbelly. Not the dark secrets of the corrupt local elite, but the fishermen and working-class families living on the proverbial wrong side of the tracks. The cops spun their wheels in emptiness. Kids were hassled, hapless junkies were caught and released, local bar toughs were strong-armed to jail. Nothing came of it. Then the anonymous letters started.

Everybody got them. Royce and Amy Cavendish, the media, the police, the mayor. They weren't letters per se. They were scribbled notes dripping with vulgar accusations. Amy was accused of more turpitudes than Marie Antoinette at the revolutionary tribunal. The news articles reproduced the documents with the obscenities blacked out. Graphology experts were called in. Every media outlet had their own and they all contradicted each other. A cursory look at a few samples convinced Declan that the notes were written by different people. It was either a conspiracy or a sick prank.

Declan's eyes were glazing over when a name shook him awake. Michael Hannigan. Twelve years old. Who in their right mind could imagine a boy that age cutting a little girl's head off? Mike was in the news for a week. They gave him a lie detector test. It was a recipe for railroading. Luckily, common sense prevailed and the kid was released.

Around the end of September the nuttiness started to abate. Everybody was exhausted and there was baseball to watch. By October, the media coverage had dried out.

Man is the most vicious animal. Ella and what happened to her was forgotten in the onslaught. Her fear and suffering weren't worth a sidebar. The day trippers that clogged the roads leading to Old Mapleton received more news coverage than the girl. Declan wondered how much the town profited from the event. The media, the cops, the ghoulish tourists had to be fed and lodged and their cars had to be gassed. The local chamber of commerce must have seen a silver lining in all the attention.

Declan closed his tablet and finished the wine. He thanked the café owner for her hospitality. Was she in business in 92, did she feed the hordes that flooded Old Mapleton? Grandin, the fancy bakery, had been on the premises since 1953—a plaque over the door proudly proclaimed. Declan bought a cheesecake for Jean and told them he would pick it up later. He had time to kill before meeting Schulman at the gallery and walked to the marina to dream of the boat he could not afford.

He recognized Chief Halston through the smoke of his stinky cigar. Out of uniform, he was a different man. The chief sat on a low wall by the dock, with a forlorn expression on his broad face.

"You took the day off?" Declan said.

"Ayuh. Went fishing this morning. A buddy told me they were jumping, but if they were, it wasn't around my bucket." He made a funny face. "It was still a good day to be out."

"I'm going tomorrow."

"Who you going with?"

"None of these fancy beauties. The *Sea Robin*."

Halston shot him a glance from under the bushy eyebrows. "Hannigan. You like rough trade."

"He was a little sour at first, but President Grant sweetened his temper. And paddies gotta stick together."

"Hannigan is always hurting for money. His wife's illness pushed him under and he's still under. It's not what he hauls out that's gonna change his predicament. He should move away from here but he's damn stubborn."

Declan sat on the wall next to Halston. "It's hard to go any-where when you're broke."

"He could sell the *Sea Robin* and the house, pay his debts, and he'll have some left over to go to friendlier climes. He knows fishing and he understands the sea. It's in his blood. He'd get hired."

Declan pointed at the yachts. "Why couldn't he get hired here? There are enough fat cats bobbing in this basin."

"It's called Old Mapleton for a reason, son. It's old."

There's an interrogator trick. Silence. It might not work with Halston. The chief knew the trick too. Let the quarry come to you. It worked better when the silence was uncomfortable, and this was not the case. Declan took out his cigar case and Halston gave him a light.

"Marsh could have told you a lot about this town, Shaw. Knowing what he did for a living, he wouldn't have sugar-coated it either." Halston pointed at the boats. "It looks pretty, doesn't it?"

"Nature and inanimate objects. I'm a city boy. I know it's people that make things ugly."

"How hard was it to learn that kind of wisdom?"

"I'm more back alleys than country roads. In a way it makes it easier. Bad guys look the part. They don't sip martinis at the country club. They down boilermakers at O'Leary's bar."

"That's the kind of thing you don't want to say aloud when some people are around, son." Halston shook his big head side to side. It made him look like a bull bothered by a pesky fly. "I was born here. Down a dirt track, in these woods. Not far from Bill Hannigan's shack, Mike's grandpa. We didn't have much, but we had more than the Hannigans. My mom took some misplaced pride in that, poor soul. That's how it goes here, Shaw. There's a ladder and you're taught at a young age what rung you're clinging to. Raise a hand to grab the next rung and lift yourself, and you'll be tumbling down before you have time to say amen. Might be different in Texas."

"We tend to be less anchored. There's so much territory to roam. The layers still exist. Money helps poke holes in them. Your old guard would say we're mercenary, and there's truth in that."

"You're not going to try one of my cigars, are you?" Halston said.

Declan chuckled. "I don't have enough sand paper in the back of my throat yet." He shook off the ash from the cigarillo. "Carlton's death is ruled a suicide. That's okay. I don't think he would have minded. There are more important truths. In his reporting, he always went for the big story."

"You promised you wouldn't make trouble. You'll break the

promise. I don't know how yet but I can feel it coming. Please don't force me to arrest you, Shaw."

"I'll try." Declan checked his phone. Time to go. "I'll see you, Chief."

"Going to buy another piece of art?" Halston said.

"Not today. I've reached my limit. Your informants are thorough. Compliments."

"They take so much pleasure in their job that I don't even have to pay them," Halston said. "Protect your rear, son."

• • •

The gallery was dark and the sign on the door showed *Closed*. A pale light in the back suggested a presence. Isabel's desk was unattended. Declan knocked and nothing moved inside. Maybe Schulman wasn't back from the art colony yet. The prickle on the back of Declan's neck could not be ignored. He didn't want to try the door handle. He had a hunch the shop was open and he would be better off avoiding going inside. He stepped away from the door and the windows.

He pulled out his phone and called Isabel's number. He heard the ringtone inside, muffled. The call went to voicemail.

"Ms. Sanders. It's Declan Shaw. I went to the gallery. There wasn't anybody there. Please tell Mr. Schulman that I'm on my way to the marina café. I'll be on the terrace for another hour or so. He can join me if it's convenient. Otherwise, call me and we'll make another appointment. Thank you."

Declan took a different street to reach the seaside. The houses were similar in period and size to Carlton Marsh's villa. They communicated sedate wealth and longtime ownership. He hadn't seen an address for the Cavendish home. It might very well be one of these. The houses had no yards in front, but plenty of space in the back. They were set well apart and he could see children running around. He tried to imagine a brazen kidnapper sneaking between the houses to grab a child. It was risky even under the cover of trees. The investigators had to look at people close to Ella—relatives, friends. If Ella knew her kidnapper, she would go quietly into the woods. Statistics didn't support the stranger theory. Children were mostly harmed by people they knew.

The apparition of a police cruiser with Officer Craig at the wheel made Declan aware of how suspicious his behavior might appear to residents. It would make Chief Halston's day if a concerned citizen called about a strange man planted on the sidewalk who looked at backyards and kids at play.

• • •

Declan was at the marina café making his scotch and soda last when he spotted Gabriel Schulman. He didn't know the man, had not seen a picture of him, and Xandra Mohr's comments didn't qualify as a portrait, yet he was certain this was the guy.

Schulman wasn't tall. His dress shoes were designed to provide a lift and that was a sure sign he was self-conscious about his height. He was on the other side of middle age and he was self-conscious about that too. He had managed to stave off the waist spread. He was fit. The hair, without a touch of gray, was combed to cover the deforestation areas. Declan's choice of meeting place must annoy him because the sea breeze disturbed the arrangement, and his hand tried to keep the strands in place. The dark gray suit was bespoke and he wore it well, with an elegant ease.

Schulman didn't walk or stride, he glided. He reminded Declan of the contraptions that floated on the surface of swimming pools, going round and round catching bugs and leaves. Skimmers. Schulman skimmed and caught Declan. He drifted through the tables to get to the corner of the terrace. From close by, the face was pleasant, with enough strength in the chin and darkness in the eyes and eyebrows to catch female attention. The tan was trademark Florida.

Declan stood as Schulman approached. He leaned on the bistro table to hide his six foot four of bony ranginess. He didn't want to start the conversation on the wrong note.

He held out his hand. "Mr. Schulman, good to meet you."

"Mr. Shaw. Sorry for missing our appointment. The business meeting took longer than I thought."

Schulman's handshake was firm, a trifle too much so. He intended to make a point. The body language emphasized it. He held himself very straight, shoulders back. It had a military feel that made Declan curious. A familiar scent tickled his nostrils. Isabel's perfume. Declan knew it well. It was sweet, floral. He'd had his nose in it three days in a row. He perceived a hint of sex musk underneath. The picture in his mind flashed bright. Schulman balling Isabel in the storage room at the gallery while his phone call provided a rhythmic soundtrack. Did they expect him to walk in on them? What purpose would it serve? It was unlikely to make him buy more art. Schulman fucking the girl to mark his territory? The hard handshake implied as much.

"How did it go at the art colony? I imagine a project like that is complicated."

"Because artists are unreliable?" Schulman said.

He had no accent whatsoever which was a giveaway. This man had either stripped every trace of his origins from his biography, or he wasn't a native English speaker and he had excellent teachers. It made Declan even more curious.

"I don't know enough artists to make that kind of judgment," Declan said. "You manage a network of galleries and artists, and a housing project. It can't be simple."

"It doesn't matter when you love what you do. You know what I used to do, Mr. Shaw?"

"You were a real estate developer."

"I built things. Many of them everyday ugly. A few were acceptable."

Declan finished his scotch. He motioned at a passing server. He ordered a refill. Schulman asked for a vodka martini.

"How did you veer off into art?" Declan said.

Schulman smiled. It made him look smug. Most people looked better when they smiled. Schulman didn't. His expression made Declan wonder what kind of lie he was about to spin.

"I built a hotel in Fort Lauderdale and I needed decorative elements for the hallways. I stumbled upon that kid, a street artist, a tagger. He'd never put anything on canvas before. I struck gold, Shaw." Schulman relived the excitement. It coated his forehead with a shine of sweat. "It was a revelation. I had the touch. I opened the Miami gallery two weeks later."

"And now you have four galleries and an artist colony," Declan said. "Only in America, right?" It was a side remark, a throwaway. He didn't expect the reaction he got.

Schulman paled under the tan, his mouth turned into a thin hard line, and the black eyes went flat obsidian hard. "An opportunity offered to all Americans."

If Declan knew more about Schulman's background, he might understand where this defensiveness came from. The *Only in America* comment challenged him. Did Schulman take offense with the irony? Declan changed tack.

"Do you meet with all your customers, Mr. Schulman?"

"Few of my customers buy pieces that are bigger than many people's apartment walls."

"Bigger than some New York apartments. As I told Ms. Sanders, I happen to have the space."

"Are you a collector, Mr. Shaw?"

"Not at all. I have to fall in love. Most of the time, I can't afford the object of my affection. I think you priced Xandra Mohr's *Rhapsody* way too low." He grinned. "I can say it now that the sale is final."

Schulman plucked the olive out of his martini and sucked on it. "I have to consider space management, and give fair exposure to all my artists."

In other words, Xandra hogged valuable real estate. Her masterpiece was the equivalent of bulky furniture that had to be disposed of. Declan wasn't going to tell Schulman that he had a goldmine right under his nose and was too dumb to see it. Let him think that he had hoodwinked another clueless tourist.

They sipped their drinks and watched the boats come in. Declan let the silence linger. He had questions that he knew Schulman would never answer.

"You should come see my collection," Schulman said. "We'll have dinner and I'll take you to the house; it's a few miles out of town."

"I'd love to, but I'm not available tonight and out of town for most of the day tomorrow. If you're around next week, no problem. Did Ms. Sanders give you my number?"

"She did. How long are you planning to stay? The town is pretty but it doesn't take long to see all there is to see."

"You seem to find it pleasant enough."

Schulman chuckled. "I'm not a visitor. I have work to do here."

"And what makes you think I don't?"

It was a wild swing and Declan had no expectation it would land anywhere. Yet it did. Gabriel Schulman bent forward at the waist, and winced. He coughed to disguise the brief spasm.

"I shouldn't drink on an empty stomach. What kind of work do you do, Mr. Shaw?"

Even if Isabel hadn't told him, which was doubtful, he must have done his due diligence.

"I look for things, and I find things."

"Treasure hunting," Schulman said. "People pay you, or are you working freelance?"

"Contract. As much as I would love to go find a dragon to slay or a damsel to rescue, I have to make a living. I couldn't impulse-buy masterpieces if I didn't. Did you keep something from that street artist you discovered? What's he called?"

"Jerzy C. It's Polish for George. I sold everything. The money was too good." Schulman wasn't interested in chatting about a talented tagger. "What kind of lost treasure do you hope to find in Old Mapleton, Mr. Shaw?"

Declan offered a cigar to Schulman who declined. He took his time lighting the cheroot. "It isn't lost. It's hidden. You see, Mr. Schulman, I live in a big, new city. Things change all the time. People too. They get there, they move around, they leave, it's a continuous flow, constant activity. In Houston even immovable objects tend to move. Buildings are torn down, new ones rise. It's like a non-stick pan. A little soap, hot water, no need to scrub, rinse, good as new. In old cities, it's different. I used to live in New Orleans. Things don't change that fast down there. Buildings stay where they're planted and people tend to stay too. There's history and memory. Things stick. That's good terrain for treasure hunters. Old Mapleton is even better. It's small. Everybody knows everybody and has known them for the longest time. It's super sticky. It will take more than scrubbing, I might have to go at it with a scraper, but once it starts to give …" Time had slowed down. Declan was attuned to Schulman's reactions. The gallery owner was fidgety. His hand reached to fix his hair more often than the light breeze required.

"Places like Old Mapleton have a life of their own," Declan continued. "Dead things come to life again." Schulman straightened. "The camp where I'm staying is a good example. It was alive and kicking a hundred years ago, then it became a dormant ruin, and now it's back." Schulman relaxed. "It's the same with people. There are those who were born here and never left. The fishermen and their families, the old town elite that runs things. And then there are those who left and came back. Did you know that the reporter who died this week, Marsh, was from here? He was the last member of one of the town's founding families. There are these names you see everywhere. Anderson, Morton, Marsh." A pause. "Cavendish."

Schulman blinked and lifted his martini glass. All that was left in the glass was the toothpick the olive had been impaled on.

"Marsh traveled the world, but he came back home in the end. I'm telling you, Schulman, this place is stickier than glue. People come back to it. Something in the air, the water, the woods. Treasure."

Declan rambled on because his voice had a hypnotic effect on Gabriel Schulman. Before he met the guy he already knew he didn't like him. The Heyzers and Xandra Mohr had set the scene, and what he guessed happened at the gallery added to the picture. After watching Schulman's body language and his reactions to the improvised speech, Declan had the beginning of a hunch. Old Mapleton. In the past. The dead coming alive, the founding families.

Ella Cavendish?

"It's an original way of looking at things, Mr. Shaw," Schulman said after what seemed like an endless pause. "I'd be interested to know if it gets you anywhere."

Declan pointed his cigar at Schulman. "That, Gabriel—you mind if I call you Gabriel?—is a different can of worms."

"You're telling me stories. You're not close to the treasure."

"Assuming I even know what I'm after," Declan said. "Sometimes you dive for a Spanish galleon and you find a German U-boot, or you find nothing at all. You always take chances in deep waters."

"It must be frustrating."

"But when you strike gold, my friend, it's an apotheosis. Not unlike your discovery of the talented tagger."

Schulman frowned. "I bought art." He looked away. There was the sound of an engine. A yacht was coming into the basin too fast. "Dangerous behavior. Some people take unnecessary risks."

Declan turned to look. "What's the hurry, right?"

"Are you a patient man?"

"On a nice afternoon like today, I have no intention to rush anywhere." As if to contradict himself, he pulled out his phone to check the time. "I need to get to a bakery before it closes. It has been a pleasure to meet you, Gabriel. Call me, and I'll have a look at your collection. I'll handle the check."

Declan uncoiled his long frame and walked to the bar. He could feel Schulman's eyes on his back the entire way.

ELEVEN

JEAN AND BILL HEYZER kept the conversation going during dinner. Declan ate very little. He was replaying the conversation with Schulman that he transcribed the best he could as soon as he got back to the camp. The words themselves didn't matter much and he couldn't remember all he said in that long speech. He tried to capture the man's reactions and the topics that triggered them.

Jean wanted him to stay at the lodge overnight but Declan decided to go back to his cabin.

"Mike Hannigan will call at four thirty. It will be a very short night."

"I won't be able to sleep."

"Take a pill," he said.

She didn't find it funny. She handed him an air horn and a bag of adult diapers. "You hit that thing and you wear those. You want to be independent, fine, but don't make a mess."

"Jean, I'm so sorry."

"Apologies accepted. Make sure you have a trash can next to the bed."

Declan chose clothes for the morning boat ride—sweater, a pair of jeans, cap and windbreaker—and went to bed. The air horn and the phone were in easy reach. The bathroom dustbin was nearby, the diaper bag not so much.

As was often the case when you were prepared, the precautions were all for naught. His sleep was interrupted by violent shivers and stabs of pain around midnight, and he took three aspirins with a drop of whisky. The combination knocked him out and Mike Hannigan's call rang in the middle of a strange dream of airport gate changes.

"Weather's good," Mike said. "We leave at five as planned."

There was a light on at the lodge, on the second floor. Declan hoped Jean had managed to catch some sleep. The air was cool with a hint of fall and a smell of hazelnuts. Dew coated the windshield of the BMW.

● ● ●

Mike Hannigan asked for the money before allowing Declan on board. As if his passenger intended to stiff him.

"Now we can enjoy ourselves," Mike said.

The expression on his face was more mourning than enjoyment. Declan had a vision of Captain Ahab after the whale bit off his leg. The kid, Bernadette, puffy with sleep, rubbed her eyes with her fists, and handled the ropes like a sleepwalker. There were no words exchanged. Father and daughter were going through their routine as if Declan wasn't there. He stayed out of the way.

Soon they chugged out of the harbor. It was pitch black. The boat's red and green lights matched the lights of the channel markers and a flickering signal pinpointed the end of the fishing pier. By the time they were clear of the port area, when the lights of Old Mapleton glinted in the distance in the west, a thin line had appeared on the horizon. Sunrise was a half hour away but the glow spread fast. It flowed on top of the waves like a glossy dark varnish that the prow of the fishing boat cut through neatly. In the back, the propeller wasn't as delicate. Even so it didn't take long for their wake to disappear.

"Are we fishing, Da?" Bernadette said. "It looks good today."

"Might as well." Mike turned to Declan. "Watch the kid, you might learn a thing or two."

The girl knew the job and she wasn't sleepy anymore. She checked the fishing lines and signaled to Mike to lower the outriggers when she had assured herself that the gear was positioned as it should. Declan admired her dedication and fastidiousness. The lines had to be just right and she jiggled pulleys to adjust them.

"All good," she said. "Steady."

"What do you think?" Mike said, with a wink in Declan's direction.

"You have a competent first mate. How do you manage on school days?"

"I have a helper. He's not as good as Bern and he gets a share of the catch. Everybody has to make a living. It happens to be meager. Hey, Bern, what about coffee?"

"I'll get it," Declan said.

They trolled for a while. Two big bluefish and a large sea bass took the bait. Bernadette handled them deftly. She released the smaller fish.

"You don't use nets," Declan said.

"Too much bycatch." Mike scowled. "I've seen folks run afoul of authorities and the environmental people. In the end, it's counter-productive. I do piecemeal and my buyers know that I'm responsible. They can advertise that. I'll never get rich but I sleep well."

In his chosen field, Declan did the same. He didn't take dubious cases and he didn't bend the rules he set for himself. They didn't always align with the strict letter of the law, but he was confident they were true to its intent.

"How do you know Kate Redmont?" Mike leaned on the control board, the compass on a steady course east.

"I don't." Declan grinned at Mike's puzzled expression. "I went to the harbor and I was fascinated by that striking woman who cleaned fish like some people do calligraphy. She made me want to go fishing with her. She was not interested in taking me aboard and sent me to you. How do you know her?"

"She was born here."

"You've known her all her life." Declan got a cigarillo and offered the case to Mike who took one.

"Not exactly. Her family left when she was little, then she came back after the divorce. I helped her buy a boat and get comfortable with it."

"You taught her how to clean fish?"

Mike smiled. "Yeah, and she's better than me. I'm always in too much of a hurry."

"I'm starving," Declan said. "Anything to eat that isn't raw fish?"

Mike pointed at the small cabin. "Enough to make sandwiches in there. Make a stack. Bern has an appetite."

"Aye, aye, Captain."

Declan wanted to push harder on Kate Redmont and Ella Cavendish but Mike was skittish. He had made some inroads and built a modicum of empathy. This required patience. It was all right, they had all day.

Over the next couple of hours, the outriggers were raised and lowered several times. The haul wasn't massive but Mike declared it was respectable and they switched to recreational fishing. Despite what he said about the tourist trade and his disdain for it, the equipment was on board. Bern rigged four sturdy rods and Mike cut the engine. Folding chairs appeared, and a cooler stocked with beer and sodas. Declan made more sandwiches.

The sun was warm in a clear sky. The sea lulled them to napping with a gentle bob. Bern fell asleep in her chair, mouth open and limbs loose. Mike's body was relaxed but his eyes remained watchful. Declan put his feet up on the side of the boat.

"What do you do for a living, Declan?"

So far it had been Mr. Shaw. Of course, Mike could have checked, and a lie would forever blow Declan's credibility. He opted for the truth. It was easier to stick to.

"I'm a private investigator."

Mike nodded. Declan was glad he told the truth. The man had looked him up.

"People hire me to find what other people want to keep concealed. It must be one of the oldest professions. With whores and spies. Detectives are mud stirrers."

"What mud are you stirring up in Old Mapleton?"

"What mud is there to stir up?"

Mike chuckled. "Quite a bit."

He was saved from having to say more when one of the rods bent at a dangerous angle. Bern, shaken awake by the clang of the rod in the holder, jumped to her feet and grabbed the pole. She took it out of the holder but the fish was too strong for her and she slammed against the side. She yelled in pain but didn't let go of the rod. Declan was out of his chair in a flash and came to the girl's rescue. He had to brace himself.

"Holy mother! What is this?"

"I hope it's not a shark," Mike said. "Hold on." He pulled on leather gloves and went to the cabin to drag out an old fishing chair. He sat down and used the side of the boat to secure his feet. "Hand me the rod. There are gloves under the sink, bring some for Bern too. You okay, Bern?"

The kid rubbed her bruised backside. "Like he knew the rod wasn't in the holder anymore. Sneaky smart."

Declan leaned overboard to see what they were dealing with. "How big do you think it is?"

"It's not the size, it's the fighting spirit." Bern sounded much older than ten. "I could have handled it. He took me by surprise."

"As surprised as he was when he found out he was caught," Declan said.

Mike shot him a squinty dark look. He gave the line a little slack before reeling it in slowly.

"Albacore," Bern said. "That's super good eating, Mr. Shaw. Da knows how to cook it."

"We haven't got it yet, kid. Gotta get it on the boat before it goes in the pan."

The albacore fought for a long time. It weighed in at 45 pounds. It was a gorgeous fish, so glossy it looked enameled.

"Do you ever throw these back in?" Declan said.

"When I have enough, I stop fishing. That catch and release thing is for the marina folks. I catch fish to feed my family."

Mike was proud, and proud of the struggle. Declan shared the blues but not the fatalism. Mike was more Irish than he was, more inclined to brood in that poetic tradition of the cliff dwellers. Declan was too impatient to waste time moping, and too cynical to look for solace in poetry.

"I'm done with fishing for today, if that's okay with you," Mike said.

"Why do you stay in Old Mapleton, Mike?"

It was as if he had uttered the ripest of obscenities. "I was born here, my parents, my grans, and their parents before that. It's my home. Why would I go?"

"Find a better life, see the world."

Step out of this box that crushes you, get away from people who spit on you.

"I'm not a wanderer. I need roots." Mike got a beer from the cooler and handed one to Declan. "And I spend my life on the water." He pointed in the direction of the invisible coast. "Past the town line, I'm embarrassed with my own two feet. It's like I don't understand the language anymore." He squinted. "You feel you belong anywhere, I guess."

"It's circumstances," Declan said. "We moved so often when I was a kid that my most lasting memory is taking a poster off a wall and being very careful to pocket all the thumbtacks."

"Don't you think it's sad?"

"Those were the good years." They had been too short. Declan took a sip of his beer.

"What were the bad ones?" Mike said.

"Eleven years in New Orleans, most of them hellish because I was stuck. Then I dropped anchor in Houston and that's been very good. I wouldn't call it roots. What I've grown is too portable to be called a root system."

Mike leaned forward to clink the neck of his bottle against Declan's. "To each his own."

"To Kate," Declan said. "Make a move, dude."

Mike sighed. "She's even more rooted than I am."

It was a weird thing to say about a woman who had gone from Old Mapleton to Melbourne and back. The question was why she came back.

"Then maybe she isn't what you need," Declan said.

"Do you suggest I bang the gallery girl? Perky little ass. Any tips?"

"All ye who enter here ... Isabel is in the business of Isabel. The flesh yields but the heart, my friend, is a different matter. And as to the soul ..."

"People say you bought something."

"You think she was the promotional item? The toy in the kids' meal. I should suggest that to Schulman next time I see him. He might go for it. He's a piece of work." Declan balanced his beer on his knee. The sea was as flat as a calm lake. He had not imagined the Atlantic that meek. "What do you think of that guy? Just curious."

"Schulman? He got here twenty years ago. Cash-loaded. He bought a shop in town. I can't remember what it was before the gallery. Then he bought land from Maxwell Morton—not cheap, old Max is greedy—and he built cabins on it. I worked on the construction. It was good money. The *Sea Robin* wouldn't be afloat without the dough I made that year. My Pop was ecstatic. New engine, new rigging. We overhauled the old bucket bow to stern. It doesn't mean I like the bastard, but I have to be grateful for the opportunity he gave us, you know."

"I didn't realize he made his fortune that young," Declan said.

"He wasn't too welcome in town at first. They're pretty tight-assed at the country club. Then there were articles in the papers and a TV crew from New York, and there was talk of art exhibitions and auctions. The city council dreamed of the next Van Gogh discovered in our woods. That nonsense. I thought Schulman would be a flash in the pan, a con man, here today gone tomorrow, but he stayed. The fuck I know why." He blew air in his beer bottle. "You're here for him?"

"I met him yesterday and I got a bad vibe."

"Why are you here, Declan?"

"I had a contract to do research for a friend and it fell through. Now, I'm on vacation, but I can't help it, I have to sniff around and Schulman is very fragrant."

This wasn't the place to talk about Carlton Marsh. The reporter's book was dedicated to Ella Cavendish. Mike was in love with Kate, Ella's sister, and he was a murder suspect when he was about Bernadette's age. It was as intricate as some sailor's knots.

Mike wasn't ready to drop the topic, however.

"Vacation, my ass. They chatter about you in town. People saw Craig Blaisdell arrest you in front of Marsh's house, then you came back with the chief and went in there, didn't look like you were going to jail. Folks thought you were one of Marsh's boy toys. God knows there was a parade of them. But you're screwing the gallery bimbo, so that's out."

Declan lit a fresh cigarillo. "What does the gossip mill say now?"

"They think you're a reporter, snooping around. They love to jabber to the press in these parts." He snickered. "Don't be surprised if people start whispering secrets in your ear. Pretty sweet spot for a detective, I'd think. What secrets are you after, Declan?"

Mike had experience with toxic rumors. And reporters. He obviously hadn't forgotten any of it, the wound of thirty years ago still hurt.

"Not now, Mike, not here. Let's talk over dinner. I don't have a kitchen worth a damn at the camp, but I might convince Jean Heyzer to lend me hers. I could cook us a meal."

"You're inviting me to dinner with the fish I caught?"

"I'm not suggesting you bring the fish as a date."

The sun was gentle, the beer cold, and the sea smooth. They had been up since before sunrise. They were all drowsy. Bernadette was asleep for good, crumpled on a bench in the prow of the old boat.

"Tell you what," Mike said. "Bern is right. I grill the best albacore steaks in town. You come to my place tonight and we'll have a feast. And yes, we'll talk. You'll stop beating around the bush and tell me why the fuck you're in Old Mapleton."

As straightforward as you could make it.

TWELVE

DECLAN DROVE BACK to the camp, tapped out by the sun, the sea air, and more beer than he had ingested in one sitting in a long time. He kicked off his sneakers and dropped on the bed. He was snoring before he was asleep. For only a few minutes, it seemed, until the persistent ring of his phone cut through the snooze.

"I've tried to reach you all day," Isabel said.

"Why didn't you leave a message?" Declan didn't want to talk to her. Smelling her on Schulman had sent his lust-meter into the freeze zone.

"I'm on my way."

How did she know he was back at the camp? Declan took a shower to get rid of the sleep dust and the beer sweat. He didn't have much time for Isabel. Mike expected him at his place in less than an hour.

Isabel walked right in. She was dressed for serious seduction. The very short dress was at least two sizes too small and the heels were at least two inches too high. The make-up was all glossy lips and dewy eyes. If Declan hadn't suspected her

113

of double dealing, it would have been a slam dunk and Mike's grilled albacore would have gone straight to leftovers.

"I missed you so bad." She launched herself at him, arms open for the embrace.

He stepped aside and she teetered on the treacherous heels. "How did you manage the path on those ankle breakers?" He pushed a chair behind her knees and she plopped down, too surprised to resist.

"Please take a seat. Would you like a cup of tea?"

"Declan?" She bit her lower lip and blinked furiously.

"Don't," he said. "I believe you're a good enough actor to be able to produce tears at will. I don't need a demonstration. I didn't call because I didn't want to see you, Isabel. If you wanted to tell me that you arranged the shipment to Houston, you could have texted me or left a voicemail."

"I … we …"

He opened the door and leaned on it to light a cigar. Jean Heyzer didn't want people smoking in the cabins. "We fucked. You went above and beyond. If Schulman sends me a feedback form, I'll give you top marks."

She jumped out of the chair and ran at him, not for a hug this time, but with fire in her eyes. Declan received her hard in the chest, wrapped an arm around her and held her tight against him.

"What were your instructions, Isabel? I'll give you the benefit of the doubt for the first night. Your interest seemed genuine and the dope fit scared you. But after that, other considerations intervened, right?"

A tear hung from her false eyelashes. She blinked and it rolled down her soft cheek. She was pretty and fresh despite the cosmetic travesty that she didn't need. The mask gave the plot away. This was Isabel on a mission. If she'd come to him in jeans and a T-shirt, he could have doubted. A little. Her sugary perfume filled his nostrils.

"What are you talking about? Let me go." She sniffled.

He stuck the cigar in the corner of his mouth and searched his pockets for a tissue. "Blow your nose." She did. She was such a cute temptation. "Did he order you to get all dolled up?" He could feel the warmth and softness of her. "No more games, girl, you're not here of your own free will."

She buried her face in his shirt. She muttered. "He came to my place after meeting you at the café. He said you were a dangerous man. That what he did to help people, the artist colony, it would all be lost."

Declan released his grip, and she leaned into him even more. She moved her body and it increased the heat. She had a direct connection to his pleasure nodes. He decided to let it ride.

"He sent you to find out why I came to town?"

"Yes." It came out in a long warm sigh. "He scares me."

He must have scared her into bed. The thought of Schulman and Isabel thrashing on the storage room table put an icy damper on Declan's desire.

With the speed of gossip in town, Schulman would know by Monday afternoon that Declan stayed in town because of Carlton Marsh's death. He would be seen at the police station with Andy Hulten and Jennie Watts retrieving the writer's belongings. Then they would go to the house together. If Schulman had anything to do with the so-called suicide, he would get nervous and nervous people made mistakes. The gallery owner had been twitchy at the café and sent Isabel for a pillow talk séance. Schulman could be needled.

Declan dropped his cigar and crushed it under a boot heel. "Let's go inside."

Isabel started to unzip her dress the moment he closed the door.

"Not tonight, sweetie. I have to be somewhere in half an hour."

Her eyes went down to the bulge in his jeans and she raised an eyebrow. "We can be quick."

"No, we can't." He noticed the greasy smudge her lipstick left on his shirt. There were traces of mascara too. "I wish you'd dispensed with the stage tricks."

She sat on the bed and watched him change shirts.

"I'm here because Carlton Marsh hired me."

"He's dead," she said.

"If he'd died of a heart attack, I would already be back in Houston. He happened to kill himself, which is not in character, hence dubious. Dubious events intrigue me."

"Why would anybody want to kill that old man?"

Old man. For Isabel, anybody over fifty was already mummified. The rich and adventurous life of Carlton Marsh would forever be incomprehensible to her. It made Declan angry. It was a pointless anger. She had no notion of what made men like Carlton do what they did. She was an ambitious, self-centered young woman living in a selfish world. She had survival smarts and liked sex too much. He doubted she was as careful as she should be. Mistakes of the young. He'd been there.

"Carlton wrote a book," Declan said. "Some people might not have been too happy with what he had to say." He sat on the bed next to her, ran a hand down the slope of her back, toyed with the zipper.

"Can somebody get killed because of a book?"

There were enough historical examples. "Words have power, Isabel."

"Do you have to go, can't you stay a little bit longer?"

"Dinner with a friend. I won't be back until late." He grabbed his jacket, his phone and his keys. "I'll see you tomorrow. Close the door when you leave."

. . .

Mike's house was in a part of town Declan had not explored yet. Down a warren of winding dirt roads, deep in the woods, a neighborhood out of sight that the town elite wanted out of mind. There were no elegant villas or quaint cape cods, it was shack and trailer territory, the non-picturesque side of America. Compared to Texas, the dwellings were a little more warped and moldy because the weather didn't help. As an old French song that popped in Declan's head went: *La misère est moins pénible au soleil.* Poverty is less unbearable in the sun.

Mike's house wasn't the worst of the bunch. A two-story colonial with gables, a little crooked. Parts of the siding needed to be replaced and the entire structure screamed for a fresh coat of paint. It had a cheery disheveled charm.

Bernadette answered Declan's knock on the door. He handed her the two bottles of Chablis he bought at a liquor store on the way.

"Wine, wow. Can I have some?"

"Put them in the fridge, kid. It's better cold."

She pointed at the back of the house, through the kitchen. "They're outside."

They? The only vehicle parked in front was a battered truck.

Mike stood by the barbecue. Kate Redmont sat in a cane chair padded with cushions.

"Ms. Redmont," Declan said. "Thank you for the recommendation. It was fun out there with Mike and Bernadette."

"Mr. Shaw. I had a feeling you two would get along."

"You want a drink?" Mike said.

"The sun and the beer knocked me over. What are you having?"

"Whiskey. I'll fix you one."

They watched the barbecue, talked about boats and fishing, and the end of the good season. It was pleasant and superficial.

Bernadette set the kitchen table with mismatched plastic plates, stainless steel knives and forks, and lemonade glasses with Looney Tunes characters, the kind gas stations used to give out. The glass bowls with the salad and the mashed potatoes were more sophisticated and Declan guessed they were Kate's contribution to the dinner.

"Mr. Shaw brought wine, Da," Bernadette said.

Mike rummaged through three drawers before finding the corkscrew.

"Can I have some?" The girl looked anxious.

"Have a sip of mine," Kate said. "It isn't sweet."

The girl took a tentative sip and her face scrunched up. "How can you drink that?"

"It's like coffee and booze, chick," Mike said. "You grow into it, to the point you might have trouble growing out of it."

The fish was delicious and grilled to perfection.

"How much did you get out of it?" Declan said.

"We'll have good eating for a while. It's in the freezer."

"And the rest of the catch?"

"Sold to a restaurant in town. They don't take big loads off my hands but they pay fair prices." Mike raised his lemonade glass. "With your fee for the trip, it was a very good day. I wish I had more like that."

There it was again, the wistfulness.

"I told you about the guy who wants his boat taken down to Florida," Kate said. "It's a good deal and he'll pay for the plane ticket back. You should do it, Mike."

"I can't take Bern out of school."

"She can stay with me. I'm not due back to work until January." Kate turned to Declan. "I'm a professor. I took a sabbatical."

"What do you teach?" He already knew.

"Sociology. I took a leave of absence to work on a publication, a lengthy one. I knew I wouldn't manage to complete it if I stayed in the city and taught at the same time."

"How's it going?"

She made a face. It wasn't unlike Bern's reaction to the wine. "It will be longer than I thought it would be."

"You'll get a book out of it. What's it about?" Declan smiled. "I won't steal your idea. I'm not in the academic papers business."

"What *is* your business?"

"Didn't Mike tell you? I'm a private detective."

"You asked questions about that shady character, Gabriel Schulman," she said.

"You don't think he deserves to be investigated?"

She shrugged. "If you're after common criminals."

"Few people are unlucky enough to cross paths with uncommon criminals. They represent a very small percentage of the prison population."

Kate looked away. "You said something about research for a friend."

"For Carlton Marsh."

She reacted as if she'd been punched. She pushed her chair away from the table as far as it would go, against the kitchen sink. The legs screeched on the linoleum floor and Bernadette jerked awake. Her head had dropped down between her arms as the adults talked.

"He was your *friend*?" Kate was out of the chair now. Her eyes were wild, her voice a scream.

Declan didn't expect that kind of outburst. "What's going on?"

Kate barked. "Get out." Her face was flushed. She shook with anger. "You tricked us. You're a liar."

Declan was on his feet too now. He raised his hands in a calming gesture. He turned to Mike who was still seated, frozen. "I don't understand."

"Da?" Bernadette said.

It broke Mike's paralysis. "Go to bed, Bern. It's nothing. A discussion. Say goodnight."

The girl was too shocked to be curious. She gave a kiss to Kate who was rigid with repressed fury, and shook Declan's hand. "Good night, Mr. Shaw. I hope we'll go fishing with you again."

"So do I, Bern." Right now it didn't look like he would be invited ever again.

The kid's footsteps on the stairs were loud in the silence.

"I'll leave if you want me to, Kate," Declan said. "But I'd like to know what the hell I did wrong."

Kate leaned on the sink. There was only darkness on the other side of the kitchen window. Nothing to see. The forest blocked the lights of the road and the neighboring houses. "Your *friend*—she spat the word—is a monster. He killed my sister. He tortured her." She banged her fists on the metal sink. It made a sound like a drum. "He had to pay for what he did. But the coward killed himself. There's no justice."

Declan was stunned. He asked Mike. "You believe this?"

"It's true. There is proof."

Carlton wasn't a murderer. He exposed murderers. "What kind of proof?"

Kate reached under her hair to unclasp the chain she wore around her neck. Her hands shook. She dropped a medallion on the kitchen table. A silver seahorse; its eye was a small red stone. "It belonged to my sister. She had it on that day. It disappeared."

Declan remembered reading something about the necklace in the articles he'd gone through. Some kook made a big deal out of the magical symbolism of the seahorse. "Where did you find it?"

"In the bottom drawer of Marsh's desk." Kate spat the name like a curse.

"I was there when she pulled it out, Declan," Mike said. "Marsh knew what it was, all right. He knew he was caught. That's why he killed himself that night. He knew we were going to the police in the morning."

"How convenient." Declan opened his cigar case and took a cheroot out. He barely glanced at the white pill stashed in there. "How did you know it was in the desk?"

Kate bristled at the question. "It was in the letter."

Declan blew a thin strip of smoke. "Ah, a letter. Of course. Anonymous, I presume? Like the nasty stuff that turned this town into one of the circles of hell thirty years ago."

It got Kate's hackles up. "The medallion was where the letter said it was. That's all I care about. I received a series of letters. They said that people lied to the police. A man testified he wasn't in town the day of the murder when he actually was. A man had a fight with my mother that day, and she never told anybody because she was too scared of him. That man was Marsh." Words tumbled out, steeped in hatred. "You think I swallowed that like the word of God, without questions? I called my father and he confirmed. Marsh was in town and had an argument with Mom. Dad refused to tell me what it was all about. He said it had nothing to do with Ella's death."

"Your dad suspected Carlton?" Declan said.

Kate shivered, hugged herself tight. "Dad said he was with Marsh in New York at the time of the kidnapping." She spoke with her head down. "Everybody's lying."

Declan opened the kitchen door. The atmosphere in the room was sticky with suspicion. He took a long drag off his cigarillo. As if he'd been given permission to puff, Mike produced a crumpled pack of cigarettes.

"You really think your father lied to you, Kate?" Declan said.

She stood hunched, arms crossed and grabbing her shoulders as if bracing against a bitter wind. She turned her back on Declan and Mike framed by the open kitchen door.

Mike came to Kate's help. "Marsh said nothing to defend himself. He just stood there. Innocent people protest."

Like you protested when the cops hooked you to a lie detector, Declan thought. He had no trouble picturing the scene between Kate and Carlton Marsh. Whoever scripted it was very slick.

"Would you have believed him, Kate? You doubt your own father." *But you believe anonymous letters.* "People who write anonymous letters are rarely well-intentioned." It was so quiet, he could hear the crackle of burning tobacco, from his cheroot and Mike's cigarette. "Somebody used you, Kate."

Mike jumped in again and Declan had to resist an urge to knock him out cold. "The medallion was where the letter said it was."

"Because the letter writer put it there." Declan tapped the end of the cigar outside the door. "Carlton didn't kill himself, he was murdered. Until tonight I couldn't be sure."

That stopped Kate's tremors and Mike's interferences.

"Carlton asked me to help with research for his book. He was tracking a Salvadoran war criminal. I don't know if he'd figured out the man he was after also killed Ella. Maybe he suspected it. When you produced the medallion, he knew. It must have shocked him. The killer was so close he could hide Ella's necklace in his desk. You wonder why he froze, Mike?"

"Why didn't he say anything?" Kate pleaded. "I would have listened."

Was the killer watching, right now? Declan felt the cold in his bones.

Kate clasped a hand on her throat. "I'm going to be sick."

Declan wanted to go to her but Mike beat him to it. He led her back to the kitchen chair and gave her a glass of water.

She buried her face in her hands. "If I accused an innocent man …" Mike reached for her and she squirmed.

"That's nonsense." Declan wasn't going to let her wallow in grief for Carlton Marsh, right after she called him a monster. "A mass murderer killed Carlton, not your little social call." His words acted like a cattle prod on Mike whose fists clenched in sync with his jaws. "You're getting tiresome, buddy. I'm setting your girlfriend straight. Take a seat, and chill." Kate looked at him between the tears. He liked the flash of anger in her eyes. It showed grit. "Get a grip, both of you. Carlton hired me to find that son of a bitch. I might need your help, Kate."

Mike exploded. He had to release all that coiled tension. "There's a killer loose and you want to involve her?"

Tiresome, indeed. God protect us from lovestruck fishermen. "I don't plan to go to El Salvador to search for mass graves. This is about Ella."

Kate regained her balance first. "He's right, Mike. I lost my head for a moment. What do you hope to find after thirty years?"

"The murderer wrote to you. That's in the here and now. I need to talk to your parents." Declan handed her his cell phone. "Give me the number."

"Dad lives in Melbourne."

"And your mother?"

"I was ten when she died. Older than Bernadette when Brigid …"

"She suffered longer," Mike said, and it was unclear who he referred to—Kate, Kate's mother, or his wife.

"I went to Australia, to live with my dad." Kate emptied her wine glass. She wiped the condensation off the side, rubbed her fingers on her jeans. She took the wine bottle and poured some. "A freak manipulated me. I'm not smarter than the people who believed the crazy letters thirty years ago, and accused everybody and their dog."

"A stupid dog like me," Mike said.

Kate reached for his hand across the table. "This town has more than its share of rotten people. Maybe we should both take that boat to Florida."

Declan thought it was a splendid idea. "Did it look like the letters were written by the same person?"

"They were made of pasted strips, like blackmail letters in movies. They were addressed to Katherine Cavendish."

"Why do people write anonymous letters?" Mike said. "Not the ones Kate received, they were sent to frame Marsh, but the others."

"Like the letters that accused you?"

Mike's face turned red, darker than the freckles. He shifted in his chair and the linoleum screeched again. "My grandfather was a tough bastard. He pissed off a lot of people."

"That's the most common reason," Declan said. "A grudge, envy, or jealousy. A coward's revenge against enemies. In a small town like this, rancor and hatred fester. The murderer might have written the first letters, as a diversion, then copycats joined the game. There are famous cases. Like *L'Affaire Gregory*, in France. There was a slew of anonymous letters."

"And a slew of suspects." Kate nodded. "It's a classic. A four-year-old boy kidnapped and murdered. The investigation went back and forth. It's still unsolved, I believe."

"Soon everybody involved will be dead," Declan said. "There are similarities with Ella's case. Contradictory and recanted testimonies."

"What are you going to do?" Mike said.

"Talk to Kate's father, and track the people who worked the case. I also need to make myself scarce around here." He shot them a crooked smile. "If I appear to doubt the police conclusion that Carlton killed himself, a stray bullet might find me. People who clean their guns in preparation for hunting season, oops."

"I have a revolver you can borrow," Mike said.

"Thanks, but no. I'm allergic to guns."

"And you're a detective? In Texas?" Mike snickered.

"Yeah, it's funny," Declan said. "I have to go. Splendid dinner, Mike. Be careful, you two, we're after a smart and dangerous criminal. It will help if you behave as if Carlton's death is a relief to you, Kate."

"It won't be easy," she said.

Declan gave her his phone number. "Call me if anything happens, okay?"

THIRTEEN

THEY SAT IN THE KITCHEN for another hour after Shaw left, rehashing what he told them. Kate was angry at herself for having been so gullible, so eager to believe the worst about a man who was a friend of her father's.

"You didn't know Marsh," Mike said.

He tried to find excuses and she didn't want to hear any. She was a researcher, analytical, thorough, and she had been bamboozled. There was no other word for it.

"It was about your sister," Mike insisted.

A sister she didn't remember. A sister she never knew. A sister who was a case study.

"Shaw asked the question I should have asked. He didn't have to rack his brains, Mike. He saw the wrinkle right away. *How did the letter writer know the medallion was in there?*" She couldn't believe how stupid she'd been.

"Maybe the person who wrote the letter saw it in the drawer. There's no proof he put it there. Shaw is smart but he doesn't know everything."

Kate had heard that touch of jealousy in Mike's voice before.

Mike was protective, which she tolerated even if it annoyed her, but he was also possessive, and that drove her nuts.

"Shaw knows more than we do. You don't believe he gave us the full story, do you?"

Mike stubbed his cigarette. "He's sneaky. I trust him and I don't." He sneered. "He's screwing the gallery girl."

Kate was getting more irritated with Mike by the minute. "You mind taking me home?"

"You can stay. I would like you to stay."

He was more insistent than usual and Kate pondered her answer longer than usual. Shaw's irruption in their lives had put Mike on the defensive and she didn't want to hurt him. For all his windswept roughness, he was surprisingly thin-skinned.

"I have a lot on my mind tonight. I've been trying to keep Ella out of my paper, and it was a mistake. She's the reason I'm here."

Mike didn't insist after that.

• • •

The key stuck in the lock and Kate had to pull at the door hard to make it catch. The familiarity of these automatic actions was reassuring. She was safe now behind the thick stone walls of the old customs house. A fortress more than a house, compared to the place where she was born, all pastel-painted walls and chintz-curtained windows.

Four years ago, she drove to Old Mapleton after a speaking engagement in New Haven, and had a look at the Cavendish house. She felt no shivers of retrospective dread, only a diffuse disappointment that her parents had once lived in such a conventional place. Her father's house in Melbourne was modern, bright, and open to the outside, the polar opposite of this cloying Victorian pastry.

The small town didn't impress her either. On a beautiful spring Friday, tourists crowded the narrow beaches. Cars clogged Main and South Street, the two major arteries. Parking was at a premium. Kate had been lucky to find a narrow spot near the commercial harbor, between a rusty pickup truck and an overflowing dumpster.

She noticed the crumbling stone structure at the end of the jetty on her way back to the car. A rusty metal board identified it as the Customs House. A newer sign warned of the danger of falling stones. Kate took pictures, with the harbor in the background. The ruin was the most interesting thing she'd seen in Old Mapleton.

Over the next few weeks, she looked at the pictures often. The simple beauty of the abandoned structure appealed to her. She called historical societies and town officials. A month later, she was the proud owner of what the mayor of Old Mapleton described as 'a pile of rubble.' Rubble with conservation strings attached. The pile nobody had cared about now needed to be either preserved as is, or restored to its original aspect. It took time and money.

She met Mike Hannigan and bought a boat. Then she decided to write a paper on the events of 1992 that had been in the back of her mind for years. Her restored stone fortress was the perfect work retreat. She would be on site, where the drama unfolded. Not Ella's murder but the frenzy that surrounded the case, a social studies subject that she could analyze with appropriate detachment.

Or so she thought.

Kate was fooling herself.

She went to the sitting room without switching on the light and sat in the corner of the sofa. She wrapped herself in a plaid. Inside the thick walls, she needed a cocoon.

The time was right for calling her father in Australia, but he would ask questions and she wasn't prepared to answer them. Her fingers hovered over Shaw's contact information. It was well past midnight, and what could she tell him anyway?

She tapped the number.

It rang for a long time. Of course, the man was asleep. She should leave a message.

Then he answered.

"Kate? What is it?"

His voice sounded weird. Reedy, hesitant, out of breath. Well, she woke him up, unless she interrupted a session with the gallery girl. She shouldn't have called.

"I'm sorry, Declan. I should have waited till morning."

He cleared his throat. "It's okay … I wasn't asleep."

Oh dear, he was with the girl, how embarrassing. "I apologize. This is so rude of me. I'll call you tomorrow. I mean, today."

He let out a little chuckle. "Don't you dare. Give me a minute."

Kate heard a dragging sound. He coughed and it sounded painful, then he was back. His voice was still shaky. "What's bugging you?"

"I'm confused," she muttered.

"I threw disturbing stuff at you. Carlton, war crimes, a book, murder. It's a lot to take in."

That wasn't it. "I'm not an impulsive person. I think things through. Usually. The first anonymous letters didn't bother me. I thought they were a prank, from a colleague, maybe."

"Why a colleague?"

"Because of the subject of my paper. I planned to write about Old Mapleton in the aftermath of Ella's murder. What made an entire community go bonkers. How the anonymous letters stoked the fire. I thought it was somebody's idea of a joke."

"Pretty sick joke."

"You'd be surprised at what faculty members pull off. Anyway, the letters got more precise and I thought some nutcase in town was trying to frighten me, using the same tricks as thirty years ago. Then came the accusations against Marsh. I talked to Mike and we decided to confront Marsh. That was stupid. If he was the killer …" She pulled the plaid up to her neck.

"You didn't believe the medallion would be in the drawer," Declan said. "You must have been as shocked as Marsh."

"Tonight I realized something else." Kate was inching closer to the root of her discomfort. Shaw was a good listener. Even through the phone she could feel the empathy. It helped that his voice was normal again. Was the gallery girl asleep by his side? She pushed the thought away. "Me and Ella."

"You were two years old. Whatever memory you have isn't really yours. It comes from photos and news articles."

"My mother's rants," Kate said. "She resented me. Why was I alive instead of Ella. She was busy with me when Ella was taken. It was all my fault. I heard it so many times, Declan. I hated the invisible sister who made my life miserable."

"Your mother heaped her feelings of guilt on you. It's tragic because she didn't do anything wrong. The media and the townspeople bear a huge responsibility."

"I never saw my mother happy," Kate said. "My clearest memory of her is the array of medications by her bed and in the bathroom. I don't think she cared what she took, as long as it made her numb."

"How's your relationship with your father?"

"I love Dad. I didn't understand why he didn't live with us, why I couldn't live with him. I spent the holidays in Australia. It was such a relief to be allowed to run outside. I didn't want to go back to New York. I remember all the goodbyes and being devastated each time. It's a terrible thing to say but when Mom died, I was relieved."

"And now you're writing a paper to understand what destroyed your family," Declan said.

"I only understood that tonight. I was all wrapped up in that academic research nonsense and missing the point. Which explains why I haven't written a line in weeks. I've been taking the boat out every day to go fishing because I suffocate in town."

"Now that you got it off your chest, it should be smooth sailing. Skewer this bunch of hypocrites."

"There's murders to solve."

"That's my job, Kate. Go to bed now."

FOURTEEN

DECLAN HAD BEEN RELIEVED to find his bed empty. All the way back from Mike's, he feared Isabel might have decided to wait for him. His back-up plan was to leave her at the cabin and retreat, with his tail between his legs, to the lodge and Jean Heyzer's maternal care.

The withdrawal crisis came soon after he turned off the bedside light. It required the bucket. He was soaked in sweat to the point that he needed a shower.

Sirens wailed some distance away, either in town or on the road. He was too exhausted to care. When the phone rang he was shivering with the fake fever of dope hunger. He considered letting the call go to voicemail.

It was Kate Redmont. He braced for the worst.

All she needed was for him to listen. She didn't have anything significant to contribute to the case. It helped her to talk through her feelings, and it helped settle his frayed nerves in the process. After they hung up, he shoved a chair under the cabin's door handle. He didn't want any surprises, from a loving woman or a murderous war criminal.

• • •

In the morning, Declan got a text from Andy Hulten. The publisher should be in Old Mapleton, with Jennie, around eleven. Could they do lunch? Was there an acceptable eatery around?

Ah, the refined palate of New Yorkers! The marina café would have to do. It was close to the police station. He could picture Hulten's reaction to Chief Halston's Tudor office.

It was way too early to call Melbourne, they were fast asleep on the other side of the world. Declan studied his notes on Ella's murder. He looked for the names of the detectives that worked the case. He ignored the local cops. Two senior officers had come from New Haven. A quick search revealed that one of them was dead and the other retired. FBI agents had joined the locals after Ella's body was found. The news articles mentioned the lead agent. Thomas Cardiff. Also retired.

Declan had contacts at the Bureau. Instead of going to voicemail, his call rolled over to another number.

"Special Agent Barnstable's phone," a male voice said.

"I'm Declan Shaw, is Keith available?"

A pause. FBI agents didn't have first names. "*Special Agent* Barnstable can't take your call right now. Can I take a message?"

Declan smiled. Breaking protocol was a sin. "Please tell him to call me back." Barnstable already had his number but he gave it anyway. "It's about a murder. A cold case. Something surfaced."

The voice tone changed to restrained excitement. "Can you tell me more, Mr. Shaw?"

"That would not be appropriate at this point." If that didn't get Barnstable out of whatever meeting he was stuck in, nothing would.

Before Barnstable returned his call, however, Bill Heyzer knocked at the cabin door.

"Hi, what's going on?"

Bill wasn't in charge of the guests. That was Jean's job.

"You didn't hear the ruckus last night?"

"I had dinner with friends and I came back late. I had one of my, uh, episodes, and I fell off the planet. What happened?"

Bill closed the door and dropped in the armchair. "It's pandemonium in town. Police and fire departments from twenty miles around. Sirens went on for hours overnight."

That awoke a vague memory. "I remember hearing sirens," Declan said.

"You missed a spectacular bonfire. Not much the firemen could do. The place burned like a house of cards."

"What burned?"

"Our fairy tale police station, and a couple of boats in the marina that were hit by flying debris. The cop on night duty is in the hospital. He got out in time. Smoke inhalation. It's lucky it happened when it did. The cleaning crew wasn't in yet and the guy on patrol was out on a call."

Very fortunate timing. Declan wouldn't be surprised if the fire started near the evidence locker. "Do they know what caused it?"

"It looks like a space heater was left switched on in one of the back offices."

A space heater. Mid-September.

"Police departments do a lot by computer nowadays but they still produce a huge amount of paper, and the building was old. Halston complained that it was a rabbit's warren. It used to be a small hotel. It sure wasn't designed for efficient police operations."

"How is Chief Halston?" Declan said.

"Mighty pissed off. He almost came to blows with the mayor. Halston told him he was responsible, because of all the budget cuts. He's right, it's a scandal."

"I should go down there."

"What good would that do? Breakfast is ready if you're interested."

"I'll be at the lodge soon. A few phone calls to make."

• • •

Andy Hulten decided to come to town anyway. The computer and the documents might be gone, but they could still look at Carlton Marsh's house.

"Somebody resorted to extreme measures, looks like," he said. "As far as I'm concerned, that's all the proof I need that Carlton was murdered. Can we nail the bastard?"

"Meet me at the marina café. You'll see the disaster area from there."

FBI Special Agent Keith Barnstable hadn't called yet when Declan left for the lodge. Jean didn't have much to add to Bill's report, except that the owners of the destroyed boats planned to sue the city for negligence.

"Two law firms called already. They booked three cabins for a week. I shouldn't rejoice. If they bleed the city, our taxes will skyrocket."

Declan didn't tell her the lawsuits would be voided if the investigators could prove arson.

The scene at the harbor was chaotic. The entire block where the police station used to be was cordoned off, as well as a portion of the marina, and a row of offices behind the incinerated building where all the windows has been blown out. Emergency lights flashed and investigators searched the site. Chief Halston stood where the front door of his station used to be, chewing on an unlit cigar. He must have realized that striking a match in the vicinity of his charred headquarters sent the wrong message. He spotted Declan and waved at him to come through the tape.

"At least I know you didn't do it," Halston said.

"Yeah? How?"

"My night patrol guy spotted you coming back home around eleven."

"I have a stake in the contents of your evidence locker. Marsh's laptop is of no use to me flash fried."

Halston chewed harder. There was a brown shine of tobacco on his lips. He removed the stogie and spit the juice out. "That's what you think, eh? That it's all about Marsh. A bit single-minded, I'd say. What kind of nutjob torches an entire police station for a computer? We don't even know if there was anything valuable in it. Rather radical."

"As radical as putting a bullet in a writer's head. Somebody plays for big stakes, Chief. Your Tudor horror is small potatoes." Declan didn't mention Marcia Cartwright. She was cremated in her house to destroy Carlton's manuscript. Would Halston consider that radical too?

Halston pointed his cigar at him. "Don't mock, son. There was stuff in there, irreplaceable."

"Like the albacore."

A moan. "Don't remind me. Bigger than the one you caught yesterday."

Jesus, what did he use, a fleet of spy drones? "All these informants on your payroll, and none of them has anything to say about the fire?"

"No. It disturbs me. Unless it's really an accident." It was obvious he didn't believe it was. "I'll have to shake a few trees. See what drops. What's your back-up plan now that the computer is kaput?"

"Carlton's house. Before an accidental firebomb levels it."

"The keys were in the same drawer as the laptop." Halston caught Declan's crooked smile. "Of course, you have your wily ways."

"Carlton's publisher and lawyer will be at the marina café soon. Join us." Then he added: "Please. They would appreciate it."

Halston grumbled an inaudible oath. He stuck both hands in

his pockets and trudged toward the ruins of his office. Declan was sympathetic. It was an ugly building but it was more home than the place where he slept, and he probably slept at the office more often than he should.

Declan was at the marina café for ten minutes, long enough to order a glass of wine, when Hulten and Jennie walked in. They were out of place among the tourists and marina habitués. Hulten, bald and bespectacled, the ultimate nerd, and Jennie who reminded Declan of Saint Germain des Prés, circa 1950, with her skinny black jeans and dark looks. Declan hoped she smoked unfiltered cigarettes and could carry a jazz tune.

"How's the food here?" Hulten pushed his rimless glasses up his nose.

"It's a disaster zone," Jennie said, more on point.

"I recommend the lobster rolls and crab cakes, and yes, it's a mess. Barring a miracle, my genius hacker won't have anything to test her talents on. Our adversary believes in scorched earth tactics. On the positive side, Chief Halston is mad and will raise hell."

"For the good that will do," Jennie said.

She ordered the crab cakes and a side salad. Hulten and Declan had the lobster rolls. A Sauvignon Blanc in an ice bucket appeared.

"This is pleasant," Hulten said. "Who are the millionaires anchored in these waters?"

"They don't anchor, Andy, they tie up. The better seafaring men and women are in the commercial harbor." Declan pointed to the right. He'd left the sea view to his guests. "But you're not interested in fishing, are you?"

Jennie chuckled. "He won't go near the fish tank in a restaurant."

"That's vile," the publisher protested. "I can't point at the fish that'll end on my plate."

"Enjoy your meal, Andy. You'll never come eye to eye with the lobster in your roll. How did it go in New Haven, Jennie?"

"The memorial is set for Wednesday. I'll text you the time and place." She pulled a folded piece of paper from her jacket pocket. "Carlton's contacts. I also have an extensive bio with Carlton's family antecedents and schools. I went through it. I doubt there's anything usable in there but I emailed it to you."

Declan glanced at the list. "Who are they?"

"Apart from Marcia Cartwright, they're AP contacts, a college dean, a librarian in Boston, his physician. Nobody with a connection to El Salvador," Jennie said. "They haven't seen Carlton's manuscript. I checked."

Declan leaned back in his chair. How did the murderer zero in on Marcia Cartwright? He must have had a direct source of information. The killer knew that Carlton finished the manuscript and sent it out to his beta reader. He also had access to the house as the seahorse medallion proved.

They finished their lunch. Chief Halston hadn't joined them. They walked to Carlton's house.

"You have a key?" Hulten said to Jennie.

"Oh, shit, no. How are we …"

Declan had his lock picks out. Jennie leaned on the side of the door to watch him work.

"These things are legal?" Hulten said.

"They are in Texas. I don't know about Connecticut."

"I deputize you as temporary locksmith." Chief Halston's voice rumbled behind them.

Hulten jumped. For a big guy Halston moved like a cat.

The door opened with a satisfactory click. Declan did the introductions. "Andrew Hulten, Jennie Watts, Chief Halston."

"I'm sorry for your police station," Hulten said.

"Not as much as I am," Halston croaked.

"I suggest you go upstairs with Jennie, Andy. The chief and I will tackle the sitting room."

"What should we look for?" Jennie asked.

"Documents, journals, photographs, notes. Look for stuff taped on the underside of furniture and drawers. Don't forget the top of armoires, lift the carpets."

They went to the bedrooms, and Declan went to the sitting room. The curtains were still closed. He pulled them open.

"You want to keep an eye on me, don't you?" Halston said.

"Works both ways, Chief. Our objectives might not be a perfect match. You have an entire City Council eager to shove embarrassment under the rug."

"Hard to do with the rubble out there." Halston pointed at the loaded bookshelves. "Are we supposed to look through all these books? Wouldn't the killer have checked already?"

Declan ran a finger on a shelf. "And sprayed dust afterwards?"

He went down on his knees and started with a bottom shelf. It contained the heavier volumes. Art, geography, photography. He pulled the books out, verified that nothing stuck out, ran a hand along the back and the sides of the bookcase, and replaced the tomes. It was repetitive work that Declan was familiar with. Halston had little patience for it. He focused on drawers and filing cabinets. Since Declan's visit, the cops had boxed the documents that were on the desk. There had been no reason for them to look any further. All the stuff they seized was now ashes.

"Interested in appointment books?" the chief said. "Eight years-worth of them."

"Yes, please."

Halston dropped the stack on the desk. He commented on what he found. Binders with invoices and bank statements. Fan letters. Conference programs. School curricula. "I had no idea he was such an in-demand speaker. Does it pay well? I mean, he's not a former president."

"Jennie would know how much he made a year. He went on TV when they needed somebody knowledgeable about Central America. He sure didn't do it for free."

138

Declan was midway through the first bookcase when he found the journals. They were leather-bound to match the classics that surrounded them. Declan put them on the desk next to the planners retrieved by Halston.

The chief's phone rang. "Halston. Yeah?" He listened and color drained from his face. "Be right there."

"Problem?" Declan said.

"They found a body."

"I thought all your people were accounted for."

"I gotta go."

Who was the victim? The arsonist? Declan sneezed. He was disturbing a lot of dust. Behind a row of Shakespeare plays, he found a manila envelope with photographs and letters. If it was valuable enough to be hidden … He completed his circuit of the room then brought a chair from the kitchen to look on top of the bookcases. An entire family of dust bunnies caused another sneezing fit but his dedication paid off. Against the wall sat a flat lacquered box, dust-covered. Whatever it was, Carlton Marsh hadn't looked at it in ages.

Declan used a corner of the curtain to clean the box and sat at the desk to look at his find.

Jennie appeared at the door. She carried a stack of notebooks. "We're not done yet, but these look promising. Where's Chief Halston?"

"He had a call. They found a body in the rubble."

"My God. A cop?"

"No. What have you got?"

"Journals. I leafed through a few pages," Jennie said. "It looks like a catalog of sexual encounters. They were under a floor board. I'm not sure I want to read them. I doubt Carlton intended to show them to anybody."

"Let's gather the stuff down here. I found journals too. Thanks, Jennie."

Declan felt a tingling in his fingers. He wanted to look at the box and he wanted to be alone when he opened it. Jennie shot him a probing glance. He had been too eager to dismiss her.

"I still have to go through the desk." Declan lied. Halston had raided the desk already.

Jennie went back upstairs.

• • •

The lacquered box contained letters, still in their envelopes, and a stack of faded color photographs. Declan spread them on the desk like cards for a game of solitaire. Group shots and portraits. He recognized a young Carlton Marsh, more from his attitude—chin forward and head held straight—than from physical traits. The pictures didn't capture the intensity of the clear blue eyes but it was definitely his college professor. He must be early twenties in these shots. Another young man featured in all the photographs. Tall, rangy, dark, with a crooked nose and a big smiling mouth. Devil-may-care. Declan felt an unexpected heart pinch. In two of the pictures the young man was kissing a girl. She was dark-haired too with strong black eyebrows.

Declan had seen her before. He had emailed a couple of links to himself during his web search, links to articles on the Ella Cavendish case. The pretty woman with the remarkable eyebrows was Amy Cavendish, Ella and Kate's mother. She didn't look pretty in the news coverage, but it was the same woman, no doubt about it.

The young man had to be Royce Cavendish.

Ella's parents. Kate took after her father.

One photograph had undeniable artistic power. It showed Royce, asleep on a striped beach towel. One arm was above his head, the other covered his forehead. He was naked and exposed, vulnerable in his abandonment. The erotic charge was powerful. The shadows were kind, they draped him.

Kate said that Carlton had been in Old Mapleton on the day

of the murder, that he had a fight with her mother, that her father knew about it but refused to tell her the reason for the fight. Carlton and Royce Cavendish?

Jennie had seen the box and would ask what was in it. Declan opened the manila envelope. The letters and photographs were interesting in a different way. Burnt villages, mass graves, letters in Spanish. Echoes from the war-torn areas Carlton reported from. Declan could say they were in the box. They fitted inside.

He gathered the pictures of Royce and Amy and shoved them in the inside pocket of his leather jacket. He heard Jennie and Andy Hulten upstairs, going through the rooms. He couldn't read the letters now. They were addressed to Carlton Marsh at various locations, hotels and PO boxes, all in the same tall, slanted handwriting. Carlton had scribbled notes on the envelopes, in the hurried, barely legible script that Declan was familiar with, from long ago in New Orleans when Professor Marsh commented on his writing assignments in big strokes of red pencil.

Stop pulling punches, Declan.

He remembered the day he didn't.

FIFTEEN

"I'M IMPRESSED with what you produced in one week," Professor Marsh said.

He read the article submitted by Sarah Layton. She interviewed the owner of a shrimp boat, a Vietnamese immigrant, who had transferred his South-Asian savvy to the waters of the Gulf. It was a strong piece and Declan listened, rapt, to the tribulations of the Nguyen family.

"This has background, local color, and a political angle that will make it attractive to the magazine market," Marsh said. "My only comment is that you should bring it to the present. What issues does Nguyen face here? As it stands, it looks like his is an ideal life. Conflict in the end would force people to think."

"But what if this life turned out great for Nguyen?" Sarah said, and Declan loved that she challenged the famous reporter. "I don't want to create drama for the sake of it. It feels artificial to me."

"If it's a happy story, sell it around Christmas." Marsh raised a hand to silence the laughter in the room. "I'm not suggesting that you hype it, Sarah. We have a commitment to truth, but look hard at that silver lining, make sure you're not being sold a fairy tale."

Fair enough, Declan thought.

Fifteen students were assembled in Carlton Marsh's sitting room for a Wednesday night review session. Marsh had selected them from articles submitted to his regular class. All were prepared to take on extra-curricular work. Declan had weighed the pros and cons. His free time was precious. His work schedule was gruesome. Between college classes and his various legit and less legit activities, he didn't get nearly enough sleep. But submitting work to Marsh-the-legend was irresistible. He took a pay cut to be here. That made him a harsh critic.

Marsh reviewed three more articles. He was tough. Students took frantic notes. He gave them the kind of candid tips that didn't fit in his regular lectures. The time allocated to the meeting was almost spent. Declan was resigned to not being critiqued tonight. It meant he wouldn't have to break his back on a new assignment for the next session.

"Then we have this UFO," Marsh said.

Declan's heart hiccupped. He recognized the cheap flimsy paper.

"I have questions, Declan. Is this a fiction piece?"

"Hell no." Fiction? Was the man out of his mind?

"Is this about a real person?"

"It's right there, in the first paragraph. I said I changed the name. For privacy."

"Is the central character a composite?" Marsh said, to ominous silence in the room. "Is there more than …"

"I know what composite means. It's a real person, and that's what two days in the life look like. I cut out the trips to the john and the treks to the burger joint, for brevity, but it's written in sequence."

The silence was heavier, if that was even possible.

"You can compress events. That's allowed. But this piece

raises a problem that reporters are bound to face," Marsh said. "Questions from the editor. Is this person real? Can you confirm your sources? People have gone to jail for that. What about your sources, Declan?"

"It's a real person," he said.

Marsh stared at the ceiling. "I won't read this piece aloud. It's very well written, and it's raw. If I read it the censors could come down on me." He winked at the audience. "Your parents might sue me." A grin. "Declan gave us a snippet of a whore's life."

Catcalls. Was she a dish, Dek? With big tits? How much did she charge? Marsh raised a hand again to silence the group.

"The piece is about an eighteen-year-old male prostitute. Gary. You chose him on purpose, Declan?"

"I won't write about a fourteen-year-old hustler, Mr. Marsh. If I witnessed underage sex, I would have to go to the cops. That would be a different kind of report."

"But that kind of thing happens, right?"

Of course it did. "I'll wait till the *NY Times* hires me to go that deep undercover."

He got the laughter on his side on that one.

"What would you do if your editor asked you to prove this story was true?" Marsh said.

"I would produce a copy of the affidavit Gary signed. With his real name blacked out, of course. I'd give my editor the phone number of the lawyer who held the original document."

"You did all that?"

"I don't have time for that. But if you ask for it, I can get it."

Marsh straightened in his chair. "I think we learned a few useful things tonight. When you tackle sensitive subjects, cover your ass. Have a lawyer friend. I'll see you all next week."

It was an abrupt dismissal. The rattled students gathered their papers.

"I want to talk to you, Declan," Marsh said.

Sarah shot him an inquiring glance and Declan mouthed *I'll be fine*. The students filed out.

"You could get this published in a heartbeat," Marsh said. "I could send it, with your own byline. It'll fetch three hundred at least."

"Can I have my copy back?"

Marsh gave him the pages. Declan pulled out his lighter and lit the stack of paper. He dropped the article in the fireplace and watched his text disappear. He didn't feel anything. That was the problem. No personal commitment. No emotion. He didn't give a shit about Gary and his predicament and he knew he should, because, with a different roll of the dice, it could have been his own.

"That's a pointless gesture," Marsh said. "You can rewrite it from memory. It might even turn out better." He went to the sideboard. "Would you like a drink?"

"Scotch," Declan said. "Neat."

It gave Marsh pause. "How old are you?"

Declan sighed. "Old enough." He downed the scotch and used the poker to crush his blackened article. It was always better to say less than more. The streets taught you it was smart to keep your mouth shut.

Marsh was behind him and he felt a hand on his shoulder. Squeezing. There wasn't much to grab there. Raw bone. It was such a clumsy attempt at intimacy that it brought tears to Declan's eyes.

Marsh's hand slid down Declan's back, stopped at the waist, slinked sideways to his hip. It was clear where it would go next. Time to stop the pilgrim's progress.

"Don't do this," Declan said.

Marsh's hand retreated and Declan returned the poker to the fireplace set. He could feel the professor's eyes on the back of his neck.

"My wallet is on the desk," Marsh said. "Take what you want." His voice was thin.

"Why the fuck would I do that?" Declan turned around.

The famous professor's face was coated in sweat. He sat on the sofa. "I just want to watch you," he muttered. "You can do whatever you want." There was a plea in his eyes. "You're terribly handsome. I'm … uh, enticed." He wiped his face with his handkerchief, seemed to get himself under control, somewhat. "The way you speak is different from the way you write. It's … exciting. You don't have to do anything. Just stand there." He looked away. "I can help you. Don't you need the money?"

Declan leaned on the fireplace, hipshot. He extracted a flat cigar case from his jeans' pocket, flicked the lighter and lit a cheroot. "Do I look hungry to you?" He took a puff, exhaled, eyes closed. He dropped the tough sharp speak and reverted to his natural low tones. "I'm not as hungry as you are. Not the same hunger." He looked at Marsh's troubled face, studied the stamped-tin ceiling of the old apartment. "I'm not like Gary, or the other lost ones."

Marsh sipped his drink. "You're a street kid. Like them."

"I've always had a roof over my head, however crumbling or unpleasant." Declan grabbed his leather jacket. "The streets don't own me, Professor. I take from them what I need, like I take from your class what I need. I thought I might try my hand at journalism, but I'd rather stick to my original plan. I want to be a lawyer."

Marsh went to the desk. He pulled banknotes out of his wallet. "Law school is expensive."

"If I ever accept money from you, Professor, it will be for real work. Not for strutting around in a drawing room comedy of errors. Be careful out there. The Mississippi delta is teeming with sharks."

"I've been to a lot worse places," Marsh said.

"You knew the locale and the players. You were acclimatized."

He said it with an exaggerated southern drawl and a wink. "Call me in a few years. Declan Francis Philip Shaw. You'll find me."

He walked out and quietly closed the door behind him.

SIXTEEN

CARLTON MARSH CALLED the agency, out of the blue, at a time when Declan struggled to make ends meet, juggling low-paying cases, trying to get recognized as a legitimate private investigator. Tough beginnings that tested his resolve. There had been no work assignment from Marsh, only candid conversations. They met occasionally, when Marsh's travels brought him to Houston, between planes, long enough to catch up over dinner or a couple of drinks. Neither of them ever mentioned the seduction attempt in New Orleans. Marsh always asked when Declan's non-existent legal career might take flight, and he always found an opportunity to slip in that Declan would have made an excellent journalist.

Well, he was an investigator, so Marsh had a point.

Declan was leafing through an appointment book when Hulten and Jennie walked into the sitting room.

"What's in there?" Jennie pointed at the lacquered box.

Declan pushed the manila envelope with the letters and pictures toward her. "The photos look like a typical Central American village. There's no identification."

"It could be the site of a massacre." Jennie scanned the letters. "Written in the late nineties. No addresses. Signed Rico, Maria, Eusebio. It'll be a headscratcher."

"Where's the fun when it's too easy," Declan said. "We have other investigation avenues. The journals can't all be cock and bull."

Hulten sighed. "From what I've seen, cock is most of it. I'm no prude, but boy oh boy."

"Hot under the collar, Andy? Carlton was a good writer, no matter the subject. Do you mind if I set camp in the house for a few days, Jennie? I don't want to lug all this paperwork to my cabin in the woods."

"Fine by me."

"You two stay here while I go get my stuff. We shouldn't leave the documents unattended."

• • •

Jean Heyzer was upset to see him move out.

"It's temporary," Declan said.

"What if I need to reach you?"

Declan kissed her on both cheeks. "You have my number. I'm not that far. I'll be staying in Carlton Marsh's house for a few days."

"A house where a man died."

Declan could imagine her crossing her fingers behind her back to keep evil at bay. "He was my friend, Jean. He won't pull on my blankets at night to frighten me."

As he carried his bag to the car, his phone rang. It was Keith Barnstable, from the FBI.

"Just in time," Declan said.

"I do my best. What kind of muck did you step in this time?"

"A friend of mine supposedly committed suicide. I won't get into my doubts about that. I have reasons to believe his death is related to a 1992 Connecticut murder. A seven-year-old girl, decapitated." Barnstable cursed. "Yeah, nasty. Thomas Cardiff was the special agent in charge. He's retired. I need to talk to him."

"A cold case," Barnstable said.

"Ella Cavendish's kidnapping and murder case is still open."

Barnstable said he would look into it.

• • •

Jennie and Hulten were deep in the journals. They looked embarrassed when Declan walked in. There was a deep flush on the publisher's cheeks. Jennie's lips were pinched into a thin hard line.

"I never imagined my job would include perusing porn in Connecticut," she said.

"How far have you got?"

"Multiple orgasms on repeat. I'm exhausted." Jennie pushed the journals away. "Knock yourself out. I'm done."

"Me too," Hulten said, sheepishly. "I can guarantee that I won't publish Carlton's personal papers anytime soon."

Declan took the chair behind the desk. It felt good, comfortable. He could swivel and look at the sea. It was a good place to work and reflect, but he needed to be alone.

"Go back to New York, handle the journalistic community. Stall. This will come together." He looked out of the window. "I think you should go now."

"You're odd," Jennie said. "No wonder Carlton liked you."

• • •

Declan was alone in the big silent house. The sun went down and he didn't switch on the lights. He looked at the horizon, at the open curtains.

The curtains were closed when the housekeeper came in and found the body. That didn't mean they were closed when Carlton was shot. Declan called Mike Hannigan.

"A question. When you went to visit Marsh with Kate, do you remember if the curtains were closed in the sitting room?"

"What are you talking about?" Mike said.

"The windows that look out to the sea, in Marsh's sitting room. Were the curtains open or closed?"

Mike was silent for a while. "Open. I think. Does it matter?"

"It might. Thanks, Mike."

Declan examined the windows. They were the kind that had to be unlocked from the sides before they could slide down.

The gunshot residue on Carlton's right hand proved he fired the gun. It was the linchpin of the suicide ruling. If he'd been down on the floor, disabled, the murderer could have put the gun in his hand and shot him point blank. But the blood spatter indicated that Carlton Marsh was standing when the killing shot was fired.

There was another possibility. The murderer could have shot Carlton, point blank, put the gun in his hand when he was on the floor, fired the gun a second time, and reloaded the gun, leaving one empty slot.

But where did the second shot go? The walls and the ceiling were intact.

The curtains were open. The windows. The killer could have fired through an open window. At that time of night, with wind and rain, there wasn't anybody on the beach. And nobody reported hearing gunshots that night. The killer wore gloves. No prints on the window latches, no latents on the curtains.

Dead end. Forensics would be no help.

Now was a decent time to call Australia. Declan had read the letters from the lacquered box and Carlton's scribbles on the envelopes. They didn't tell him anything he hadn't already figured out by looking at the photographs. Carlton Marsh and

Royce Cavendish were lovers. For a long time. Through college and Royce and Amy's marriage. All the letters predated little Ella's murder.

He was about to dial the number Kate gave him when the phone rang. It was Barnstable calling back.

"I have bad news and a workaround," the FBI special agent said. "Thomas Cardiff was diagnosed with early-onset Alzheimer's five years ago. I'll text you his address, in case you want to visit him anyway, but I suggest you talk to his partner, Dominique Lagarde. She retired last year. Brilliant career. Remarkable agent and teacher. She punched through quite a few glass ceilings. She lives near Providence."

"Rhode Island. That's next door. Thanks, Barns. What do you think of the case?" Declan knew his friend went through the file. Barnstable was thorough.

"Gruesome. I've worked one kid case in my career and it sticks in my head. You know who did it?"

"I'm hunting a shadow. All I see is the trail of destruction this guy leaves behind. I know he watches me. I have that nerve tingle. I'm not close to catching him. If I was getting warmer, he would have come after me already and he doesn't hold back when he's threatened." Carlton, Marcia Cartwright, the anonymous victim at the police station.

"How many murders are we talking about?"

"Too many. Where are you right now?" Declan said.

"In D.C. for a couple of days. Seminars. My butt hurts."

"I'll go see Ms. Lagarde. I need to offload some of this. Off the record."

Barnstable agreed it was a good idea, in case something happened to him.

• • •

It was surreal to imagine the ring of a phone in Melbourne,

Australia, where it was a day later and the morning, while Declan had a whiskey and watched the sky turn a dark velvety blue in Connecticut.

A woman answered the call.

"Good morning. I'm Declan Shaw. I'm a detective. Is Royce Cavendish in?"

A pause. "What is this about?"

"I'm calling from the U.S. ma'am. Mr. Cavendish's daughter, Kate, gave me this number."

"Just a moment."

Cavendish came on the line. "Is Kate all right?"

"She's fine. We had dinner together yesterday. Mr. Cavendish, can we connect via video conference? It would be easier. FaceTime, Zoom, Skype, whatever is convenient for you."

"FaceTime works," Cavendish said.

"I'll call you back right away."

Royce Cavendish's face was lined and suntanned but the same dark eyes that smiled at Carlton, half a century ago, stared at Declan through the distance of time and miles. He looked even more like Kate in real life than in the photographs.

"I'm intrigued, Mr. Shaw," he said.

"I'm a private detective and a friend of Carlton Marsh," Declan said. "I'm in Carlton's sitting room in Old Mapleton right now."

Cavendish's expression hardened. "What do you want? Where's Carl?"

"I have bad news, sir. Carlton Marsh died last week."

Cavendish pushed away from the indiscreet computer screen. "How?"

"That's the reason for my call," Declan said. "It appears to be suicide. Appearances can be misleading. I need your help, Mr. Cavendish."

"Oh, God." He looked away from the screen. "Give me a minute. I have to shut the office door." He was back quickly. "Why do you think I can help? I haven't set foot in the States in years." Then a sudden flash of worry. "Is Kate involved?"

"Sideways. I'll lay it out for you. It will take a while."

Declan summarized the events of the recent days. He touched on Marsh's book project and the suspicion that the reporter was hunting a war criminal. "I believe he got close, Mr. Cavendish. So close it caused his death."

"Carl's always been a devoted dragon slayer. He risked his life many times because he stuck his neck out too far. What can I do?"

"The seahorse medallion," Declan said.

Cavendish stared at the screen. "It was lost. The police thought ..." He looked away.

Declan told him about the anonymous letters sent to Kate, with the last one revealing the location of the medallion. "I'm convinced the man Carlton was chasing killed Ella, sir."

"You think I know who it is?" Cavendish said. "I told the police everything I knew, so many times." He ran a hand through his hair, closed his eyes. After all these years, the pain was still sharp.

"You lied to the cops. Carlton lied too. Tell me about that day. Please."

Royce Cavendish's eyes strayed from the screen. "It was between Carl, Amy and me. Two of them are gone now. I guess it doesn't matter anymore." He started, haltingly. "Our relationship. Our affair. Whatever ... It would have ended sooner if Carl had been more present in my life, but he was always on the move, flying into war zones, being shot at, hooked on danger, impossible to pin down. He surfaced at random, without warning, and I was a complete idiot, I ran when he whistled.

"The day before Ella's disappearance, Carl called my office. He was in New York for a few days, before going back to El Salvador to report on the aftermath of the Chapultepec Peace Accords signed earlier that year. He came to my New York apartment. We, well … it was the same as it always was. Carl knew how to push my buttons. I worried about Amy, and I told him I couldn't spend the night, that I had to go home. He got upset. We argued and I left, angry. He came to Old Mapleton that night, to apologize."

They met in the house Declan was calling from.

"Amy walked in on us." Cavendish described the ugly scene. Ultimatums. Screams and slammed doors. Tears. "I chose Amy and the girls. There was no doubt at all in my mind. That was where my responsibilities were. And a big chunk of my heart. I left very early in the morning. I couldn't stay in the house a moment longer. I had work to do in the city, meetings. I sleep-walked through them."

"Carlton stayed in Old Mapleton?" Declan said.

"He went to see Amy. I learned about it later that day and I was appalled. He told me he pleaded with her. She knew about the two of us, from before we were married. I had promised her we were through and I betrayed that promise. Carl was so naïve when it came to relationships. He was so smart about everything else. He couldn't see why we couldn't find an arrangement. We didn't hurt anybody, that kind of thing. He was in town maybe once or twice a year, and it all seemed so simple and logical to him. Amy went berserk."

It was the fight Kate told Declan about. No wonder Cavendish couldn't tell his daughter.

"You all lied to the cops about Carlton's presence in Old Mapleton," Declan said.

"It didn't matter. Carl was with me in New York when Ella was taken. He had nothing to do with it. We were in a hotel bar, drinking too much. There were witnesses. Carl tried to patch things up. I knew it was over between us."

"Why did the police and the media focus on Amy for so long? I read the articles. The attacks were relentless."

"Amy gave off all the wrong signals," Cavendish said. "She

couldn't cope with the questions and the attention. She was already on the edge and Ella's death sent her over. She hadn't been well for a while."

He told Declan that the problems started when they found out Amy was pregnant with Kate. It had been difficult from the beginning. Morning sickness crippled Amy, and she was prescribed bed rest for the last three months of the pregnancy. She resented the baby that caused her so much pain. Ella hadn't been like that. Ella had been easy. A dream child.

"Amy almost died," Cavendish said. "She hemorrhaged during delivery. She was in the hospital for weeks. I took Kate home and cared for her and Ella. By the time Amy came home, I had figured how to organize things. I managed my job as best I could. At the time, I did a lot of work on the phone anyway. It might have added to Amy's problems. She didn't feel needed or competent."

"There were mentions of post-partum depression," Declan said, cautiously.

"You don't have to dance around it, Mr. Shaw. Amy was depressed and her condition didn't improve with time. She took care of Kate, but she didn't love her. Not like Ella when she was a baby. And she was brittle, short tempered, always tired."

"She was already broken before Ella disappeared."

"My wife was spiraling, Mr. Shaw, and I was helpless. I had to cut her access to our bank accounts. She was erratic and irresponsible."

"What do you mean, cutting access?"

"She took money out of our accounts. It wasn't much at first, a few hundred here and there, but then it turned into thousands."

"Did she say what the money was for?"

"I questioned her. She threw a fit. Called me abusive, said she needed the money. I couldn't figure what she needed it for. She could have buried it in the yard, for all I know. I opened new accounts and closed the old ones. I couldn't trust her with the money."

"How much did she siphon out?"

"About three hundred thousand in six months, from our checking and investment accounts."

Could Amy have been blackmailed? "When did you cut her off?" Declan said.

"I don't remember exactly. In late spring of that year, I think."

"I know this is painful, Mr. Cavendish, but try to go back to these days. You said Amy was on edge. Was it about Carlton and you?"

"No, I hadn't seen Carl in over a year."

"Did you exchange letters?" Declan had one of them in front of him.

"He wrote to me at the New York address. Amy never came to the apartment."

There was something. Declan could smell it. "Could she have been afraid of somebody?"

"Amy never said anything. Wouldn't she have told me?"

"Not if she was scared into silence. How did you meet Amy, Mr. Cavendish?" The picture of Royce and Amy kissing was on the desk, next to Declan's whiskey glass.

"She was working for an ad agency in New York. I was with a brokerage firm at the time. 1980, clubs, parties, we bumped into each other at every corner. She was fun and pretty. The most interesting girl I ever met. We married a year later."

"And Carlton?"

Silence.

"What does that have to do with anything, Shaw?"

He wasn't *Mr.* Shaw anymore, a line had been crossed. Backtracking was in order. "I'm sorry, sir. Carlton was a friend but I didn't know much about his life, apart from the frontline reporting."

Cavendish nodded. Apologies accepted.

"Can I ask you about Old Mapleton?" Declan said.

A little wave of the hand. Proceed.

"I understand that the Cavendish and Marsh families have a long history in the area."

"You want to know about old feuds because the town turned against us." Cavendish sighed. "I don't know why they came after us. As kids, Carl and I spent all our summers and holidays in Old Mapleton. We hung out with a bunch of other kids, went swimming, sailing, fishing, explored the woods. All the families seemed to get along. When Ella was born, my parents decided to relocate to Florida and we moved into the family house. I commuted to New York. Amy quit her job to raise Ella. We went to parties at the country club, donated to local charities, socialized with the neighbors, got library cards."

It was said with a hint of sarcasm. Royce Cavendish must have often wondered how his Norman Rockwell little town turned into a snake pit.

"We didn't have close friends in town. There weren't many families with young children in Old Mapleton that were permanent residents." He made a face. "Not in our social set anyway. It's probably still the same today. Damn rigid up there."

"What about family?" Declan said. Nowhere in the media coverage had he seen any mention of relatives coming to Royce and Amy's defense.

"No family to speak of," Cavendish said. "My father passed before Kate was born, and Mom was in a retirement home in Fort Lauderdale. I'm an only child. Pretty thin on the bloodline."

"And on Amy's side?"

"Her father died when she was still a baby. Her mom came to our wedding, with her second husband, Oscar. All the way from El Salvador. Wonderful people. They're long gone."

El Salvador. Declan's breath caught and he took a sip of whiskey. "Amy's mother lived in El Salvador?"

"She was from there. Amy was born in San Salvador."

That was the connection. No doubt about it. Declan's throat felt dry and he gulped more whiskey. It went the wrong way and he coughed it all over Carlton Marsh's journals. "Excuse me." He leaned over the tablet to make eye contact with Cavendish. "Carlton was writing about the Salvadoran civil war."

"That was his lifelong beat," Cavendish said. "Central America."

The man didn't realize what this meant. "Carlton was after a Salvadoran war criminal, Cavendish. A man who killed girls in the jungle. A man who killed your daughter in the woods. Your wife was from El Salvador. She knew him."

The story was tumbling through Declan's mind. Amy saw the man. She knew what he was, who he was. She could expose him. He killed Ella to shut her up.

"That's utter nonsense." Cavendish spoke through clenched teeth. He was angry. "Amy's dad worked at the U.S. embassy in San Salvador. He met Amy's mom, Nita. After his death, Nita remarried. Amy left El Salvador to go to college. She never went back to Central America. Look at the fucking timeline, Shaw. She wasn't there during the civil war. How could she know a war criminal?"

Declan blinked, reconsidered his hypothesis. War criminals weren't born fully formed like Athena from Zeus's head. They were kids once. Did Amy cross paths with a monster in the making?

"Who did Amy's mom marry?" Declan said.

Cavendish's hackles were still up. "I resent that, Shaw. Oscar was a great guy, kind, generous. You're out of your mind."

"I just need a name, sir."

"Oscar Balaguer. You're barking up the wrong tree. Oscar and Nita left El Salvador, right after our wedding. The place was turning into a nightmare. They settled in Buenos Aires."

Carlton Marsh wrote countless articles about the violence that tore up the country. People with means left. The poor were left behind. "Did Amy have brothers and sisters?"

"God! You're relentless!"

"Please, sir. Amy's siblings?"

Cavendish rolled his eyes. "A half-brother, Gael Balaguer. I never met him. He didn't come to our wedding. There was a rift in the family for some reason. Oscar and Nita were tight-lipped about him. I know he didn't go to Argentina with them."

"Thank you, sir. You've been very patient. I apologize for taking so much of your time. Can I ask a last question?"

Cavendish groaned. "Is it really the last?"

"The murder investigation went on for months," Declan said. "What happened afterwards?"

"We packed and left. We couldn't stay in Old Mapleton. Amy was hospitalized for a while and Kate and I lived in the New York apartment. When Amy was released, I thought we could make things work, but it was impossible. We divorced. A few months later, I was offered an opportunity to work in Australia and I took it."

"Amy got custody of Kate," Declan said.

"I fought it and lost. Amy appeared competent and the courts tend to side with the mother. I made sure Kate had a reliable nanny."

"Kate told me about the time she spent with you. How hard it was to come back to New York."

"I wanted to keep her with me. I had started the procedure, it was very slow going, then Amy died." Cavendish looked tired suddenly, older.

"Thank you, sir," Declan said. "This isn't easy."

"The older you get, the less you need to pretend. Sadness and passion fade equally."

Declan wondered how Royce Cavendish would react to the picture Carlton took of him on the beach. Passion might have faded but he should feel at least the echo of desire.

SEVENTEEN

DECLAN HAD NEW NAMES to search for, both online and in Carlton's journals and calendars.

Nita and Oscar Balaguer.

Gael Balaguer.

Especially Gael Balaguer, Amy Cavendish's half-brother, estranged from his family for reasons his parents didn't want to talk about.

Declan ordered a pizza and appropriated a bottle from the dining room wine rack. He called Dominique Lagarde, the retired FBI agent, while he waited for his dinner to be delivered.

"Ms. Lagarde, my name is Declan Shaw, I'm a private investigator. Special Agent Barnstable gave me your contact information. I'm interested in a case you worked back in 92."

"Give me Barnstable's number," she said. "Can I reach you at the number you're calling from? I'll get back to you. Maybe." Call ended.

Declan had to smile. Lagarde didn't have a little chip on her shoulder, she carried a two-by-four.

She called right back. "You have a reputation," she said, and he detected a tingle of amusement. "Barnstable also said you were a pain in the neck."

"I'm the persistent kind. It's about the Ella Cavendish murder. I'm in Connecticut. I can visit."

She chuckled. "Can't we do this over the phone?"

"I'm afraid not. What about tomorrow?"

"Persistent *and* in a hurry. What's the rush? The girl has been dead for thirty years."

"My friend Carlton Marsh died last week, as did his friend Marcia Cartwright. Carlton was in Old Mapleton, Marcia in North Carolina. None of these were accidental deaths, Ms. Lagarde. The Old Mapleton police station burned down last night with the evidence from Carlton's case inside, and a body, still unidentified as far as I know, was found in the rubble. I believe there is quite a rush."

There was an audible intake of breath. "All right. Is early afternoon okay for you?" She gave him road directions. "It's a small place. GPS is sketchy."

Declan was opening the first of Carlton's journals when the pizza arrived. One bite of the pizza and one page in the journal and he decided to tackle the desk calendars first. They were much easier to digest.

It was routine stuff. Doctors' appointments, flights to various American college towns for conferences. The book for the current year was missing; the police took it. It was now ashy dust like Carlton's laptop and the rest of the seized documents. Declan took pictures when he encountered names he couldn't identify. He would send them to Hulten and Jennie for verification. A significant number of appointments came with first names only and phone numbers. Carlton used the desk calendars to keep track of assignations. Very few were repeats. A Jack C. appeared in October. Jack Corvill? If it was him, he lasted much longer than his colleagues. The relationship wasn't exclusive. Other names were sprinkled through: Jamie, Rico, Larbi,

Isaac. Carlton cut a large swath. Declan felt let down. After his conversation with Royce Cavendish, he had formed an image of Carlton Marsh that was more romantic than what he contemplated now.

Time to tackle the journals. Declan refilled his wine glass and moved from the desk to the sofa.

The first pages raised his temperature. Carlton was a very good writer. He brought sex prose to new heights. He might have missed his calling when he decided to go into journalism. After ten pages, Declan's interest subsided. After twenty pages, he yawned. The repeated descriptions of intercourse made him sleepy.

He scanned the pages diagonally, looking for changes in topic and paragraphs that stood out.

Here was one, notes on a trip to the border between El Salvador and Honduras where a massacre took place. Peasants who tried to cross the border were shot at by Honduran soldiers, then attacked by Salvadoran troopers coming from behind. Carlton scribbled: *include in chapter on refugee camps*. He came under fire and his photographer was wounded. They had to scramble to get back to their vehicle and make it out of there.

The fragment gave Declan hope. Maybe the sweaty purple prose wasn't a complete waste of time.

At two in the morning, he had to stop. A monster headache pounded and he was two wine bottles in.

By then he had collected names and references, mostly from a ten-year-old journal: Captain General Gerardo Barrios Military Academy, commanders of Atlacatl battalion, collaborators of Roberto d'Aubuisson, El Mozote massacre, El Gato (several mentions, once with a short description: young, smart. And this question: *Where is he now?*), CIA involvement, U.S. military advisors, and this line: *Check in Miami*.

Ten years ago, Carlton had just assembled in one volume all his AP articles on Central America, from 1980 on, when he was first drawn to the tumultuous region. It was a companion piece to his extensive research on the Iran-Contra scandal, that was published in the early 2000s.

Carlton was already thinking about his next book—the manuscript, now lost, that Andy Hulten expected to receive by year-end. The focus was clearly on the Salvadoran armed forces and the role of the military in the violence that devastated the country, and the U.S. involvement in the conflict.

The three chapters of the manuscript Declan had read set the scene and summarized the case. It was all there. Carlton hit hard, from the get-go, and kept hammering, piling evidence. It made him an extremely effective investigative reporter.

But he needed Declan's help to find El Gato. That wasn't investigative reporting, it was slinking in the dark, claws at the ready. Cat on Cat.

Declan hauled himself to bed. There were three more journals he hadn't gone through yet. He would take them with him on his road trip tomorrow. He was exhausted and fell asleep immediately.

And woke up three hours later, with the shakes and the shivers, sweat-soaked again and his stomach in a vise. He stumbled to the bathroom and made it in time to puke a few glasses worth of red Bordeaux. This ordeal was as tiresome as Carlton's porn. He ran the bath as hot as he could stand it and sat in the tub. When he started sliding to the bottom, overcome by sleep, he stepped out, wrapped a towel around his middle and went back to bed. Compared to the previous crises, this one was mild.

• • •

Dominique Lagarde said she could see him early afternoon. It was about an hour drive to Providence. The morning was halfway spent when Declan emerged. He checked his face in the bathroom mirror. It wasn't too bad if he ignored the dark shadows under the eyes. He guessed he had dropped a few pounds. The jeans felt loose and he tightened his belt one more notch. All that nocturnal barfing did wonders for his waistline and wreaked havoc on his pipes and teeth. It was high time it stopped. He shoved the planners and journals in the desk drawers, and took the three journals he had not examined yet. They went in his backpack with his travel kit and a change of clothes, in case he decided to spend the night in Providence.

There were supplies in the fridge—eggs, muffins, and orange juice—and he fixed breakfast before checking his tablet. A message from Jennie confirmed she would get on the names he sent, ASAP.

Declan called her to ask if Carlton had traveled to Florida and when. It was the kind of research he would have asked Moira Perkins to carry out if this had been a regular agency case. Jennie sounded happy to contribute to the investigation. Like the good lawyer she was, she didn't ask why he needed the information. Plausible deniability.

Isabel called while he was on the phone with Jennie and he let her message go to voicemail. Did she call for herself or on behalf of Schulman?

Declan used the next few hours to run a search on Amy Cavendish's relatives. There were a few articles in Spanish about Oscar Balaguer's ownership of a renowned restaurant in Buenos Aires. He had hired a famous chef. Declan understood enough Spanish to gather that the reporter was excited about this addition to the Argentine culinary scene. Data on Gael Balaguer were sparse. He was listed among the Salvadoran Military Academy graduates of 1978, with a mention of his selection for training in the U.S.—talent, family connections, or a combination of both. He reached the rank of lieutenant in 1980 and was in the elite Atlacatl battalion when it was formed in 81.

The civil war was heating up and the young man was in the thick of it.

Gael. El Gato? Carlton Marsh wrote: *Where is he now?*

The dates matched, and the military career. Young and smart. And he was connected to Amy Cavendish.

Declan grabbed his backpack and left the house. It was still too early to drive to Providence. He went to the harbor to try to catch Chief Halston. Instead he ran into Officer Craig, who looked both bored and desolate.

"I'm looking for the chief," Declan said.

"He'll be back soon. He's at city hall trying to wrangle a couple of trailers from the maintenance crew. For temporary quarters, you know."

"The season is over," Declan said. "Tourists are gone. Lots of available rentals in the area."

"Budget's tight. The trailers are free. Ah, here he comes."

Halston looked flustered. "You'd think I wanted to move into the mayor's basement. We got one double-wide, Craig. I have no idea in what shape it is. It's in the parking lot of the Northside Clinic. You think you could get your brother-in-law to bring it here with his truck? We'll set it next to the DPS office."

"I'll go see about it."

"Good boy." Halston looked at Declan, at the backpack. "On a hike?" Stared at the cowboy boots. "Ain't the right footwear."

"An errand out of town. Any news about the body?"

Halston blew out air. "A fifteen-year old kid. No idea why he was in there. He lives next door to Hannigan. Gives him a hand with the fishing."

"He isn't one of your little spy mice?"

"What makes you say that?" Halston was startled.

"I was poor and fifteen once. I jumped on any job for a buck."

"I plan to talk to the kid's brother. You want to come along?"

"I can't today. I would ask the brother who the kid did chores for. Good luck with the trailer." Declan turned on his heels to leave.

"I may be a thick-headed small-town cop, I can still smell when things start sliding sideways. Be careful, Declan."

Declan doffed an invisible cap. "You too."

They were after the same nastiness. They were undeclared allies. Sometimes those were the most reliable.

• • •

Dominique Lagarde's directions were impeccable. Declan parked the BMW next to her Land Rover an hour and a half after hopping on the freeway outside Old Mapleton. Her house was a small cottage, homey. It belonged in the hilly landscape.

"How was the drive?" she said, as soon as he got out of the car.

"Easy. Thanks for the coordinates."

She was of medium height, squarish, with broad shoulders, and a no-nonsense attitude that must have served her well in the field. Her gray hair was cut short and looked as practical as the rest of her.

"Come on in. You're a tall drink of water. Basketball player?"

"Can't stand it. High stakes poker."

"Exotic. Let's sit outside. It's nice on the back porch." She grabbed a crystal ashtray and gave it to him. "Coffee? How do you take it?"

"With nothing in it." How did she guess he wanted a smoke? He smiled. Beware of the profiler.

They settled on the porch with big mugs of coffee and Declan lit one of his cigarillos.

"What caused the sudden interest in the Ella Cavendish murder?" Dominique said.

"Carlton Marsh's book. He dedicated it to her. *For Ella and all the innocents slain by soulless men.*"

Dominique Lagarde remembered Marsh. "We interviewed him. He was with Cavendish in New York. They were each other's alibi, and witnesses confirmed their whereabouts. We excluded both of them right off the bat. How much do you know about the case?"

"I read the published stuff. I also talked at length with Cavendish, his daughter Kate, and Mike Hannigan. I know how things connect."

"There isn't much I can add then," Dominique said.

"My focus is on the mother, Amy. I believe she's the fulcrum."

"We thought so too. It didn't pan out." Dominique sipped her coffee. She watched him over the rim of her mug.

Declan blew a little cigar smoke to blunt her inquisitive stare. "Amy was a wreck, even before Ella's kidnapping. You couldn't get a grasp of her because her head was somewhere else."

"My senior partner, Cardiff, had very little patience with her. I never believed she could have killed her daughter in that gruesome manner. Cardiff disagreed. He was convinced she was a basket case and capable of anything."

Declan switched on his tablet. "Please read this. It's the beginning of Carlton Marsh's book. We don't have the full manuscript."

He watched her, interpreted the ripple of emotions on her face, the change in her breathing, the look in her eyes.

"Jesus," she whispered. "You think …?"

"No published article went into the graphic details of the massacre; Carlton's piece was censored. Nobody had the stomach for decapitated girls and heads hanging from clotheslines. He was the only reporter on the spot when the Salvadoran army moved in. The scene was sanitized, houses razed to the ground, bodies buried in mass graves."

"What are the odds? I mean … Girls in El Salvador, and a kid in Connecticut?" She raised her hands in a silent question.

"Amy's mother was Salvadoran and Amy lived there before she came to the U.S. for college."

Dominique frowned. "It says here that the village massacre happened in 82. Was Amy Cavendish in El Salvador at the time?"

"She'd been living in the U.S. for eleven years by then," Declan said.

Dominique leaned forward. "Were the girls in El Salvador raped?"

Declan was taken aback. "I don't know. Ella was?"

Dominique nodded.

"It was early for DNA but the case is still open," Declan said.

"Tests were done later." Dominique stood up. "Give me a minute to get my notes. I pulled them out after you called."

She was back quickly with a thick binder. "All investigators are pack rats and an unsolved case is like the red cape for the bull. Can't let it go. We were talking about DNA. Let's see."

She ran a finger on the binder tabs. Declan had visited with retired cops. Most kept files in moldy, dusty boxes. Few were as organized as Dominique Lagarde.

"A spot on the dress was traced to her baby sister," she read. "Saliva. A long blond hair belonged to the girl she was playing with that afternoon. No semen. The killer might have used an object, like a sex toy. The lack of fluids clinched it for Cardiff. He was even more convinced it was the mother."

"The link with El Salvador is solid," Declan said. "The killer decapitated Ella and hung the head by the hair in a tree. That is distinctive enough to be a signature, Ms. Lagarde."

"Dominique." She pulled her legs under her and curled up in the chair. "It's an interesting theory."

"You're a tough one, but you don't scare me. I have more." Declan held up one finger. "Carlton's book dedication and the gruesome display of the heads." Two fingers. "Amy's connection with El Salvador." Three fingers. "Carlton's conversations with his publisher and his lawyer implying he was after a Salvadoran war criminal. He expected the hunt to be strenuous. That's why he hired me."

Dominique tapped her binder. "Tell me why the killer in here is the mass murderer Marsh was trying to catch. That's the clincher and you don't have it."

"I planned to walk you through the process, but fine, we can shortcut."

She let out a long breath. "Stop jerking me around."

"I talked to Kate Redmont, Ella's sister. She received a series of anonymous letters."

Dominique threw her hands up in the air in frustration. "We were swamped with anonymous letters. You want to see them? I have copies right here."

"The letters addressed to Kate suggested Carlton Marsh was the murderer."

"That is utter nonsense."

Declan doubted she was that outspoken when she worked for the FBI. She must have found the compulsory restraint asphyxiating. "Hear me out. The letters said Carlton and Kate's father lied to the police. That Carlton and the mother had a fight on the day of the murder." Declan crushed his cigar in the ashtray. "That's true. I talked to Royce Cavendish and he confirmed. None of it had anything to do with Ella's death. Kate questioned her father and he was evasive. It made her suspicious. When the last letter hit her mailbox, she was ready to believe."

"An attempt to frame Marsh wouldn't have gone anywhere," Dominique said.

"The last letter described a medallion Ella was very fond of. She wore it all the time."

"The seahorse," Dominique said. "It was never found."

"The letter claimed it was in the bottom drawer of Carlton Marsh's desk. Kate went to see Carlton."

Dominique leaned forward. "And she found the medallion in the drawer?"

"Tell me, Special Agent Lagarde, does that clinch it or not? Carlton allegedly and conveniently committed suicide that same night."

"Overcome by guilt, no doubt. Ridiculous. The entire play with the letters is overkill. Marsh is hot on the killer's trail, he's dangerous, he got *suicided*. Why involve Kate Redmont?"

"Because the killer is a sick fuck; because he wants Carlton to know that he's coming for him, that he's close enough to get into his house, rummage in his desk drawers. Because he wants to show he's smarter than the celebrated reporter." He sighed. "I don't know, Dominique. You're the profiler."

"You're doing a fine job. What about the other deaths?"

"Marcia Cartwright, from Jefferson, North Carolina. She died a few days after Carlton, in the fire that destroyed her house. She was his beta reader."

"She saw the manuscript," Dominique said. "Dear God."

"The motherfucker is mopping up. The Old Mapleton police station was torched Sunday night. Carlton's laptop and documents were in there. The arson investigators found the body of a kid. Accomplice, collateral damage? I don't know. But the body count is mounting."

"Would you like something stronger than coffee?" Dominique said.

"Is it that time of day yet?"

"Who's checking? You dumped a load on me, Declan. Why don't you go in there and fix us a drink. I want to go through my documents. See if there's anything that jumps at me."

Declan understood. Investigations were fluid. New clues changed the perspective and he had shifted the case onto a different plane. "What would you like?"

"Impress me. The bar is in the sitting room."

She had a good selection of spirits, and something Declan hadn't enjoyed in a while. He went back to the porch. "Do you have limes?"

"Fridge, bottom drawer. I warn you, I have no patience for drinks that come with paper umbrellas."

"I think I have you pegged, Dominique. I should tell you about my bartender days."

She was deep in the binder, leafing through text-heavy pages when he came back with two frosted glasses.

"Sláinte."

"*Santé. Comme on dit chez nous.*"

"*Et où est le chez nous de Dominique Lagarde?*"

She stopped with the glass an inch from her lips. "You're full of surprises. La Gaspésie, Sainte-Anne-des-Monts." She took a sip. "Oh, I love this. Planter's punch?"

"Ti' Punch. Not many people have *rhum agricole* as a bar staple."

"Celia must have given it to me. She's from Martinique. My daughter-in-law. A wonderful woman. Chris, my son, is a bit of a doofus. He did much better than I expected in the wife department."

Declan lit another cheroot. "Tell me about yourself."

She ran her tongue on the rim of her glass. "This is addictive. Will you let me into the mystery of your gumshoe life?"

"Deal," Declan said.

She gave him a slight bow. "I went to law school in the U.S. where I met my future husband. He was JAG. I had language abilities on top of the law degree and the FBI was interested. We had two boys, Christopher and Kevin, two years apart. An IED on a road outside of Kabul made me a widow fifteen years ago. I'm not bitter, or angry. It could have been me. I've been shot at. Took them in the vest, very lucky. Your turn."

"Born in Austin. My dad came ashore straight from Ireland. Mom was from an old New Orleans family—that's where the French comes from. I was eleven when they died in a car crash. I was shipped to my grandmother in *La Nouvelle Orléans.* Muscled through college, history and pre-law. I needed money for law school and tried to make some in Houston—bigger city, better opportunities. I helped a shop owner nail a couple of thieves, helped a guy find his daughter, and without further ado I was a detective and I enjoyed it. A friendly cop told me to get legit." He raised his glass in salute. "I'm still at it."

"Compelling," Dominique said. "You've done well for yourself. Not many private dicks have buddies in the FBI."

"My first meeting with Special Agent Barnstable was contentious. He didn't have time for me and I hate procedure. We locked horns. We were both smart enough to realize it wasn't productive."

"How much does Barnstable know about what you're doing in Old Mapleton?"

"That it's about the Ella Cavendish cold case."

Dominique drained her glass. "You've convinced me. It's the same killer."

When a comment started that way, Declan knew what came next. "But?"

"The question that bugged me all through the investigation is still bugging me. Why Ella? This was not a crime of opportunity. It was planned." She tapped the binder. "It's all in here. The nanny was sent on a fake errand, the neighbor was distracted. The Salvadoran angle only reinforces the assumption that it wasn't a random kid grab."

"We're back where I started, back to Amy Cavendish," Declan said.

"Poker player, eh? Does that involve hiding cards in your sleeve?"

Declan chuckled. "That's cheating, ma'am. It'll get you in trouble."

"Knock it off. I've been dealing with smug smartasses all my life, and I don't have the patience for it anymore. Spit it out."

Duly chastised, Declan puffed a couple of times. "I know who the guy is. He's the only character that checks all the boxes.

But ..." He dropped his cigar in the ashtray. He should slow down. He was smoking way too much. "I still can't answer your question. Not to my complete satisfaction. Why Ella?"

Dominique raised her glass. "Make me another one of these."

"They're treacherous," Declan said.

"I'm not going anywhere."

A few minutes later, Declan set fresh cocktails on the table.

"Gael Balaguer, Amy's half-brother." When he said the name aloud, he knew it was right. It had that ring. Pure, like the perfect golf shot. The sweet spot of the golf club, the center of the tennis racket for maximum power. True. The precise angle for the race car to negotiate the curve.

Declan listed the facts. Born in 1957 in San Salvador. Graduated from the Military Academy in 78. Sent to the U.S. for additional training in 79. Served with the notorious Atlacatl in 81.

"He must appear in U.S. government documents," Dominique said.

"If he's what I think he is—a death squad commander—his stint in the U.S. must have been erased. And if his CIA buddies facilitated his extraction when the winds started shifting in 89, after these Jesuit priests were killed in San Salvador, all documents are long gone. The murder of the priests made worldwide headlines. The U.S. government tried to disengage. It was the beginning of the end for butchers like d'Aubuisson. Gael Balaguer was under his command. Carlton covered the entire thing, and kept writing about the country, long after everybody lost interest. El Salvador is still in deep trouble. Hell doesn't relinquish its hold willingly. Why do you think all these Salvadorans risk their lives trying to come here?"

"Don't turn into Carlton Marsh now. Keep the politics for the op-ed pages," Dominique said. "Why do I know that name. Balaguer."

"You're thinking of Joaquín Balaguer, the Dominican Republic president," Declan said. "Not a relative, as far as I know."

"You realize your theory relies on the CIA protecting their assets." Dominique was smiling.

"Protecting their asses might be more accurate. The U.S. government granted citizenship to the loyal instruments of its Central American policy. Cold War. Block the Reds. Realpolitik. Gael Balaguer is somewhere in the building, Dominique. He didn't leave like Elvis."

She stretched. She rolled her shoulders and cracked her neck to work out the stiffness. "I'm hungry. Let's have dinner. My son came yesterday and I made a mess of spaghetti and meatballs. It's always better left over. The least you can do is help me finish it."

● ● ●

The meal was delicious and the wine that went with it was perfect. They refrained from discussing the case while eating. Declan talked about his hosts in Old Mapleton, Jean and Bill Heyzer, and described their restored camp. Dominique mused about retirement and the adjustment from intense and challenging work to plenty of time to ponder and reflect.

It was getting too late to drive back to Old Mapleton. Declan tried to remember if he had passed a motel on the way.

Dominique read his thoughts. "The guest bedroom is at the end of the hallway. We're not done with the story, are we? "

"I can't stay, Dominique. I have to find a hotel."

"Why? I'm old enough to be your mother. You can't spend the night under a widow's roof? Is that some Old West thing, cowboy? These rakish boots. You're such a show off."

"Nothing like that. I have, uh, a condition."

"You're a bed wetter?"

She was quite something. "I have night seizures. They're noisy and messy."

He didn't fool her for a second. She held out her hand, palm up. "Give it to me." She made that come-on finger gesture. "The dope, boy."

"I haven't touched it for almost a week. That's the whole point. If I took it, I wouldn't have the shakes. You must understand."

"I do understand. Give it to me anyway. You'll get the stuff back tomorrow."

"It's unnecessary, Dominique. I'm in control." She made that gesture again and he handed her the silver cigar case.

She turned it upside down, looked at the engraving, an art deco geometrical design. "Pretty." She opened the case and pushed the smokes aside. There were two pills inside. "Where are the others?"

Declan was defeated. "In my travel kit."

"Go get it. You need to bring your bag in anyway."

The pill bottle joined the cigar case on the kitchen table. They both contemplated the objects in silence.

"What happened? Does it have something to do with that little hitch in your step?"

"The surgery was tough. I needed the prescription. I weaned myself off. Then I had a few long stake-outs in Houston. After the flight to get up here and the drive, the pain got unbearable. I took a pill. The next night was worse."

"The dope's got its hooks in you again," Dominique said.

"I can handle it but I don't need an audience."

"Pride can be a bad thing to cling to, Declan. It isn't weakness to accept help."

That wasn't it. He accepted Jean Heyzer's help. It had to do with Dominique, with who she was. An Officer of the Law. Retired, but still.

"Help doesn't bother me. Judgment does."

She shot him a dark glance. She cleared the table, went to

the sink and loaded the dishwasher. She spoke with her back to him. "I'm sorry. Please take your things back. I have no right to ask for them."

"I'm too prickly. It's part of the problem." He took a towel and dried the pot she had finished scrubbing. "When I was a kid, my best friend was a user. I loved him and pitied him. I vowed never to be like him, never to let the need own me. I didn't touch the stuff, not even a joint."

"You were cleaner than me," Dominique said. "Your bartender experience didn't turn you off hard liquor."

"You need some vices to fit in the private detective mold." He felt a tingle in the leg and it reminded him he had to loosen up and move. "I should go for a walk, doctor's orders."

"Does the doc require that you walk solo?"

Declan switched footwear and they set off at a good clip. There was an air of fall in the light, different from Old Mapleton where the sea dominated. They went around the square in front of the town hall. The shops were the usual mix of pseudo-antique stores, coffee shops, arty and curios displays, New England neat and prosperous.

"We get business traffic from Providence," Dominique said.

She had an uncanny talent. "Do you always know what people think?"

"I'm a logical person. You're looking in the windows, this is a small place and you wonder how anybody makes a living. Ergo … I can't guess what you're still not telling me about the case."

"Why Ella," Declan said. "Only the murderer knows. Amy Cavendish is dead. Her husband has no clue. Carlton's journals mention *El Gato*, a young Salvadoran officer. Carlton might have had sources in Florida. If he had contacts in the CIA, I don't know who they are."

"He knew enough to get murdered," Dominique said.

"If I were a war criminal in hiding, I'd be paranoid too."

Dominique stopped in front of a historical marker affixed to a clapboard structure that was leaning ominously. The plaque said something about this being the location of the first school operating in the county.

"Maybe Amy recognized Gael Balaguer and had to be silenced," she said.

"I thought about that. It doesn't make sense. There's no indication she knew what her half-brother did in El Salvador. She must have been aware of the rift in the family, with the parents having cut all contact with him. Gael didn't come to her wedding. The worst of the violence over there was still to come. I don't think Amy could have been a threat to him."

They resumed walking. Dominique waved at a couple of neighbors but didn't stop to chat with them. She was too absorbed in their conversation. "Let's say Gael got in the U.S. around 1990. His CIA handlers gave him a new identity. Why would he risk damaging his cover by approaching his half-sister? In a town as small as Old Mapleton, where gossip is endemic."

"It has to be money," Declan said. "The universal motivator. The Cavendishes were well-off. Gael must have pressured Amy. She made multiple bank withdrawals in the months before the murder. Her husband questioned her, and she refused to tell him what the money was for. It got so bad, he blocked her from the accounts."

"We looked at the family's finances. The withdrawals weren't large enough to raise suspicion. Cavendish said he made a few bad bets. We didn't pursue. We had so much on our plate. That case was a clusterfuck, Declan. Suspects left and right, denunciations, letters, false confessions."

Declan recalled the news articles. Slime oozed between the lines. The investigators lost their bearings. "It's always easier in retrospect and we have Carlton's first chapters as a compass. Cavendish blocking Amy's access to the money could have been the trigger. Gael might have been threatening her for months."

"Killing a little girl to hammer a point?" Dominique said.

"How much restraint do you expect from a sadistic freak?" Dominique sighed. "Let's go home. It's getting chilly."

EIGHTEEN

ISABEL CONTEMPLATED the two suitcases in her closet. The seasonal carrousel between New York, Miami and L.A. took a toll on the wheels. Another month and she would fly to Florida to go sit behind another desk as drab as the one in Old Mapleton, and peddle pseudo-art to sunburned tourists. Miami had better weather and better entertainment but from a professional perspective it was worse. At least here she had the art colony and its crew of eccentrics. They weren't all talented but they were amusing. And she was close to New York.

Miami was disturbing in other ways. It was Schulman's favorite residence. He popped in and out of the shop at all times, and dragged her to countless parties and business shindigs. It had been fun at first, but by now it had gotten old. She had her fill of middle-aged, potbellied investors with roving hands. The new crop of slick operators who spoke English with soft Spanish accents pleased her even less. Their hands were as hard as their eyes. When he was around them, Schulman dropped all pretense of courtesy. He treated her like merchandise.

Like in the storage room.

She lifted the larger suitcase and unzipped it on the bed. There was a leaflet from a Los Angeles gallery in there. She recalled talking to the woman who ran the place. They had hit it off. The woman said she was thinking of moving to Las Cruces, New Mexico. The desert appealed to her.

Isabel thought the desert would be a huge improvement.

She grabbed her phone and called Declan again. He didn't pick up.

He didn't want to see her, that much was clear.

She dropped on the bed. What was it with her? Why couldn't she tell Schulman, the graying investors, or the young men with stone eyes to go fuck themselves? She was a wind-up toy, and really easy to wind up too. She went all out and regretted it. Even with Declan, when she knew better. That mindless fuck on the desk at the gallery was all wrong. He pretended to shrug it off but it bothered him.

"Because he lost control," she muttered. "And he hates that."

That was her problem. The root of all her problems. She loved to lose control.

She put the L.A. gallery leaflet in her purse and started loading the big suitcase. She heard the key in the door. It scared the shit out of her that Schulman could walk in at any time of day or night. She grabbed the suitcase and shoved it under the bed.

"Shaw is not answering my calls," she said before he could ask. "His car is no longer at Marsh's house and he isn't at the camp. I have no idea where he is."

"You better find him. If you can't deliver Shaw, you are of no use to me, Isabel."

NINETEEN

DECLAN'S NIGHT WAS A REPEAT of the previous one. He had taken the precaution to cover the pillow and the bottom sheet with bath towels to avoid making a mess. Dominique's room was upstairs and he hoped he didn't disturb her, but when he ran the shower, she came down to enquire.

She knocked on the door. "Declan, you all right?"

He padded through the bedroom, cracked the door open. "Sorry for the water works. I'll sleep straight through from now on. It's always like this."

"You look gray. I'll make you some tea."

Gray? She put it kindly. He looked like a ghost. The shivers didn't help. "Please, don't bother."

She waved his objections away. "I won't be a minute."

The herbal tea was hot and fragrant. The sweetness of the honey gave him a welcome kick. He could feel the warmth spread from the top of his head to his toes. "Thank you."

"You wouldn't get that in a hotel."

"I don't want to get used to ladies tucking me into bed with an infusion."

"Shut up, I'll see you at breakfast."

• • •

After eight hours of sound sleep, Declan felt and looked human again. Dominique was on the phone, notepad in her lap, and she mouthed *breakfast's in the kitchen* before resuming her conversation with a: "Yes, okay, I have that. Thanks for taking the time. Yes, I'll keep you posted."

Hot coffee and crispy croissants in a bread basket.

"Do you want eggs?"

"No, thanks. This is wonderful. I want to marry your baker."

She riffled through the pages of the notepad. They were covered with bulleted scribbles. "People drive miles for his baguettes. I've been at work for you already."

"Uh?" Declan's mouth was full of croissant. He swiped the crumbs in a little pile. "Work?"

"The Marcia Cartwright case. Jefferson, North Carolina. I talked to the local sheriff. Nice woman, upset at the events that rocked her community."

"It is foul play, no doubt about it?"

"When fire starts on all four corners of a house as well as two bedrooms on the second floor and an office nook, it's definitely arson. When the body of the owner of said house shows traces of physical restraints, it's murder. The sheriff told me that the place still reeked of gasoline after the firemen doused the ashes. They questioned the neighbors—they're not nearby, it's rural. A white van was spotted in the area. It had some lettering on the doors but nobody was close enough to see what it said."

"The inevitable white van," Declan said.

"I didn't tell the sheriff it might be related to a suspicious suicide in Connecticut, but I told her that there was a possible connection with a cold case that I have an interest in. It helps to be ex-FBI. I still have some sway." She ripped off a page from the notepad. "Here's the sheriff's name and number."

"I love working with pros."

She refreshed his coffee. "I have more, but if you share what I'm going to tell you with anybody, they'll rip my head off. What they'll do to you, I don't even want to imagine."

"Who's they?"

"Spooks. Hush-hush people. I called an old friend who's still in the loop. We've helped each other out of sticky situations. He's NSA."

"Jesus, Dominique! These people are up to their eyeballs in the kind of political crap that got us where we are. They covered for the likes of Gael Balaguer for years."

She leaned on the table. Her chin rested on her steepled hands. "Don't you want justice?"

"I want to nail a psychopath. I don't want a fight with the U.S. government. I don't want to have to call Keith Barnstable at midnight to ask him to drop me in some remote country that doesn't extradite Americans. And I like my name too, no witness protection program, thank you very much. Dominique, that was a bonehead move."

"Your name was never mentioned."

Declan took the pill bottle that was where they left it last night and shook it. It rattled. There weren't many left in there. Still more than enough for an end run.

"I told my friend I had a blast from the past," Dominique said. "A guy who was involved in the worst case of my career just killed himself. When I said it was Carlton Marsh, my friend situated him right away. Damn good reporter, pain in the ass. My friend remembered that the Iran-Contra book gave people cold sweats."

She told her NSA buddy that Marsh worked on another controversial book, about El Salvador this time, and was after a death squad commander named Balaguer.

"He didn't ask how you knew all this?" Declan said.

"He didn't try to pump me. It isn't the way it rolls between us. We trust each other, no questions asked. I didn't have to tell him to keep it confidential."

"That's the way you left it with him?"

"He said he would call back," Dominique said.

Declan wasn't reassured. He could feel Gael Balaguer's breath on his neck; now he would also have to watch for federal agents getting underfoot. "I should go."

"I'd like you to be here when my friend calls."

"You're confident he will."

"I've known him for longer than you've been breathing."

Declan took his coffee mug to the sitting room. He had three of Carlton's journals to go through. He doubted another dose of pornography could take his mind away from Dominique's NSA contact.

He went through the pages quickly. Toward the end of the first journal, a section stuck out. Mass graves dug by the death squads. Declan still wasn't used to find descriptions of atrocities in the middle of breathless transports of lust. Did Carlton use this patchwork technique to mislead eventual snoops? Unless it was stream of consciousness and he wrote thoughts down as they occurred to him. Journal number two contained more mentions of El Gato, together with a tally of political murders and the execution of foreign journalists. R. d'A. was mentioned. Roberto d'Aubuisson, notorious for his death squad connections, died in 92, and escaped being held accountable for his actions. The last journal was more of the same, except for a scribble: *Samuel and Antonia, Miami,* followed by a cryptic note on the need to keep eyes open and mouths shut. Did Carlton suspect he was under surveillance? The painter boyfriend, Jack Corvill, was a prime spy candidate.

Declan was checking email when Dominique waved at him. She had a finger on her lips and her phone to her ear. Obviously, she couldn't put her correspondent on speaker. She did the next best thing, she wrote key words on a legal pad.

"They must have marked the bills and recorded the numbers," she said. She wrote the answer. "He was prepared. He had a plan." She went uh-uh. "Thanks, darling. Will you act on the information I gave you?" More scribbling. "Of course, yes. Me? Are you kidding? I'm very happy away from all the cloak and dagger stuff. When do *you* retire?" She chuckled. "Can't be too soon. Right. If you're ever in the neighborhood ..." Then *goodbye* and *take care.*

Declan remained seated by her side at the kitchen table, the legal pad in front of them.

"They lost him," he said. "With all the king's horses and all the king's men."

"He wasn't a priority target," Dominique said. "You understand my notes?"

"Mostly."

"It's not pretty. Gael Balaguer was granted U.S. citizenship in 91. He transited through the Dominican Republic and landed at night in one of the Keys. Passport, driver's license and social security card, plus two thousand dollars in an envelope. He became Antonio Merida, 31, born in El Paso, Texas. He said thank you and vanished. The spooks couldn't attract attention to him and besides he was one of them. They followed the marked money, and that didn't pan out."

"He found a poker game in Miami." Declan pointed at an underlined sentence. "Paper to chips to paper again."

"The assumption is that he connected with a network of Salvadoran immigrants. He ditched the Merida persona. He must have switched IDs multiple times and in quick succession. The spooks didn't care and they didn't have resources to waste on him anyway."

"Good riddance," Declan said. "I imagine not everybody in the agency agreed the U.S. should be involved with this garbage."

"My friend didn't say who arranged the deal. But Balaguer is a problem now, because of Carlton Marsh's suspicious death and his book project. I didn't tell my buddy that the manuscript was destroyed." She smiled. "It never hurts to light a fire under bureaucratic asses."

"Your friend didn't know about Balaguer before you called."

"Intelligence agencies share only when they can't afford not to. Marsh knew people in D.C. and had a habit of kicking the hornet's nest. Now the spooks have a serious issue. They need to locate Balaguer before the subject of Marsh's book becomes public. And it doesn't matter that the manuscript is missing. The three chapters I read are devastating, even if they don't mention Balaguer."

"I should call Carlton's publisher. He's in the line of fire," Declan said.

"The agency trying to strongarm the estate of Carlton Marsh, that'll be entertaining."

Declan didn't think Andy Hulten would see it that way. "They'll focus on Balaguer and shove everything else under the historical rug. God knows, they've done it many times before."

"You're closer to Balaguer than they are," Dominique said. "In the agency's book, the guy's been in the wind forever."

"Part of me hopes they find him before I do. They can cut his throat in a back alley. I won't insist on a public execution."

"Hang on to that thought. My advice is to let it ride. They'll find Balaguer and dispose of him discreetly. Much safer for you."

She was right and it was an option if he drove to Newark and hopped on a plane to Houston. He couldn't do it. Kate Redmont would not understand.

"I can't drop it."

"Of course you would say that. Do me a favor, because I like you and your cowboy boots, talk to Barnstable. Set a trap, be the bait. At least you'll have the FBI as a back-up, and they can play interference with the other agencies."

Barnstable could be hard-headed but he would see a good case when one was presented to him, and they had worked together before. "I'll do that."

Dominique was relieved to find him so accommodating. "Do you carry?"

"I don't like guns."

"I'm tempted to give you one. He's a killer, Declan, and he acts fast. You don't go into a situation like that naked."

Declan leaned to the side and extracted the hunting knife he kept in his right boot, in a special pocket. "I'm not toothless."

"Won't help if he takes potshots at you."

"He'll want to get close."

TWENTY

JENNIE WATTS CALLED as Declan was leaving. She had organized a small farewell ceremony for Carlton Marsh, and he decided to go straight to New Haven and meet her at the funeral home.

Jennie was happy to see him. Hulten was in a strategy meeting and couldn't join them. She didn't want to be alone when the casket disappeared behind the velvet drapes.

"He had such an outsize personality. There should be a crowd here to pay tribute."

"It will happen," Declan said. "We'll do it right, I promise."

"By the way, Jack Corvill called me. He's back from Canada. He said he couldn't come."

"What a surprise."

"He gave me a reason." Jennie's face scrunched up. "He can't attend funerals because they ruin his creativity. He's a painter of *joy!*"

"He's an even bigger prick than I thought. Let's get a drink."

They found an Irish bar to send off their friend the proper way.

Not one to snooze on the job, Jennie had brought documents. Printouts from Carlton's accountant with lists of his recent trips.

She had also identified most of the names Declan flagged in the desk calendars.

"Old Mapleton councilmen. Country Club types. Chamber of Commerce. Dinners and social niceties. What about the journals? Apart from the sex."

"There was a lot of that." Declan chuckled. "If I fucked that much, I wouldn't have time for anything else. And he managed to write a book. He had remarkable stamina and exceptional time management skills."

"There must have been a fair amount of fantasy woven through. If I wrote about atrocities all day long, I would need some kind of relief too."

She hadn't seen the desk planners. The appointments were real, not Carlton's imagination. Declan didn't make her wise.

"He traveled a lot," Jennie said. "I marked the speaking and teaching engagements. Five trips didn't have an academic purpose. He went to Miami and D.C. twice, and to New Orleans once in the last six months. I can go back further."

"No, that's perfect." Declan leafed through the stapled attachments. Were *Samuel and Antonia, Miami* in there? "Hotel and restaurant bills, limo service, rental cars. That's useful. Another round?"

"Shouldn't we order food? I have to face New York traffic."

"I suggest we find a hotel, have a nice dinner in Carlton's honor, and get hammered. He would approve."

She looked at him, a trifle suspicious. "Are you hitting on me, Declan?"

"On a wake night? God help me, lass. I have principles."

She exploded in a gale of laughter. His repartee wasn't that funny. He reached across the table and held both her hands in his.

"Jennie, Jennie. Today is nothing. I don't believe he had a lot of reverence for these ceremonies. He'll be vindicated when we nail the bastard. He'll pop the bubbly with Saint Peter."

She freed a hand to get a tissue. When she was done wiping

her eyes, she returned her hand to his. "Do you know your way around New Haven?"

"Not at all. There should be beds for rent and feeding troughs near Yale, but I've no idea where that is from here."

"Not far. Our cars are at the funeral home. Are you fit to drive?"

"I'm the typical male. I always think I'm a capable driver."

Jennie handled navigation. She got them to a hotel without a hitch even if her eyes had trouble focusing. Declan booked two rooms on the same floor. The restaurant was pleasant and the bar cozy. By the time they made it to the elevator, Jennie needed a strong arm around her waist. She had slipped out of her lawyer persona like a snake shedding its skin. She hung on Declan's neck with a floppy arm.

"I love you," she muttered.

"Of course you do, I'm very lovable." He swiped her key card and half-carried her to the bed. He struggled to undress her. If he'd been sober, it would have been no problem at all. Soon, she was tucked in and already asleep. He landed a kiss on her forehead and almost toppled forward.

"I haven't been that drunk in a while," he said, to nobody in particular.

It was tempting to just spread out on the king size bed. He left Jennie's room to stumble into his own.

· · ·

The dope didn't give a damn that Declan was drunk. The pain raced through his body with the violence of a nor'easter. He reached the bathroom on all fours. He didn't mind hugging the toilet. It would save him from the mother of all hangovers. He didn't have the energy for a shower and stuck his head under the faucet.

In the morning, the towel was still wrapped around his head

like a turban. His first thought was for Jennie. He called reception and secured a late check out. After a shower and a shave, he was again in respectable shape.

He grabbed his backpack, and the documents Jennie gave him spilled out onto the bed. On both trips to Miami, Carlton stayed at a hotel in Coconut Grove. He collected bar tabs and restaurant checks from the same neighborhood. On one restaurant bill he had scribbled *Noto & wife*. Were they *Samuel and Antonia*? There were copies of car rental agreements and chits from gas stations. Declan set aside the predictable receipts for filling up at the airport. On the second trip, Carlton stopped twice for gas. Once in Marathon. He went to the Keys. On the trail of Balaguer/Merida? It was a flimsy trail but Declan had a new name to look up: Noto.

He pulled out his tablet and went online. Noto. Coconut Grove.

A necrology appeared on top of the search results. Samuel Noto, died in June, age 82, in Coconut Grove. Survived by his wife Maria and sons, Angelo and Felix. Other relatives were listed. No Antonia. A phone number search gave him Angelo Noto, insurance broker.

A female voice answered. "Ange Noto. We care. Can I help you?"

"I would like to speak to Mr. Noto," Declan said. "It's about his father, Samuel."

"Oh. Don't you know? Mr. Samuel …"

Declan cut in. "Yes, I know. I'm sorry. It's why I'm calling. Is Mr. Noto available?"

"Who can I say this is?"

"Declan Shaw."

He could picture the office. The receptionist calls the boss, Angelo hesitates, and eventually acquiesces.

"Ange Noto." The voice was firm.

"My name is Shaw. I'm a private investigator. Your father's name appeared in documents related to a case I'm working on."

"What kind of case?"

"I would much prefer to do this face-to-face, Mr. Noto, but I'm in Connecticut. Does the name Carlton Marsh mean any-thing to you?"

"How do I know who you are?"

"Look me up online. Shaw Investigations, Houston, Texas, and call the number on the website. My partner Moira Perkins will confirm my cell phone number. You can call me back and we'll go from there."

"I'll do that."

Declan called Moira right away.

"Will you tell me what's cooking?" she said.

"As soon as it's safe to do so. Right now, you're better off not knowing." He could tell she didn't like it. It wasn't the first time he'd gone on a wild goose chase. "I won't be away much lon-ger, Moira."

"Some vacation. Careful in the dark. Bye."

Noto called back five minutes later. "I know Carlton Marsh. He was a friend of my father."

"I apologize if this sounds crude, Mr. Noto, but how did your father die?"

"Heart attack. Papá lived large. He'd had alerts. There was nothing suspicious."

"That's reassuring. Carlton Marsh died last week. There was nothing natural in his passing."

Silence. "It's about El Salvador, isn't it?"

"What do you know?"

"Family lore. I was a boy when we ran. All I remember is that I was scared all the time. Florida was paradise."

"What about Carlton?"

"He helped us escape. He was always welcome at home. Mamá cooked a feast when Tío Carlos visited. Later I learned that he was a famous reporter. I read the articles. His heart was in the right place. Is that why he died?"

"Yes." Again, Declan felt that thrill that rang so true. "He went after a monster."

"And he was defeated. Did Papá help him?"

"Carlton traveled to Florida twice recently. In January and March. In January he had dinner with your father and your mother. Maybe she'll remember what they talked about. In March he drove to the Keys."

There was a knock at the door. Declan ignored it and the door opened a crack, blocked by the security lock. He went to it, phone in hand.

"It's vague," Noto said.

Declan peeked through the door opening. A room service guy with a loaded cart and Jennie by his side.

"Breakfast delivered," she said, brightly.

Declan let them in and moved aside. He motioned to Jennie to give him a minute. "I'd be grateful for anything you can find. Is there an Antonia either in the family or among your father's friends? Carlton mentioned her."

"I can't think of anybody but I'll ask. Mr. Shaw?"

"Yeah."

The room service guy did the unveiling ceremony with the breakfast goodies. Jennie signed the room service receipt and closed the door behind him.

"Why are you involved in this?" Noto said.

"Your tío was a dear friend of mine. Let's talk later. I have people in here now."

"I'll see what I can find out. I'll call you back."

Jennie was back in lawyer mode. The excesses of the night had left no traces. Declan shot a glance at his bed and remembered hers. He had taken her shoes off, peeled off her clothes, and unclasped her bra. It was an underwire, uncomfortable to sleep in.

"Thanks for getting me home." Jennie was composed.

"You helped me navigate through town."

"I was referring to the sleeping arrangement."

"You were out," Declan said. "I wasn't much better."

She perused the breakfast items, and buttered a slice of toast. "My car is at the funeral home."

"I will need your help to get there. The entire map is blurry." Declan dragged an armchair to the breakfast spread. Eggs Benedict. Yoghurt and fruit. Freshly pressed juice. He downed the juice and munched on a muffin. The eggs were a little much.

"You undressed me."

"I can't say I have a clear memory of the events."

She smiled. "It might have been me doing you the favor, if my alcohol tolerance had been a mite better. I guess we're real friends now."

"We're drinking buddies." He filled her coffee cup.

Declan's phone buzzed and it reminded him of a loose end. "Can you give me Jack Corvill's number?" Jennie raised an eyebrow. He smiled an apology and answered the call. "Shaw."

It was Noto. "I talked to my mother. She didn't want to tell me, at first. She was scared."

Maria Noto recalled that all her husband ever talked to Marsh about was El Salvador, the massacres, and the constant fear of the death squads.

"All she wanted was to forget, Papá wanted justice."

"Did he mention somebody in particular?"

"A nickname, El Gato. I could hear the fear in Mom's voice. I felt bad for putting her through it."

"If I text you a picture, can you show it to your mother?" Declan didn't have a picture of Balaguer yet, but he knew somebody who might have one.

"Is it necessary?"

"I won't ask you if I find another way. What about Antonia?"

"Mom said it must be Toni. She worked with Papá in San Salvador. He helped her get out; we were already settled in Miami then."

"You know her?"

"I didn't realize her name was Antonia. She's always been Toni to me. We had lunch last week-end."

"You have a phone number?"

"I'll text it to you. If Toni can help you, you won't need my mother, will you?"

"That's right. Thank you so much."

"It's for Papá."

"Who was that?" Jennie said. She had a healthy appetite. She started on the second egg as Declan hung up with Noto.

"Checking on names from the journals." He was reluctant to share with her. She would tell Hulten and the less people knew about the Noto family the better.

"I texted you Corvill's number," she said.

"I better get it over with." Declan used the hotel phone for this particular call. The ringing went on for a long time and he hoped it would go to voicemail. He didn't feel like talking to the guy.

"Whassit?" A sleepy voice. At eleven in the morning. Somebody else had a late night.

"Uh, Jack Corvill?"

"Yeah, whosit?"

Declan was tempted to end the call. "My name's Dunoit. I'm a friend of Carlton Marsh. I'd like to see you about unfinished business."

"What kind of business?"

"His book. You're in it, Jack." The lie came easily. "There's, uh, money involved."

"That bitch lawyer said there wasn't any."

Declan winced. "Carlton knew how to keep secrets."

"Okay." Corvill sounded hesitant. "Where are you?"

"In New Haven. Are you at the art colony? I will need directions."

Corvill gave them. "I'm in bungalow six. See you around three." He hung up.

"What was that accent for?" Jennie said.

"Monsieur Dunoit is from New Orleans, dahlin'. He will enter Jack Corvill's life bearing gifts, for as long as it'll take me to extract a confession from him."

"Corvill was in Canada. He had nothing to do with Carlton's death."

"Somebody informed on Carlton's book progress and I doubt it was the housekeeper. Jack hung around for much longer than any of the boyfriends in the rotation. I believe he had to work hard to keep his prime spot in Carlton's life. Why would he do that? Not for love. Jack's a hired hand."

"Carlton had money," Jennie said. "Corvill was upset there wasn't a penny in the will for him."

"Why did he come back to Old Mapleton? The Montreal gig was a big success, I heard. Someone wanted him back and he's not in a position to refuse." It was a hunch that might not lead anywhere. Jack could have come back because he had nowhere else to go. Or he played hard to get for the benefit of a new sponsor. If Corvill was involved in the plot against Carlton, he had completed his assignment. He might be on call for another one.

"You're in charge," Jennie said. "I'm just a lawyer. We should pack and go."

"Take your time. We have the rooms until two. I asked for a late check-out."

"He thinks of everything." She gave him a peck on the cheek and left.

Next on Declan's agenda was a search for a picture of Gael Balaguer and a call to Antonia in Miami. She didn't answer and he left a message, with Angelo Noto as a reference. If she was as cautious as he had been, she would confirm with him before calling back. He sat at the table, nibbled at the breakfast leftovers, and went online for another deep dive search. Predictably, the

Salvadoran army didn't publish pictures of its commanders. The Military Academy wasn't as skittish. Declan found a picture of the class of 78 graduates. The names were underneath in alphabetical order. Gael Balaguer was somewhere in there under a stiff peaked cap that made all the young officers look alike. He selected a good photograph of silver-haired Oscar Balaguer and compared it to the picture of the academy graduates. Nothing jumped at him. Of course there were no pictures of El Gato. He would have to go back to Dominique. A passport and driver's license had been issued to Antonio Merida.

Dominique answered right away. "I don't know if I can swing that. The documents must have been destroyed."

Next, he called Kate Redmont and left a message: "Do you have family pictures that I could look at?"

Jennie knocked at the door. "I'll take a taxi to the funeral home to get my car. You're busy and I have to go back to town."

Declan protested that he could drive her and she shushed him. "Your meeting with Corvill is not for another two hours. I'll take care of the hotel bill. Be careful. You're about to enter dangerous waters."

Declan had felt the same prickling when he met Dominique Lagarde. He was taking direct steps against Gael Balaguer. The man was bound to notice. Old Mapleton could turn into an obstacle course. Or a shooting range.

Antonia Morelli, Toni, called as Declan gathered his belongings. She had checked with Noto. "I went to the Keys with Carlton Marsh. Sam was recovering from a health scare and couldn't do it."

"Where did you go?"

"Lower Sugarloaf Key. It's beyond the long bridge toward Key West."

"You had a lead?"

"The Salvadoran community is chatty. There's a lot of hearsay, but when it comes to the death squads, people are tight-lipped. When something seeps through, it has to be serious."

"About El Gato?"

"Carlton Marsh was focused on him. I don't know why he was so bent on catching that guy, they were all murderous bastards. There was talk that El Gato had come in through Florida. People were nervous. We tracked him to Sugarloaf Key. No way to know where he went from there. Thirty years ago, good luck."

"Do you know what he looks like, Toni?"

"I saw him. It was a long time ago."

Declan could feel the weight of that past encounter. He wished he was with her in Miami.

"It was a miracle, Mr. Shaw. I shouldn't be here. People died around me. I was left for dead. I crawled out before the bulldozers came to dig the mass graves."

"I'm in charge of the hunt now," Declan said. "Carlton was my friend. I'm going after this man. Anything you can tell me about him will help."

"He was terrifying. The soldiers were brutes. They looked like brutes. You knew what they would do. El Gato …" A long pause. "He was young, handsome. Mid-twenties. Not very tall, slender, and he moved like a cat. Very quiet and then very quick. He deserved the name. He was dark. The hair, the eyes. I will never forget the eyes. They burned. He wasn't dark in the face. You could tell he was upper class, not a peasant like the others. He had a soft voice. Educated. I didn't know people could be crazy and look like that."

"Toni, if I text you a picture—not a picture of him, I don't have one—but a picture of a man I believe is his father, could you tell me if you see a likeness?"

"I can try."

"Did you find anything in Sugarloaf Key?"

"An old guy remembered that he gave a man a lift to

Islamorada. He remembered because of the way he was dressed. In a dark suit and tie, at midnight, in August."

It correlated with the info from Dominique's NSA contact.

"I'll send you the picture. If I manage to find a better one, would you mind …?"

"I will help any way I can, Mr. Shaw."

It was time to get on the road back to Old Mapleton and meet Jack Corvill. Not knowing what he would face at the art colony, Declan transferred the hunting knife from the backpack to his boot, and replaced the oxys in the cigar case with a couple of sedatives. Hopefully, it would be all the protection he needed. He also pocketed his lock picking set, just in case.

TWENTY-ONE

DECLAN WANDERED DOWN country roads and reached the art colony from the back. Number six was surrounded by trees. The unit didn't have a sea view like Xandra Mohr's. A white Kia was parked under a tree.

He knocked on the door of the cabin, didn't hear a sound, and knocked again. If Corvill wasn't home, he would have to break in. It was too late in the game to waste any more time.

Declan was pulling out his lock picks when the door opened.

He set eyes on Jack Corvill.

A buck-naked Jack Corvill who sported a massive erection.

Declan could confirm to Jennie that Carlton's journals were not fantasy at all. He was rendered speechless and his own equipment shrunk, intimidated.

"Uh, I … I can come back later." The hesitation was welcome, because he forgot to switch on his pretend southern accent.

"Come in," Corvill said. "I'm working. I always work in the nude." He closed the door behind Declan and preceded him into a large studio.

Looking at the man's muscular back and firm buttocks was

less distracting than the full frontal. Jack Corvill was a well-built specimen, not tall but very fit. Those lats took time and discipline.

"My art is sensual," Corvill said. "I have a physical contact with the canvas when creativity surges. I throw everything I have in what I paint."

Declan bit his lips to stifle a fit of laughter. "I see." He almost lost it right there. This guy was a riot. Carlton must have kept him around for comic relief, on top of his obvious endowments.

Corvill stood in contemplation of a work in progress propped on an easel. "I've been on it all day. It's an exultation."

The studio layout was different from Xandra Mohr's. One big room, a kitchen to one side, a bathroom to the other. It was messy. The bed was unmade, the sheets rumpled. Two empty bottles of bubbly and two smudged glasses on a dingy credenza completed the picture. An unopened bottle of champagne sat in an ice bucket drippy from the melting ice. Whoever had frolicked with Jack hadn't left long ago. It was obvious that to get Jack to talk, Declan would have to make a personal investment that was out of the question. It was easier to slip him a pill, search the place, and pocket the dirty glasses.

Corvill caught him looking around. "Don't mind the clutter. I just got back from Montreal. I haven't had time to clean up. When creation calls, I have to answer. Nothing else matters. It's life and death."

What a pompous ass. "Inspiration is fleeting," Declan said, in his New Orleans by the way of Savannah purr. What was not fleeting, however, was that monstrous boner. Declan had not yet looked at Corvill's face. Couldn't have described the guy, couldn't draw a sketch. The body was spectacular; the rest was disappointing. Corvill's head was too small for the pile of muscle. A small nose, a small mouth, little eyes set too close, and a low forehead. A rodent's head on Apollo's body. Nature had a wicked sense of humor.

"Come, come, look at it."

He meant the canvas.

Corvill must believe that a painting needed to have a lot of paint on it. Thick layers on top of each other. The *oeuvre d'art* must weigh a ton. Maybe he priced his pieces by the pound.

"Do you have a name for it?" Declan would call it *The Bruise*. It was the purple color of a fresh shiner, with an undertone of red for burst blood vessels. There was even a touch of bilious yellow, appropriate for vomit or pus. Declan was glad he skipped lunch.

"I showed a series in Montreal called *The World Outside*. This will be the first of *The World Inside*."

Declan didn't want another look at the inside of Corvill's world. "Ambitious."

"It is, it is. Are you a collector?"

"Not at all."

"Ah, what do you do?"

"I'm a *financier*." In French, *s'il vous plaît*. It helped him get back into his Dunoit-from-the-Deep-South persona.

"Does that have something to do with finances?" A glimmer of interest in the little beady eyes.

Carlton Marsh hadn't picked this magnificent piece of ass for his brains.

"Investment deals."

Corvill looked at Declan's outfit. The leather jacket, the black jeans, the cowboy boots. "Is this how they dress on Wall Street these days?"

"That is not where I make *my* deals, *mon ami*. Let's talk about the deal I have for you." Declan pointed at the champagne bottle in the ice bucket. "I wouldn't mind a sip of that, to start the conversation."

Corvill trotted to the credenza. He noticed the dirty glasses. "I'll get fresh ones."

"I'll open the bottle." Declan slid the two dirty glasses to the side. Out of sight, out of mind. The cork popped with no symbolic spillage.

"You know how to do that. I always get foam all over."

I bet you do. Declan pulled out his cigar case. He took out one cheroot and the two sleeping pills. It helped to have card-shark-trained nimble fingers.

"You can't smoke in here." Corvill brought the glasses. "Paint and turpentine. Vapors."

"Oh, of course, sorry." The case went back in Declan's pocket. He filled the two lemonade glasses. The pills sank in the froth.

Corvill was very close now. His hip brushed Declan's leg.

"You were a friend of Carlton's, you said."

"We have that in common." Husky enough to suggest the visit wasn't solely about a financial arrangement. Declan knocked his glass against Corvill's. His eyes traveled down. "Isn't it uncomfortable? Shouldn't we do something about it?" The man was a flag pole. Declan sipped the bubbly. Piper Heidsieck. Not too shabby. Fit for what kind of celebration?

"I can hold it for a long time when I'm in creation mode."

"Convenient. I'm afraid I can't. Drink." Declan took off his jacket and started unbuttoning his shirt. The pills were fast action; he shouldn't have to strip all the way.

Corvill drained his glass. "What about that deal you were talking about?"

"Pleasure before business."

"You read my mind." Corvill grabbed Declan's crotch. The button fly puzzled him and he removed his hand.

"Nothing beats the classics," Declan said. "It slows things down. More fun."

He put a hand on Jack's ripped chest and pushed him toward the cruddy bed. The painter's eyes had started to take the glazed shine brought on by the roofies. It took longer than usual. The muscle mass slowed the process. Had to seep through all that meat. Corvill sprawled on the bed, eyes sleepy, but not sleepy enough yet.

Declan popped his jeans' buttons and sat on the edge of the bed to remove his boots. He took one off in slow motion as Corvill drifted gently into mellow Neverland. The reliable miracles of chemistry.

Corvill's eyelids flickered. He was out.

Declan fixed his clothes, pulled on a pair of latex gloves and set to work.

The grimy kitchen was first. Jack Corvill was a slob. There was nothing worth an investigator's time in there. For the sake of thoroughness, Declan went through the garbage. At least Jack had emptied his trash can before leaving for Canada. Catalogs, flyers. Declan moved to the bathroom. Hydrocodone and condoms, a couple of used ones in the bin. Considering the time it took to get a DNA analysis, gathering a sample was pointless. The case would come to a head well before lab results came in.

He searched the studio thoroughly. He knocked on the walls, the baseboards, and the floor. He looked behind the stacked canvasses. It was overkill. Jack Corvill didn't have secrets that warranted that level of precaution.

Declan found pictures in one of the credenza drawers. A stack of shots from events and exhibitions. They featured an inebriated Corvill hanging onto girls and boys with the same enthusiasm. A couple of pics showed him with Gabriel Schulman. Corvill was less interesting with his clothes on. If Declan had been his agent, he would have steered him toward the adult movie market. The bottom of a drawer delivered a letter from Carlton Marsh, with the now familiar outpouring of lust. It dated from the beginning of their relationship, when Jack C. first appeared in the desk calendars.

Corvill snored, flat on his back on the bed.

Declan found a contract drawn between Schulman's Isthmus gallery and Jack Corvill. It was similar to what Xandra Mohr described. Free lodging for exclusivity. Percentage on sales. Jack didn't have a special deal. The document predated Carlton's letter by a month. Declan had assumed Jack was a long-time resident of the art colony but he was newer to the place than Xandra. Among invoices for art supplies, he found a slim file labelled TAXES. Last year's documents were gathered in a plastic folder; the current year's were loose. Corvill kept track of expenses, no surprise with his consumption of pigments. Five receipts from Isthmus itemized with commendable transparency the sales price, gallery share, and artist's portion. Declan scanned the bank statements. Corvill's account showed little activity before the agreement with Isthmus. His revenue came from outfits with names like Academy Thorens or Studio Melba. None of these payments amounted to much. After he signed with Isthmus, he started receiving a monthly two-thousand-dollar stipend from an organization identified by the acronym M.G.I. and a bank account number. Declan took pictures. That would have to do. The turpentine vapors gave him a headache.

He inspected the room one last time for the sake of thoroughness. He wrapped the smudgy champagne glasses in a clean kitchen towel, wiped off the champagne bottle to remove his prints and washed his glass. He returned it to the cupboard. Jack's lemonade glass, carefully rinsed to remove the sedative residue but not the fingerprints, joined the others in the towel.

Declan recalled all his moves from the moment he came in. He had touched very little. Corvill snored. His cock, at rest, was still impressive.

• • •

Somebody—Schulman?—paid a pension, or equivalent, to Jack Corvill. What did the painter do to merit the reward? Unless it was a shakedown scheme. Always possible when sex was involved. Dominique Lagarde might be able to identify the owner of the bank account, she had contacts in the right places, or Keith Barnstable. Declan had to get in touch with him anyway; he promised Dominique.

He considered saying hello to Xandra but he didn't have anything new to tell her. Bernie Mellon had acknowledged his email, saying he would get in touch with the artist, but that was all.

Declan's phone rang as he drove out of the compound. It was Isabel. She deserved a courtesy return call. He should tell her their little adventure was over. If she demanded to know why, he wouldn't hesitate to bring in the romp with Schulman in the storage room. He hoped it wouldn't be needed.

● ● ●

Declan had to brake hard to avoid slamming into the road block. The police had positioned themselves after a blind curve. Great for surprise, risky for the cruisers' bodywork.

Two troopers, hands on their holsters came toward the BMW, one on each side. A third one was positioned behind one of the police cars, with his gun aimed at Declan's windshield. He didn't raise his hands; it was safer to not move at all. The guys looked tense.

One of the troopers motioned at him to lower the window.

"License and registration."

"My wallet is in my back pocket." The cop acknowledged and Declan shifted in his seat to reach for the document. He kept one hand on the steering wheel. "The car is a rental. The contract is in the glove box."

The cop looked at the driver's license. "Get the contract. My colleague is watching you."

The warning was unnecessary. The colleague was at the passenger side window.

"Texas DL. What are you doing here?"

"I'm staying in Old Mapleton." He answered the questioning glance. "At Bill and Jean Heyzer's camp."

The trooper studied the car rental contract. "Have you been at the camp since you got here?"

"What's going on?"

An eyebrow went up. "If you're staying in town, you should know."

"I was in New Haven last night and in Providence the night before."

"Verifiable?"

Declan wasn't about to rattle off an alibi to cops manning a road block. "I'll be happy to show my credit card receipts to Chief Halston."

"Step out of the car, sir." The cop moved aside, Declan's documents in his left hand, the right hand pulling the gun halfway out of the holster.

Declan got out of the car. He held his arms away from his body. These kinds of interactions could shift on an eyewink. The troopers were on edge, jaws clenched, fingers itchy. The senior cop told his partner to get Chief Halston on the radio. "Tell him we have a Declan Shaw from Texas in custody."

That was an overstatement.

The junior colleague said, "The chief wants to talk to him."

Tension slid several degrees down the scale, into a more temperate zone.

"Hi Chief."

"Get your ass to city hall," Halston said.

Declan handed the radio back to the cop. "He wants me at city hall."

The road block was dismantled and Declan drove through. It felt as if the troopers were reluctant to let him go. He was ten minutes away from downtown. He called Jean Heyzer.

"I ran into a roadblock," he said. "Why?"

Jean was a good one to talk to in an emergency. She wasn't circuitous. "Mike Hannigan is dead."

Declan grabbed the steering wheel. "What?"

"The cops aren't saying much. I heard Kate Redmont found him on the *Sea Robin*. Police came from nearby towns and scattered like a flock of birds. We've been asked to stay home. Come back here, Declan."

"Halston expects me at city hall. Where's Kate?"

"I don't know."

Declan had to park three blocks from the building. Police cars with multiple precincts and sheriff decals clogged the streets. He found his way to Halston without trouble. The word must have been given to let him through. He would have preferred if he'd been challenged; the privilege made him uneasy.

"Where were you?" Halston said, the moment Declan entered a bustling crisis command center on the ground floor of Old Mapleton's city hall.

"I went to see a friend in Providence, and I was in New Haven overnight. Carlton Marsh was cremated yesterday. What's going on here?"

"Too much dying, that's what's going on. And it started with Marsh. You'll set me straight, Shaw, or I swear I'll have somebody beat it out of you."

"I need to get in touch with a FBI buddy. I'd rather not tell the story twice."

"The feds are on their way." Halston looked ten years older than a few days ago. He had been furious then, now he was in pain. "Mike Hannigan is dead. Maybe I had something to do with it." He looked away. "I need a drink. Let's get out of here."

TWENTY-TWO

JEAN HEYZER DIDN'T KNOW Kate Redmont. She had seen her in town, and she and Bill had been interested in the restoration work at the old customs house. Another newcomer getting wrapped up in an impossible project. Kate kept to herself. She attended a party at the yacht club and Jean could feel the young woman's discomfort. She was surrounded by local dignitaries and it was obvious she would rather be anywhere else.

There was inevitable gossip when Kate bought a fishing boat. What possessed her? An answer was quickly found. She had fallen for Mike Hannigan. Talk about scraping the bottom of the barrel. Kate wouldn't be the first one to get drawn to bad boys.

Jean didn't judge. Kate Redmont seemed reasonable, and Hannigan was a single father with a young girl. More hardscrabble than outlaw, and from what she could see he taught Kate well. She knew how to handle that boat. When Bill said Hannigan would pump the woman for all she got, Jean told him to shut up.

And now Mike Hannigan was dead and the cops were frantic. Declan had asked where Kate was.

Jean gave a few calls. Her sources of information were eager to chat. One of them had seen Kate Redmont being loaded into an ambulance. The nearest hospital was Northside. Jean grabbed a jacket and her big tote.

"I'm going for a drive," she told Bill.

"We've been told to stay home," Bill said.

She closed the front door on his protest. If they turned her away at the hospital, so be it, but she would have tried. Declan called the girl Kate. And he went fishing with Mike Hannigan. They had a connection.

Jean wasn't turned away at the hospital. She said she was Kate Redmont's aunt. Bill said she could talk the toupee off a bald man. Whatever that meant.

An information desk person pointed her to the third floor.

The head nurse was a tougher nut to crack. Her name tag said *Clodagh*. She was all Jean feared in a head nurse. Tall, broad-shouldered, and firmly planted on her rubber-soled shoes.

"I'm her only family nearby," Jean said.

"She's heavily sedated."

"I'll just sit there. Please, nurse. So she can see me when she wakes up."

"When she wakes up, she screams."

"Oh, I'll call you." Jean frowned in concern. The terrible things that happen to good people in this crazy world.

Nurse Clodagh straightened her uniform and preceded her down a drab corridor painted in institutional grayish green.

Kate Redmont was in a double room that looked even more forlorn for having a single bed occupied. Her dark hair was mussed on the pillow. She was too pale and her hawkish features verged on skeletal. She could have posed for her death mask.

Nurse Clodagh checked the IV flow and tapped the monitor that beeped with soulless life measurements.

"Does she need the IV?" Jean said.

"Hydration and glucose. We dispense a sedative if she's in

trouble." She pointed at a pouch that wasn't connected. "At Northside, we only medicate when it's necessary."

Jean had seen what sedatives did to Declan. "That's very sensible."

Nurse Clodagh removed the sedative pouch and carried it out as if she didn't trust Jean near it. She left the door wide open behind her.

Jean dragged a chair close to the bed and took Kate's limp hand in hers. The pulse was regular. She tried to ignore the beeping sound from the monitor. It had a Chinese water torture quality.

"Kate. Wake up, child."

Inspirational literature told people that a loving human voice could cut through layers of unconsciousness. Maybe it was rubbish, but nobody would mock Jean for trying.

Sitting there in the relative silence of the hospital room—the nurses in the corridor were blank noise, less intrusive than the bleeps of the machine that marked the beats of Kate's life—Jean let her mind roam. Did this have something to do with Declan's investigation of Carlton Marsh's death? It looked like it. Otherwise why would Chief Halston have asked him to come to city hall. She couldn't believe Mike Hannigan had anything to do with it. The man had rough edges but he was raising his daughter right and that said a lot.

"Wake up, Kate."

The hand she held in hers didn't respond.

Time trickled.

Jean dozed. Nobody came into the room to ask her to leave. Silence was an invisibility cloak.

When Kate's hand squeezed her fingers, it happened in a half-dream, and the light touch wrapped itself around the story Jean drifted through. Then pressure on her hand increased and Jean stirred.

There was movement behind the eyelids, a change in Kate's

breathing and heartbeat, and the muffled noises of consciousness returning. Her eyes opened, too large in her thin face.

"I'm here for you, Kate." She was on the verge of a scream and Jean shushed her. "It's all right." Without letting go of her hand, she sat on the edge of the bed and leaned in to wrap an arm around Kate's shoulders.

"I'm so sorry."

Kate cried in long painful sobs. Jean got a handkerchief from her jacket pocket. She wiped Kate's eyes and runny nose. "Here, here." The tears were good, a better release than the screams that would bring Nurse Clodagh on the double.

"Where's Bernadette?" Kate muttered.

Jean patted Kate's back. Bernadette, Mike's daughter. "Isn't she in school?" But school had long let out. Was the kid with the police?

"I know you," Kate said. "You run that camp. What are you doing here?"

"I'm a friend of Declan's."

Kate sat up in the bed. "Where is he? I have to see him."

"He's with Chief Halston. He'll come as soon as he can." Jean was making promises she wasn't sure she could keep. "Could Bernadette be with social services?"

Kate leaned back on the pillow. "She called me because she missed school. Mike …" Her voice faltered. She blinked. It didn't stop the tears. "He didn't wake her up for school." She looked at the smudged window. "He wasn't at home."

"You took the girl to school. What school does she go to, Kate?"

"Sundowner Middle School. I … I dropped her before going to …" A surge of panic threatened to overcome her and she buried her face in the pillow.

"I'll call the school right now," Jean said.

A female voice came on the line. "Bernadette Hannigan? Let

me check." The woman was back a few minutes later. "She's not here, ma'am. Isn't she home? Who are you?"

Jean could hear the undertone of worry. "I'm her grandmother." She was getting good at this lying thing. "I was supposed to pick her up but I was late. She must have walked home. Thank you." She hung up. "I'd better go now, before somebody sends the cops. The girl could be hiding. If she sees the police, she might run away." She squeezed Kate's hand. "Don't worry. I'll handle Bernadette and I'll send Declan to you." She smiled. "Okay?"

Kate nodded. "I'm not going anywhere." She looked at the tubes and monitors. "I'm all tied up."

There was a hint of a smile. Brave girl. Jean liked her better than the gallery hussy.

TWENTY-THREE

THEY LEFT THE BUZZING city hall crisis center and went to the marina café. The hostess waved at Declan. He was too well-known around this place. They sat in the far corner of the terrace and ordered whisky sodas.

"It seems like forever since last time we talked," Halston said.

"You were on your way to go see the dead kid's family."

"The kid is Daryl Markus. I went to see Geoff, his brother. He was out on the *Sea Robin* with Hannigan. I waited for the boat to come in, and gave them time to handle the catch."

Halston found the fishermen drinking and smoking weed. Halston delivered the news. Daryl's body had been found in the ruins of the police station. When it registered, Geoff Markus got belligerent. The chief had to fend off both Markus and Hannigan.

"I was accused of all that's wrong in the world," Halston said. "The town never gives a chance to the working stiffs, Daryl was dead because nobody hires a kid from the woods, Daryl was pushed the wrong way, the town will have to pay for it … Hannigan blew a fuse. All the bile came out. The town was evil, there was blood in the soil. Hannigan was drunk. Fillet knives came out. I can't pretend I retreated in dignified order. I decided to tackle these guys in the morning, when I could catch them sober." Halston swirled the alcohol in his glass. "I should have called a prowler and dumped them in the drunk tank." He took a sip. "Hannigan might still be alive."

In the morning, Halston went back with his sidekick, officer Craig. Geoff Markus was sober. He didn't know what his little brother did with his free time. The kid had a hard time staying in school. The cops found an X-box in the kid's bedroom and expensive new sneakers. Geoff Markus had no clue where Daryl got them.

"It's a story that repeats generation after generation. Markus is right, the town doesn't do anything for kids like Daryl. They're left to fend for themselves. They end where they started, or lower. The class layers are granite hard. You need a jackhammer to break through them, and you're gonna hurt yourself doing it."

"You got through," Declan said.

"I'm the token punk, reminded at every turn." Halston slammed his glass down on the table and scotch spilled over. He pointed a fat finger at Declan. "You're an upstart punk too."

Declan wasn't, not completely. He was a half-punk, a hybrid. One foot in the Irish bog, another in a riding boot. No wonder he limped. "It's a big country, Chief. You can remake yourself with a bus ticket. Kate Redmont tried to convince Mike to leave. He was reluctant."

"We tend to remain stuck in these parts and our line of sight is limited, even with the sea out there."

"Why do you say you played a part in Mike's death?" Declan didn't ask how Hannigan died. Halston would get to it when he was ready. He got his cigarillos out, offered one to Halston who accepted.

"Young Daryl did little jobs for Hannigan, boat cleaning and such. I went to talk to him after my visit with Geoff Markus. He was still incensed about the previous night." Halston rested both elbows on the table. "At one point he talked about the Cavendish murder. And Marsh's suicide. He said they were related." The chief moved his drink and Declan's out of the way. To have a clear playing field. "He said you knew about it."

"I'm convinced Carlton's and Ella Cavendish's deaths are connected," Declan said. "I'd never heard of Daryl Markus until just now."

"You intended to share with me?"

"You have no time for shooting the shit. I would tell you if I had actionable proof. What did Mike say about Daryl?"

Halston ran a hand over his bald pate. It was shiny with sweat. "He said Daryl was gathering information for somebody."

"And that somebody wasn't you?"

"He said the man paid *well*. He said the man was too close to the kid. That it bothered him. Mike has a young girl, he pays attention to that kind of thing. He said Daryl was getting dark, embarrassed around him, shifty. Signs that something was going on with Daryl and that it was trouble."

"Did he tell you who the man was?"

"I pressed and pushed, and Mike got squirrelly."

"Scared?"

"Computing, like. What he could gain one way or the other. Talking to me or keeping mum. How much it would be worth. Figuring the buttered side of the bread, so to speak. I know how these guys think. Always working angles." Halston made a sliding hand gesture. "Little arrangements, betting they won't get caught."

"You think he went to the guy and tried to make a deal," Declan said.

"I think he miscalculated. Tried to bite more than he could chew. He died ugly." Halston spotted the waiter and raised two fingers for a refill. "He was tortured and sexually mutilated. His body was covered with burns. That was before his throat was cut. Somebody decided it wasn't enough to kill him."

"Cigarette burns?"

"The doc thinks a blowtorch was used."

Declan let out a long breath. He tapped off his cigar ash and got his phone. "I have to call my FBI friend."

"They must be in town by now."

"The case has wider implications, Chief, beyond local feds."

The call to Barnstable switched over, like last time, and a careful official voice, cast in the same neutral mold as the previous one, answered. Declan put the phone on speaker.

"Declan Shaw for Keith Barnstable. It's urgent."

"Special Agent Barnstable isn't …"

"Find him. Now. It can't wait, understand?"

"But, sir …"

"Tell him it's about mass murders and Blowtorch Bob. Now get Keith or I'm going all the way up to the AG."

He was put on hold.

"You know the motherfucker who did this?" Halston said.

"I know who he apprenticed with, where, and when."

The human answering machine managed to locate Barnstable.

"For fuck's sake. I was in an important staff meeting." The FBI agent fumed.

"Bureaucratic masturbation can wait. I'm with Burt Halston, Chief of Police in Old Mapleton, Connecticut. You're on speaker, Barns. This morning the body of a local fisherman was found on his boat. He was tortured with a blowtorch, his penis was chopped off, and his throat was cut. I'm sure the killer is one Gael Balaguer, native of El Salvador, former death squad commander known as El Gato." Declan felt a dark satisfaction at burning his bridges.

"Jesus H.," Barnstable said. "Walk me through it."

Declan did, in excruciating detail. He left out Dominique Lagarde. He called her *a law enforcement contact in Providence.* Barnstable knew who it was and Halston didn't need to know.

"It's still circumstantial, Dek," Barnstable said, predictably.

"Mike Hannigan knew who the kid, Daryl Markus, was entangled with. That person was Balaguer, whatever he calls himself now. He was tortured because Balaguer needed to know if Hannigan gave his name to anybody. Hannigan didn't give it to me or Chief Halston. We could have pushed Hannigan to reveal the identity of the man who paid Daryl. That's why he's dead. All we're missing, is the name the motherfucker's hiding behind."

"It's everything. Men in their early sixties somewhere in New England? If he hasn't taken a plane to nowhere already. If he's smart, he's gone."

"I don't think so," Declan said. "He's established around here, respectable. If he left now, his absence would be noticed and his cover blown. He built a cushy nest. He's not a young man anymore, Barns. He won't run unless he's forced to."

"How long do you think he's been living around there?" Halston said.

"He came to the U.S. in 91, Ella was killed in 92. So, a couple of years after that."

"How come we don't know what he looks like?" Barnstable said. "There must be pictures somewhere."

"There's one on the passport his spook handlers gave him," Declan said.

"That's been shredded by now. If there's something in the Army files, it goes back to 79, and even with the computer simulations, it's a long shot. How many people live in Old Mapleton, Chief?"

"Anywhere between a thousand and forty thousand. Depending on how you look at it. We have a large hinterland, and a ton of seasonal residents."

"We'll put our noses to the grind," Barnstable said. "We're good at that. Exclude the females and anybody under forty. Any physical description at all, Dek?"

"Medium height, soft spoken, dark hair, dark eyes, piercing

said one of my contacts, but she was scared to death and she thought he was the devil. I have a good picture of his father in middle age that we could use for reference."

"He will have changed his appearance," Barnstable said.

"There might be another way to approach it."

Declan told them about Jack Corvill, his relationship with Carlton Marsh, the bank statements, the bedsheets and the condoms, and the fingerprints on the champagne glasses.

"If we assume Balaguer killed Marsh and Marcia Cartwright, somebody must have informed him of Carlton's progress on the book. Jack Corvill was on site, as close as can be. He could have dropped the seahorse medallion in the desk drawer. It was very convenient that Jack was in Canada when Carlton died."

"Then we sweat Corvill," Halston said.

Declan and Barnstable grunted in harmony. "Make him wise, Barns," Declan said.

"If we go after Corvill, two things will happen. Corvill will be dead before he can be enticed to talk, and our quarry will vanish. I agree with Declan that Balaguer has built a comfortable life that he's grown fond of, but his survival instinct will kick in as soon as he smells us closing in. Declan's visit to Corvill might have already tickled him. We have to pussyfoot this one."

Halston grumbled. "I'm not in the mood to dance around Hannigan's murder."

"By all means," Declan said. "Keep bulldozing. Anything less would be suspicious." It came out condescending and he bit his lips.

"You're a fucking prick, Shaw."

Barnstable's cluck on the speaker phone sounded like a squeaky hinge.

"You know what I mean, Barns. Our man despises the law, local and federal. He despises the spooks who helped him; he swindled them. He's killed four people, that we know of, and has never been suspected. He's arrogant and over-confident. We want to keep him in that mood. That's all I'm saying, Chief."

"Talk about arrogant," Halston mumbled. "What do you want me to do, Barnstable? Your federal colleagues are moving in. You joining them?"

"We keep this conversation private. The Salvadoran connection remains under wraps. We handle it off the books. Officially, I'm not in this. You're caught in the middle, Chief. My colleagues will bully their way in. Nobody will wonder why you retire to sulk under your tent."

"So what, I make noises, cuss, and growl?" Halston said.

"Can you access population records discreetly, narrow down our search?"

"Yeah." Reluctant.

Declan was losing patience. "You could do the fingerprints. What about the bank account, Barns?"

"Send me the number. Get me the fingerprints, Chief, I'll run them through."

It wasn't moving fast enough for Declan. "Can't we set a trap or something?" Balaguer must have eyes on him, he was bait—Dominique Lagarde suggested as much. He showed up at Corvill's. They could do something with that.

"You've done enough, Dek," Barnstable said.

A half smile played on Halston's broad mouth. He couldn't hide his glee. The mighty FBI slapped the uppity private dick.

Declan swallowed his mounting irritation. He did all the work and he was shoved aside. Fine. He still had a card or two up his sleeve. His years in the gumshoe trade had taught him it never paid to disclose everything to the uniforms.

"Any objection if I go check on Kate Redmont?" he said.

Halston grinned. "Gonna hold her hand?"

"What else will you let me do?"

"You did a great job," Barnstable said.

Pat on the back from the government. Declan extinguished

the cheroot that he hadn't given any attention to, and finished his tepid drink. "Where is Kate?"

"Northside Hospital," Halston said. "Can I have your number, Barnstable?"

Declan listened to the two cops as they exchanged phone numbers.

"I better go," Declan said. "Hanging up, Barns."

"I'll call you right back, Chief. Thanks for everything, Dek."

"You're welcome." Declan grabbed his phone and took the towel with the glasses out of his backpack. He set the bundle on the table. "The prints on the lemonade glass are Corvill's. I'll get the check. See you later, Chief."

Halston's phone was ringing. It was Barnstable.

TWENTY-FOUR

NORTHSIDE HOSPITAL WAS HARDER to get into than the police-besieged city hall. Declan had to use all his powers of persuasion to get Kate's room number. Then he faced nurse Clodagh.

"Her aunt was here a short while ago," the nurse said. "Who are you, her cousin?"

Aunt? "I, uh, we … you know …" He shot her his best lopsided grin.

"This way."

Kate was awake. The ordeal had lined her eyes with blueish smudges and left a ring of pallor around her mouth. "Jean said you would come."

Jean Heyzer. "Aunt Jean is a rock." He sat on the bed and pulled Kate close. She wrapped her arms around his neck.

"Be reasonable," the nurse said. "She needs rest."

Declan heard the click of the door closing.

"Jean went to look for Bernadette," Kate said.

"She'll find the kid and feed her pancakes till she bursts. How do you feel?"

"Can I get out of here? I hate being like this." Kate jiggled the IV line. "What are they giving me?"

"They're keeping you hydrated. Can you stand?" He got off the bed.

Kate pushed away the covers and swung her legs over the side. She pulled on the hospital gown to cover her knees and grabbed his arm for balance before easing her feet down onto the floor. "I can't pull off these tubes without raising alarms, can I?"

"It should be okay. They have to allow for potty breaks and you're not in ICU. Where are your clothes?"

They were on a coat hanger in a narrow closet. Declan disconnected the lines and tubes. Kate averted her eyes, when he pulled out the IV and taped the puncture wound.

"You're good at this," she said.

"I have some experience." He handed her the jeans, underwear, and T-shirt. She wasn't shy about taking off the gown.

"I need help with the shoes. I can't look down; my head's swimming."

Declan went down on a knee and tied up the sneakers. Like she was a little girl. Her helplessness tug at his heart "All set. Do you have anything else, a purse, your phone?"

"Look in the night table." She was catching her breath. "I did nothing and I'm winded."

"Take it slow. Small steps." Declan took her purse. He supported her at the waist. She was no burden at all.

"They won't let me leave like this, will they? They'll call a doctor and make a fuss."

"This is a daring escape, darling. Hang on."

They paused at the door and he peered down the corridor. A nurse went into a room and the path to the elevator was clear. It would be more efficient if Declan carried her but she would resent it.

They were at the elevator waiting for the car when a call came from the other end of the corridor. "Hey, where are you going?"

The elevator arrived. The doors opened. From then on, they were in the clear. Declan handed Kate his aviator sunglasses and it made her look like a movie star sneaking out of rehab. He chuckled.

"What?"

"You look far too sophisticated for Old Mapleton."

"What the fuck does that mean?"

They reached the BMW. Declan helped her into the passenger seat. Her face was tight with the effort of fighting a fainting spell.

"I'll take you to Jean and Bill Heyzer's. You'll be safe at the lodge."

"I want to go home. Please."

He didn't argue.

Her house was off the old harbor, on a point jutting out into the bay, a two-story stone pile built to withstand winter storms. It wouldn't have been out of place on an Irish cape of tempests.

"What are you living in, a chunk of an old fort?" Declan said.

"It's the customs house," Kate said. "I can see my boat from here. I can escape to sea whenever I feel like it."

She wanted to take a shower.

"Do you mind waiting in the bedroom till I'm done. In case I … I'm a little unsteady."

Declan listened to the shower running. Not so long ago, he had crumbled in a shower stall himself. Kate emerged wrapped in a bath towel. She looked so young with her short black hair dripping wet. She teetered.

"I have to sit," she muttered.

He caught her before her knees buckled and carried her to the bed. He brought a smaller towel to dry her hair and she didn't protest at being taken care of.

"Lie down. I'll go make tea."

The kitchen was very much Kate. Every utensil in its place, dirty dishes cleared out, a well-organized pantry. Declan put a kettle on the stove and opened a can of soup—creamy chowder with potatoes. She would never admit to be hungry but it was almost seven and she hadn't had anything all day. He was stirring the pot when she shuffled into the kitchen, bundled in a fluffy robe.

"I'm making you a bowl of soup." Declan pulled out a chair. "Sit down before you fall over."

"This is unnecessary." She plopped down on the chair.

"Let me be the grown-up in the room." He gave her a mug of tea. His phone rang and he turned off the heat under the soup. It was Jean Heyzer.

"Where are you?" she said.

"I brought Kate home."

"Good. Tell her I have Bernadette."

Declan relayed the information.

"What do I tell the kid?" Jean said.

"Is she asking questions?"

"I wish she did. She's too quiet."

Declan sighed. "She knows something bad happened to her dad. Feed her and tuck her in. Stay with her tonight. She might try to run."

"I'll go to her," Kate said.

Declan didn't remind her that he wanted to take her to the lodge. "I'll bring Kate," he told Jean, "once she's a bit more solid on her feet. Tell Bernadette."

He had just ended the call when the phone rang again. It was Isabel. He didn't want to get into an argument in front of Kate, and let the call go to voicemail. There had a to be a collection of messages by now.

Kate ate half the soup and he finished it. He made grilled cheese sandwiches and they had a glass of wine with that. Color returned to Kate's cheeks.

"Who did that horror, Declan?"

"The sick motherfucker Carlton was after." He didn't have to tell her he was Ella's killer. He wasn't prepared to say that the murderer was a distant relative of hers.

"But why? Mike didn't know anything." She needed logic and reason, when insanity had none of that.

"I can't get into that man's head, Kate. He hides under a false identity. He set fire to the police station because Carlton's notes and his computer were in there. A kid died in the blaze. Mike knew the kid. So, he goes after Mike, because the kid might have talked to him."

"You're in danger too." Kate's eyes had gone wide. "You need to stop."

"I could have let it go after Carlton, and gone back to Houston, but it's too late now."

"The police are on it. They have people, technology, guns."

"And they move like a herd of elephants. They're fast when they get momentum going but it takes them a fucking long time to get going. This guy's nickname is El Gato. He'll slink away and not a leaf will flutter."

"Why do you think you can get to him?"

"The elephant herd gives good cover. He can't afford to take his eyes off them. I might slip under his radar." Declan thought about his conversation with Toni, in Miami, and the call he gave Kate earlier. "Do you have old family photos? From your mom and dad, and your grandparents."

"Why?"

Declan had to handle this carefully. "I called your father in Melbourne. We had a long conversation. I asked him about Carlton's fight with your mom. It had nothing to do with Ella. Your dad and Carlton were together in New York when she was taken. They were in a public place. There are witnesses."

"What was it all about, then?"

"Your parents' marriage was in trouble. You'll have to ask your father." Kate tried to interrupt. "Let me continue. We talked about your mother. Her health, the difficult pregnancy. I learned that she grew up in El Salvador and came to the U.S. to go to college. Her mother, your grandmother, was Salvadoran. That answered a big question I had since I started looking at the case. What drew the killer to Ella? There's a connection between your mother and the killer, a connection that goes back to El Salvador."

"I'll get the pictures," Kate said.

She had sifted through the documents, looking for pictures of her parents and their friends when they lived in Old Mapleton. Declan was interested in what she discarded. There were four boxes of it. He carried them to the dining room. The big table was perfect for spreading out.

"Can I help? What should I look for?" Kate said.

"Pictures of your mom before she married your dad." Declan knew Gael Balaguer did not attend Amy and Royce's wedding. "Shots that look like they're from Central America. We make three piles. Yes, no, and not sure."

Kate set to it with her natural determination. They worked efficiently, shoulder to shoulder. When Declan's phone rang, he gave it a distracted glance. It was Chief Halston.

The police chief was furious. "What the hell did you do with Kate Redmont?"

"I brought her home. She's fine. Do you want to talk to her?"

"God damn you, doctors have a say in this. I can't waste time listening to their bellyaching."

"Give me a number. Kate will call the hospital."

Halston grunted. "She stays put, okay?"

"She's not going anywhere."

The chief hung up, still in a huff.

"The doctors and the nurses are so stuck in their routines," Kate said. "On one hand, they want to keep you in there, and on the other they can't kick you out fast enough."

"When the insurance coverage runs out," Declan said. "Not a minute earlier."

When they reached the bottom of the boxes, they had a much smaller stack to deal with. Group shots. Family reunions. Nita and Oscar Balaguer with the kids, Amy and Gael. Could simulations develop a portrait of what Gael Balaguer looked like half a century later?

Declan arranged the pictures of Gael by age with a couple of good shots of Oscar and Nita. Gael took after his mother. He had her straight nose and high forehead, her eyes. Burning, Toni from Miami said. They burned the photographic paper.

"You think it's him." Kate held her robe closed at the neck with a clenched fist. She let off a moan and grabbed the table for support.

Declan led her to a chair. He kneeled in front of her and took her hands in his. "He's the one, Kate. Gael Balaguer. Your mother's half-brother. He was in the Salvadoran army at the time of the civil war. He escaped to the U.S. and terrorized your mother."

"He's here now," she whispered. "Why isn't he arrested?"

"We don't know what he looks like." Declan got back on his feet and plucked a snapshot from the *not sure* pile. "This is the best we have."

It was a picture of a young man dressed in jeans, T-shirt, and chukka boots, with his arm around the shoulders of another kid the same age. Early twenties.

"I've never seen him," Kate said.

Declan put the picture at the end of the family display, side by side with a close-up shot of Nita Balaguer, Kate's grandmother. The resemblance was uncanny. He studied the photos. Gael would be in his sixties now. How did he age?

How did Nita age?

The photos of Royce and Amy Cavendish's wedding were in another box. Declan upended it on the dining room table.

The photographer had taken shots of the guests arriving at the reception. Oscar and Nita Balaguer were all smiles. Nita had gained weight around the middle but time had barely touched her face. The cheeks were fuller, the forehead was smooth, the dark eyes bright under the strong eyebrows she shared with the bride, Amy. It was an attractive face with a well-defined square chin she had passed on to her son. Declan used a piece of paper to cover the top part of Nita's head.

"I'm a fucking moron," he muttered.

"What is it?" Kate said.

Thank God, Kate didn't know the man. But Isabel did.

Declan grabbed his phone and went to the voicemail messages. The tone of Isabel's voice varied. It was pitched higher from call to call. From plaintive *where are you* and *why don't you call me* to begging *I have to see you* and, more urgent, *please, please, call me, I need you.*

"I have to run an errand," he said. "I'll be back soon and I'll take you to Bernadette. Do you have a spare key? Lock the door after me and don't open to anybody."

Kate gave him a key. "Don't be long. Be careful."

TWENTY-FIVE

DECLAN CALLED ISABEL from the car. "Where are you?"

"Home. Where have you been?"

"I'm on my way. We have to talk."

"I've been calling you for days, Declan. Of course, we have to talk."

He was at her place in ten minutes. He rang the bell and she made him wait. He almost turned tail. Nothing indicated that she was in danger.

Isabel buzzed him in.

"You took your sweet time to return my calls."

She was fresh out of the shower and radiated heat, wrapped in a short silky robe that hung open in case Declan mistook her intentions. Even comatose he couldn't have mistaken her intentions. She pressed her body against his. Her free hand went down to feel his crotch. There wasn't much there and she stared at him.

"We have to work on this. I'm hungry. You made me wait so long."

Declan put both hands on her hips and lifted her. She

wrapped her legs around his waist and kissed him. Her carried her to the bedroom. She muttered endearments with her mouth buried in his neck. He deposited her on the bed and disentangled himself. The bed was freshly made. The sheets smelled of laundry soap and dryer sheets. Isabel's apartment wasn't untidy the last time he was there but a pristine bed was a little *too* neat. She grabbed his belt and pulled to bring him down on top of her. He landed on his elbows and rolled off her. She straddled him and worked on his shirt buttons.

Declan's plan had been to get her out of there, and load her and a suitcase in a cab, destination out of town. He reconsidered, and it had very little to do with her caresses. She was down to his fly and, contrary to Jack Corvill, the buttons didn't faze her at all.

"I thought you agreed we had to talk," he said.

"I have to return a favor first."

He let her go about as far as he could stand it. "Isabel, stop."

She raised her head, puzzled, wiped her mouth with the back of her hand and the childish gesture pricked his heart. For all her seductress wiles, she was just a kid.

"He was here when I called, wasn't he?"

Her eyes widened. "Who?"

Declan rearranged his clothes and sat on the side of the bed. Isabel kneeled next to him and belted her robe in a sudden surge of self-consciousness. Maybe a dip in self-confidence too. How often had she been told to hold off on a blowjob in progress?

"Schulman. Your boss. Your pimp."

She slapped him as hard as she could. Two red blotches appeared on her cheeks. "That's not true. Not. True." He dodged another slap. Her hand hit the side of his head. She screamed. "How do you dare!"

Declan grabbed both her wrists and held her close. Too close for knee action. He spoke in her ear. "He owns this place and everything in it. He tells you who to fuck."

He didn't imagine the panicked look in her eyes. "You're wrong. Let me go."

She sat on the bed. He stood a few steps away. He leaned on a credenza. He didn't want to hulk over her. "All right. How am I wrong? I care about you, Isabel." It was true. His first instinct had been to get her to safety.

"You care? Why are you saying these things to me? I'm not a …" She took a quick breath. "I'm not a whore. I sleep with you because I want to, because it's good." A surge of tears. "Oh fuck, because I want more of you. There I said it, and I'm stupid, okay?"

She was working herself into a frenzy and the excess of emotion would soon send her overboard, like when she was having sex.

Declan sighed. "You're not being straight with me." He left the relative shelter of the credenza and sat next to her. She enclosed him with arms and legs, her head in his lap. Puppy love. Kitten cute. "You know what they say about you in town, Isabel?"

"Bunch of stuck-up hypocrites."

Couldn't argue against that. "Men in cars, sweetums. You're a girl in an art gallery in a village, not a nightclub bartender in a metropolis. Of course, people will think you're on call."

She wiped her nose on her robe. "Schulman takes me to places. He introduces me to people."

"People who can be useful to him." Now they were getting somewhere.

"I don't know." Her tear-swollen eyes stared at him. "He doesn't ask me to sleep with them. I do what I want."

Schulman didn't have to tell her to do anything. Her sensuality only needed a little nudge. If he ever encountered a tender-hearted stud, Declan would send him her way. She deserved better than random hook-ups.

"I believe you," he said.

She ran two hands through her hair. She knew full well that

she made a perfect picture in the soft skimpy garment with the dim light of the lamp behind her.

"Where is Schulman now?"

"Oh, come on, enough with this puke. He treats me like shit. I don't want to hear another word about him." She pouted. "Come to bed."

"I assume he has a key. I don't want him to walk in on us." The sheepishness sounded false but she was too hyped to notice.

She tugged at his sleeve. "Forget him."

"He wanted me to walk in on you two doing it, that day at the gallery."

A bucket of ice water couldn't have shocked her more. Her mouth opened and nothing came out. Declan plucked a cigar from the case and lit it, with more care than the cheroot demanded. He blew smoke toward the ceiling and the fire alarm.

"That was … It was an accident."

"I see. His dick got inside you by mistake." He watched a crooked smoke ring disintegrate, and blew another perfect one. "Stranger things have happened. I hope he apologized."

She had gathered her legs under her, trying to make herself smaller.

"Stop it." Then she turned defiant. "What do you want? We're not engaged as far as I know. Where were you these past few days? I called and called, and you didn't bother to answer."

She was so predictable. It was time to get to the point. Kate waited and a killer was loose. "Where is Schulman?"

She made a face. "I don't know and why the hell should I care."

Declan didn't want to scare her but he had tried everything else. "He's way nastier than you think, Isabel. Stop waffling. It's important."

She considered him, eyes half closed. "You're serious." She straightened up. The robe slipped a tad. "He has several places that I know of. He could be at any of them." Declan urged her on. "There's the lodge at the art colony. I've been there a couple of times for press events. Then there's the villa on the golf course. He uses it for the country club crowd. It's posh."

Both locations were out of town. Going to and from them required crossing the police road blocks. "What else?"

"The apartment at the gallery."

"There's living space at the gallery? Why don't you use it? It would be more convenient."

"I asked. It was as if I'd demanded the moon. I've never been inside. The door has so many locks, it's like a fortress."

Bluebeard's secret chamber. "I have to get in there, Isabel."

"Didn't you hear what I just said? What's so important about that guy anyway. I want to forget him, okay?" She looked away. "He scared me today."

"What did he do?"

She discarded the robe and grabbed clothes from a chair—panties, bra, jeans, and a T-shirt. "I don't want to talk about it."

Declan took her in his arms and turned her around. There were three long red streaks on her lower back. The skin wasn't broken. "He hit you."

She freed herself. "It doesn't matter." She dressed quickly. The sensible undergarments made her look much younger. Her sneakers were in the closet and she slipped them on, without socks. "I like sex. It isn't the first time it turns a bit rough. I've seen worse. No big deal."

"You're getting out of here." There was a roller suitcase in the closet and Declan pulled it out. "Pack."

"You're over-reacting," she said. "I told you, it's okay. I can handle it."

"A man was sliced and diced last night, Isabel. A kid burned to death a few days ago. I don't want to go to the morgue to identify your body."

She shot a glance at the front door. "Because of Gabe Schulman? You're out of your mind."

"I won't waste time arguing with you. Pack. Now."

She got moving. "Are you coming with me?"

"I have a job to do."

She stopped, holding a pair of shoes. "If you're not going, why should I leave?"

"I have the FBI on my side. You're solo, sweetie. Take your passport and all the cash you got. You might not be able to come back to get your stuff for a while."

She pulled a larger suitcase from under the bed and put it next to the smaller roller. She was an efficient and fast packer. She dropped a pink bikini on top and it made Declan smile. She would find a hotel with a pool, and attractive men with time on their hands. While she was in the bathroom gathering toiletries, he checked her purse and retrieved a flyer from an L.A. gallery. Was she looking for another job? He took her phone and tablet, and switched off both. It was doubtful Schulman would bother to trace her, but he could call and there was no telling what she would say. He found her phone charger and dropped it in the bag before calling the local cab service. A couple of minutes, said the dispatcher.

Isabel got a windbreaker from the closet and he handed her the purse. She checked the contents and added her e-reader and its charger.

"Don't contact Schulman," Declan said.

"What do you think I am? A dodo?"

"Don't talk to anybody else in town either. You don't know who to trust."

She smiled. "There's you."

"Yeah, but I'll be busy." The cab honked outside. "I'll call you later." He carried the suitcases.

The cabdriver popped open his trunk and took the luggage. Declan held the back door for Isabel. She slipped in. He pulled out his wallet and extracted the bills. He gave them to her.

She pushed his hand away. "I don't need money." She looked pale in the cold glow of the street lights. A single tear rolled down her cheek. Declan leaned in and kissed her. The cabdriver stared, a smirk on his face.

"I shipped your painting today," she said, "and that fucking raven."

Declan whispered. "Come see them in situ, some day. What's the code for the gallery alarm? Where's the panel?"

"Behind my desk. 7954."

She lunged to grab his arm and he took a step back.

He turned to the cabdriver. "The road to New Haven. The lady will tell you where to go from there."

He closed the door and the cab pulled away. Isabel's little face appeared, floating in the back window. Soon the cab turned the corner and he couldn't see her anymore.

TWENTY-SIX

NOW THAT DECLAN was gone, Kate felt the anxiety creep up again. While they'd been going through the photos, he made her feel safe. His physical presence, his height, his wingspan, the way he moved, didn't intimidate her. He was somewhat wistful. Restrained, controlled. Not like Mike. She shuddered. Poor Mike who had been so in love with her that his awkwardness made her cringe. She often wished he had taken her in his arms and kissed her and gotten it out of his system. Once, on her boat, she had been a heartbeat away from leading him to the cabin. Her solid common sense interfered. Giving him what he wanted wouldn't have solved anything. He would have been even more smitten and she couldn't fake desire that didn't exist.

Declan was no Mike. Their interaction on the dock when she was cleaning fish—of all non-romantic things—had been laced with innuendo. They didn't pursue because the Carlton Marsh investigation intruded.

Kate poured another glass of wine and took it to the sofa in the sitting room. The murder investigation wasn't so absorbing that it kept him from banging the art gallery bimbo. She drank half the glass. What did it say about him that he would fall for such cheap fare? It was college all over again. Her crushes were hopping into bed for a quick fuck with the same kinds of girls. Men and their cocks.

She arranged the throw pillows. Declan's green eyes, the smile that went with them … Shit, triple shit! She emptied the wine glass.

He said he wouldn't be long. She curled up and fell asleep.

• • •

The doorbell must have been ringing for ever before the shrill sound poked through a slumber that was part wine, part emotional exhaustion. Kate went to the door, fuzzy with interrupted sleep. She peered through the side window. A police uniform.

"Please, no more bad news," she muttered.

She opened the door a crack. She knew the young officer. She'd seen him with Chief Halston. Couldn't remember his name. There was another guy with him, in a dark suit. He was too far from the porch light for her to have a good look.

"Ms. Redmont. I'm Officer Blaisdell, Old Mapleton police."

"Yes?"

He extracted a plastic pill bottle from his pocket. "The hospital gave me these for you. They thought you might need, uh, some help to get through the night."

Meds? "I don't need anything. I was asleep actually." You woke me up to give me sleeping pills, you idiot.

Officer Blaisdell looked contrite. "I'm sorry. I'm just the delivery guy."

Now she felt bad for him. She opened the door a bit more and held out her hand for the medication.

"I'm so sorry to impose on you, ma'am, but there's some business to attend to. I need your signature on a receipt for the pills, and my colleague wants to talk to you." He looked at her with a tilt of the head. "He's FBI." He separated the letters for awed emphasis.

Kate sighed. "Can't it wait till tomorrow? I'm wiped."

The man in the suit came forward. "We're dealing with a dangerous criminal, Ms. Redmont. Time is of the essence."

"All right, come in."

She led them to the sitting room and dropped on the sofa. Blaisdell handed her a pen and a piece of paper that had *Receipt* on it and the name of the prescription. She signed it.

"You're FBI?" she said.

The man in the suit wore little round glasses, like John Lennon's. They must let their agents have some way to express their personality. He was middle age, in his fifties maybe but he looked in terrific shape. No flab allowed, not like Blaisdell who was thirty years younger and had a beer gut.

"Special Agent Drysdale." He flipped out a wallet with an official card. He was prestidigitator-fast, a career-long habit of showing his credentials.

"What can I do for you?"

Drysdale sat in the armchair next to the sofa and leaned forward with his hands clasped between his knees. "Sometimes, we don't know what we know, Ms. Redmont."

His voice was soft, not what she expected from a government drone. This guy must be good. Kate wished Declan was there.

"This morning. You got a call."

"Bernadette called me. Mike's daughter."

"Why did she call you?" Drysdale pulled out a notepad and waited, pen poised.

"I'm a friend of the family. Bernadette knows me. She missed the school bus because her dad didn't wake her up. She looked for him, he wasn't in the house, and she got worried."

"Did the girl have a cell phone?"

It was a strange question. "I don't think so."

"Could you check your recent calls, Ms. Redmont? Tell me what number the call came from."

Kate was impressed. She talked to the police earlier, and nobody asked about phone numbers. This guy was thorough. She looked at the number. It was local.

Officer Blaisdell checked his notes. "That's the Hannigan land line."

"What did you do then Ms. Redmont?" Drysdale said.

"I drove Bernadette to school." Drysdale raised an eyebrow. She added: "Sundowner Middle School."

"What happened next?"

"Well …" She was embarrassed but Special Agent Drysdale looked at her with an encouraging smile. "There's a girl in town that Mike sees." She swallowed. "I drove by her place. His truck wasn't there."

"You know her name?"

Kate blushed. "She works at a bar on Main, *The Blue Fern*."

Drysdale made a note. "Keep going."

"I drove through town. When Mike gets too drunk and doesn't want to drive, he spends the night on his boat. I went to the harbor. His truck was in the parking lot."

"You went to check the boat."

She wished she hadn't. She would never forget what she saw on the *Sea Robin*. The memory overwhelmed her and she burst into tears. Blaisdell went to the kitchen to get a glass of water.

"Thank you." He shook two pills out of the container and handed them to her. "I don't need that."

Then it went bad fast. Blaisdell pressed his hand against her mouth and shoved the pills inside. He pinched her nose and poured water down her throat. Kate half-swallowed, half choked, coughed and fought back. The other guy held her, hands around her neck, and she was sure they were going to rape her, right there, on the sofa, in her sitting room.

"Relax," said Drysdale. "It'll be over soon."

Blaisdell forced her mouth open and inserted more pills, and more water. She sputtered, thought she was drowning, and it all went dark.

• • •

Kate emerged in a dim place. She was face down, tied up. She opened her eyes a slit. She didn't hurt. Just the rub of the scratchy rope on her wrists and ankles. If they planned to rape her, they didn't go about it the right way.

She figured she was on a pallet of some kind, not a mattress, not cushy, more like a futon. There was a round opening to her right, and it moved. She was on a boat.

Her boat. The *Yarra Moon*.

A soft voice came from behind her, where the sleeping quarters connected with the galley. It was Drysdale.

"You're awake. Don't pretend. I know how the pills work." He sat on the edge of the berth and flipped her onto her back. The light was behind him. It hid his face, like it had been hidden in the house. The round glasses were gone.

"What do you want?" She wasn't gagged. Didn't he worry she might scream?

"Nothing from you, dear. Nothing at all. You're what the finance people call *collateral*. A guarantee, shall we say."

"Hostage." Kate's mind was clearer by the minute. "For what kind of deal?"

"Smart girl. Do you know who I am?" Drysdale lit a Coleman lantern and placed it on the floor. The light hit him from below and turned his face into a demonic mask.

"I can't see you," Kate said.

He lifted the lantern and shaded the brightness with the side of his hand.

A cold stream seeped between Kate's ribs and flooded her heart. She knew who he was. The picture from the box she went through with Declan. The dark eyes. The eyes of a killer. "You're my uncle." She knew she was going to die.

"Half-uncle." He turned off the light. It was a relief.

"What do you want?" The rope chafed. Kate focused on it; it was less disturbing than thinking about what he might do to her.

"What if I just want to talk?"

Well, talk, motherfucker. I'm a captive audience if there ever was one. "I'm all ears."

Her tone seemed to upset him and it made her feel better.

"Don't you want to know why I cut your sister's head?"

"I was two years old. I didn't know her. I don't remember her."

It pissed him off. He jumped to his feet and towered over her. Because she was flat on her back. He wasn't tall. Not like Declan. His head didn't brush the ceiling.

"Your mother. I asked for help, and the bitch strung me along. A little money, just enough not to drown. She was wealthy, she had a disease of the rich. I pressed and she gave in. Then her faggot husband …" He raised an accusing finger. "Your fucking homo father! He closed the accounts. I had to do *something*!"

Kate wanted to go back to sleep. She didn't care about the problems that nutcase had collecting money. That's why he killed Ella? To shake down her mother? "How did that work out for you?"

He slapped her and her skull hit the bulkhead. It didn't hurt. These pills were awesome chemical pillows. Voices reached her through a muffler.

"I heard shouts. You okay?"

"Yeah. What time is it?"

"Eleven, about. You need me to stay?"

"Go check if he's still with her."

TWENTY-SEVEN

DECLAN WATCHED THE CAB turn the corner and retreated to the shadow of the building. He couldn't spot any watchers but that didn't mean anything. He decided to leave his car parked in front of the apartment. If one of Schulman's informers drove by, they would assume he was still inside.

The gallery was in walking distance.

The lock on the gallery's back door was an easy pick. There weren't any security cameras. Declan went to Isabel's desk and found the control panel to kill the alarm. He would know soon enough if Schulman was in the apartment. The stairs leading upstairs were tucked away in a corner of the storage room. He gave a passing glance at the wide table used for packing the artwork.

The apartment door was a thick metal panel with a series of complex locks. He banged on the door and got no reaction. Schulman wasn't there.

Twenty minutes of patient work took care of the door. The heavy brocade curtains were open and let in the lights from the street. Declan closed them and switched on two table lamps.

Schulman didn't hang pictures from the gallery on his walls. The art in the apartment was museum-worthy. The furniture was modern and expensive. The king size bed was in a corner, next to a bathroom with walk-in shower. The kitchen, separated from the main room by a counter with an inserted wine cooler, was gleaming metal and in too impeccable a condition to have ever been used to cook a meal. A Biedermeier secretaire with companion chair stood between two windows. There were no shelves or filing cabinets, no magazines or newspapers that would indicate when the apartment had last been visited by its owner.

Declan searched the walk-in closet. Two dark suits, five dress shirts, two pairs of black shoes polished to a mirror gleam, boxer shorts and socks in a drawer. This was an overnight stop. A leather saddle bag was tucked on an upper shelf. Declan retrieved a three-months-old boarding pass from a Chicago to Newark flight. He took a picture with his phone and returned the document to the bag. The bathroom contained grooming essentials. No medicine except aspirins. If Schulman had to leave suddenly, there wouldn't be anything here that he would miss.

The night table drawer contained a box of condoms and a paperback from an author Declan didn't know. The lurid cover implied it had crime and sex. He leafed through it. There wasn't anything stuck inside.

The desk was locked. Declan was careful not to scratch the delicate mechanism. He overturned the chair to look underneath before sitting on it to explore the various drawers and cubbyholes. Letter paper, envelopes, office supplies. One drawer contained recent utility bills, all paid through direct bank transfer. Another drawer held scribbled notes that he photographed and a postcard from Montreal signed *Love, Jack*. Schulman had stayed at the apartment while Corvill was in Canada.

Declan tested for secret drawers and nooks, and found two

empty hidden trays. He locked the secretaire and replaced the chair in the exact position he found it.

He searched the kitchen drawers and the wine cooler, before turning his attention to the walls and plinths. The safe was behind a Kandinsky silkscreen. It was complex enough to discourage an amateur. Declan was no amateur. He had expertise and patience. He took a picture of the dial before setting to work.

The safe was small. Declan took a picture of the inside. A stack of money, banded, sat on top of a large leather-bound ledger. He took the book to the kitchen counter.

The pages were covered with columns of a small, neat handwriting. Schulman used a code to hide the names. It looked like the kind of list a bookie or a money lender might keep, debit and credit. The amounts coming in were larger than those going out. The individual line entries looked too small for money laundering, even if the total came to a significant amount.

Declan took pictures and put the book and the money back in the safe. He emailed the shots to Moira Perkins at the office, with instructions to keep the pictures in an encrypted folder.

By the time he was done, it was much later than he expected. He switched off the lamps and opened the brocade curtains. He locked the door, set the alarm from the wall panel and left the gallery the way he came.

A brisk jog brought him back to Isabel's apartment. He approached it from the back, walked through the ground floor hallway and exited from the front to get to his car. He felt he was overdoing it but years of tracking and surveillance had taught him caution was never a waste of time.

• • •

Kate's house was dark. Declan used her spare key and was surprised to find the door open. It was wrong. She had locked the door behind him. He reached in his boot and pulled out the hunting knife. He stood to the side of the door and pushed the panel open with his foot.

He slipped inside and listened. Empty houses emit a special kind of silence. He went down the hallway, peeked around the corner into the sitting room. He flicked on a switch. There were no signs of struggle. An empty glass of wine was on the coffee table. His glass and a bottle of wine were on the counter in the kitchen. His sense of dread increased as he went up the stairs. Three bedrooms, two bathrooms. One of the rooms was Kate's office. The master bedroom was undisturbed.

She wasn't in the house.

Declan went down the stairs, back to the sitting room. The stack of pictures was still on the table. The photograph of the young man with his friend was missing.

Schulman. He was here. He took Kate.

She was a risk. She was Mike's friend, and she was close to Declan. Schulman could have killed her right there and then. What was one more body added to the tally? But he took her. As a hostage?

Schulman knew that his cover identity was running thin. The picture of Gael Balaguer was the clincher. From Gael to Gabriel. From Balaguer to Schulman. It was only a matter of time before the police came for him. He could have quietly disappeared, but that was not the way he rolled. Kate's abduction was a power demonstration similar to the medallion in Carlton Marsh's drawer, with identical lethal results. She would be able to identify him. He would not release her alive. He dared Declan to come for her.

Maybe she was already dead.

No. She was bait. Worthless as a corpse. Schulman would keep her alive long enough to get Declan where he wanted him. And he was certain Declan could figure out where she was held.

Not at the gallery, Declan was just there. The artist colony and Schulman's villa were on the other side of the roadblocks.

Too risky with cops in full alert. Declan's cabin at the Heyzer camp wasn't private enough.

He stood at the sitting room window and looked at the small town. Carlton Marsh's house was nearby. Schulman had been there before. Staging another execution on that carpet had a freaky logic.

Declan set off on the path that connected to the beachfront. He gave a glance at the *Sea Robin*, Mike Hannigan's boat, encircled by yards of yellow tape. The harbor was a patchwork of shadows and pale light circles under the far apart lamp posts. Channel lights blinked further out. The boats were dark floating lumps, laborers at rest for a few hours before they were called upon to go out and toil again.

Floating in the obscurity, one swinging lantern danced like the lure of an hypnotist.

Kate told him that she could see her boat from the kitchen window. She found it reassuring to have a way to escape if she chose to.

That lit lantern was on her boat.

The sea was Schulman's escape. He only had to go far enough to bypass the roadblocks. He could alight anywhere along the coast, scuttle the boat, and disappear.

A small boat is a controlled environment. Can't get on it without being spotted. Can't hide anywhere onboard. Declan hadn't been on Kate's boat but the layout had to be simple, like Mike's *Sea Robin*. A galley, a couple of berths, an engine room down a hatch. Was Balaguer alone or did he have an accomplice? It didn't matter. He was in control. His intentions were clear. He planned to wipe them both out. It wouldn't be a showy exhibition like Mike's murder. He could throw their bodies overboard at a safe distance from the coast, never to be found.

Declan sat in his car and called Barnstable. He got the stand-in receptionist again, a woman this time, and didn't insist to be connected to the FBI agent.

"Make a note. Gael Balaguer's alias is Gabriel Schulman." He spelled it for her. "He's taken Kate Redmont hostage and is holding her on her boat, the *Yarra Moon*. I'm going after him. You have that? Get it to Barnstable. Tell him to call Moira Perkins, she has pictures he'll want to see. That's all."

He called Chief Halston next and left the same message, adding that he tried to reach Barnstable.

It would cut into Balaguer's lead and make the net somewhat tighter. If the cops were fast enough, they might catch him in port.

Declan walked down the path to the commercial harbor.

● ● ●

Yarra Moon.

The lantern swung with the surge of the incoming tide. It hung above the door of the galley. The sway was a wink, a come hither from a cheeky dancer on a ballroom floor.

Declan examined the front and back decks. No gun-toting or knife-wielding sidekick hid behind the lobster traps, and the *Yarra Moon* was securely tied up. He stepped on board and slipped on the wet deck. His boots didn't provide any traction. He resisted pulling out the hunting knife. It was useless against a gun but it might come handy later. The galley door opened with a light push. Another lit lantern hanging from the ceiling swayed with the movement of the surf. The small room was empty. Declan felt like a mouse with foresight of the trap's mechanism. The moment he walked in, the gate would slam shut behind him. He had no choice but to go forward.

He stepped inside. The access to the sleeping quarters was right ahead. He didn't bother to mute the clack of his heels.

The picture was close to what he had imagined he would see. Kate, in her bathrobe, tied up on the bunk. The flat, dead look in her eyes spoke of drugs and resignation. She had gone through terror and come out the other way, all emotions expended. She had seen the butchered body of a friend; now she was captive and too doped up for pain or fear. Declan's fury surged. A monster had done this to her.

The monster, however, was nowhere to be seen.

Declan untied her. "Let's get out of here, Kate." He lifted her off the bunk.

What game was Schulman playing?

They crossed the threshold into the galley and there he was, leaning against the doorjamb. His gun was pointed at Declan's stomach.

Declan led Kate to the padded bench under the portholes. She scooted over to the farthest corner and pulled her legs under her. Tears ran down her face. Declan stood next to her. The galley was small and his head touched the ceiling. There wasn't anywhere to go. A fight in such close quarters would be like a brawl in an elevator. Schulman didn't have to aim. Wherever he pointed, he was guaranteed to hit something.

"Wasn't Isabel nice to you?" Schulman said. "I expected you around dawn or so."

"Don't let your imagination run wild. I helped her pack." It was a meager satisfaction to watch the man's face grow tense. "Put an ad in the paper for another gallery maiden."

"The Isabels of the world are a dime a dozen. It's over for you, Shaw."

"The FBI's in town and a bunch of acronym agency operators stand at the ready. You're a national embarrassment, Schulman—or should I say Balaguer? You're a liability. When politics intervene, bureaucrats get motivated. Psychopaths seldom get that kind of attention. Congratulations, you made it." Schulman's gun was steady and Declan ignored it. He ran his fingers through Kate's hair and she moved her head to lean into his hand. She closed her eyes. "You didn't have to get her involved. We could have sorted it out, the two of us."

"This gives me more pleasure," Schulman said. "I enjoy seeing you together. Watching you die together will be a treat."

His smile was that of a carnivore contemplating a feast. The years hadn't dulled the razor sharpness of the eyes that terrified Toni. El Gato. He wasn't your casually cruel domestic cat.

The rumble of the engine surprised Declan and the sudden lurch of the boat leaving the dock made him lose his balance. He reached to the ceiling to steady himself. Kate was shaken back to awareness.

"You can't take my boat!"

Somebody was messing with her *Yarra Moon*. It pushed away the drowsiness of the pills and the shock of terror.

"Well, are we wide awake and perky all of a sudden," Schulman said. "There's more to you than I thought, Kate. I'll have to restrain you again."

Without a change in his facial expression, he shot Declan in the arm.

The shot boomed in the small space. Kate screamed.

The force of the slug drove Declan back and he fell half on the padded bench, half on the ground, awkwardly, the pain magnified when his injured arm hit the edge of the bench. Schulman was on him before he could react. The butt of the gun caught him on the side of the head.

TWENTY-EIGHT

DECLAN WAS PRONE on a hard, wet, cold surface. The pain in his head radiated all the way down his neck and he tasted blood. The slug had caught him in the upper arm and the wound throbbed. It wasn't as painful as the bump on his head. His hands were tied behind his back, and more restraints bound his knees and ankles. He was in the galley, between the table and the bench, where he fell. He rolled on his side and thought his head would explode. Kate was on the bench, untied and unconscious. Her face was pale. She was naked. They were alone.

The ceiling lantern swung and objects rattled in the cupboards. The sound of the engine reached Declan intermittently, through the crash of the waves against the hull. They must be out of the shelter of the harbor in rough, open seas. A layer of water colored pink with blood covered the floor. No light came through the portholes. It was still night. The boat lurched side to side. Declan pushed against the table bolted to the floor to get to a sitting position, with his back against the bench. He glanced at his arm. The bullet had made a neat hole in his leather jacket and the shirt underneath was glossy with blood. The wound didn't appear to be bleeding anymore. He got on his knees and rested his head on the padded bench, wheezing from the effort.

"Kate!"

She didn't stir. One of her hands hung off the bench. He bumped it with his head. No reaction. She was out. He sank his teeth in the pad below her thumb. She moaned. Her eyelids fluttered. The boat rolled and she slipped off the bench. The fall woke her up. Declan scooted over to her.

She was about to scream and he kissed her. It was amazing the things you could do without using your hands. She resisted but he was on top of her.

"Please be quiet," he said. "You have to untie me. Hurry."

She looked bewildered. He turned to show her his hands.

"You're bleeding," she said.

"It'll be easier to handle when I'm free. Come on, Kate."

"I have no strength at all."

"There's a knife in my right boot. Quick."

She held the blade awkwardly. "I'll cut you."

"Put it against the rope, hold it." He moved his hands against the sharp edge of the knife and felt it bite into the rope. The useless arm made the maneuver awkward.

"I'll do it," Kate said.

Once his hands were free, he made quick work of the leg restraints. The boat was listing. "Who's helping Schulman, do you know?"

"A young cop, Blaisdell. He's crazy." She shivered. Panic was taking hold of her.

Blaisdell? It didn't ring a bell. Declan caressed her cheek. "We'll get through this." He got to his feet, hunched over, stumbled toward the berths and grabbed a sheet from one of the bunks. Kate wrapped herself in it. How long had he been out? Long enough for these freaks to assault her.

Declan sat on the bench next to Kate. The headache and the

blood loss made him swoon. The gunshot was a dull pain. "Do they know the waters around here?"

Kate reached for his arm. "Blaisdell might know. He's local. Let me look at you." She helped him out of the leather jacket. "There are two holes in the sleeve."

The bullet went through.

"I have a first aid kit. This needs to be cleaned. It'll get infected."

Declan chuckled. Big deal, they were about to be tossed overboard. There was a huge crash outside and water came in under the galley door.

"How seaworthy is this boat?"

Blaisdell and Schulman must have their hands full out there.

"It's been in worse weather. We won't capsize." Kate looked at the porthole. It was pitch black and there was nothing to see except water splashing on the glass. "We must be near Cross Point. It's always rough going around, even on a calm day. Once we're past it, it'll settle down."

Declan wished it wouldn't. "Do you have a gun aboard? Pistol, rifle?"

"There's a flare gun in the lock box." She pointed at a corner cupboard.

Declan shuffled toward it. He loaded the gun and dropped the spare cartridges in the small kitchen sink. He checked the kitchen drawers and retrieved a large chef's knife. He gave it to Kate.

"You want me to use this? I don't know if I can."

"Just hold it by your side. If one of these bastards comes for you, you hold it straight and let gravity do the job. It's not attack, it's defense. You can do it." Declan slipped the hunting knife back in his boot. He liked the flare gun. It had a nice, competent heft.

He took a couple of steps toward the galley door and a sudden roll slammed him against the metal sink. His hip connected and he stifled a cry. He didn't let go of the flare gun. As if the blow triggered something in his pain receptors, the bum leg awoke. It was worse than the headache and the gunshot wound combined. He was cut at the knees. A fit of dry retching bent him in two and the shakes slammed him against the galley cabinets. He dropped the flare gun and it slid to a corner. At least he didn't shit his pants; he was spared that humiliation. Kate screamed. It was far away, in a thick mist.

Declan tried to signal her to keep quiet, that it would pass, but the fit didn't give him any reprieve.

The boat steadied and the sound of the waves calmed down. Kate's wail pierced the sudden stillness.

The galley door opened and the cop, Blaisdell, appeared, gun in hand. He was sickly green and soaking wet. It must have been rough out there, keeping the bucket afloat and his stomach from turning over. Declan took stock of the opposition in the middle of his personal misery.

Officer Craig. The rookie.

Blaisdell was Chief Halston's inept sidekick. It made complete sense. He was Schulman's informant. Close to the source. It was like mainlining police reports. No wonder Schulman was two steps ahead of everybody. And Craig went with Halston to interview Mike Hannigan. What a clusterfuck.

Craig looked at the scene in the galley and laughed.

"Hey, Gabe, come have a look."

Schulman appeared at the door. "This boat doesn't captain itself. What is it?"

Craig pointed at Declan thrashing on the floor, puke running down his chin, helpless in the throes of the seizure. Kate provided the shrill soundtrack. She was in her own nightmare, off a thin ledge of sanity.

"How interesting," Schulman said. "Get out there and keep the boat steady. I want to observe this new development." He leaned on the doorjamb, at ease, gun held loosely. "Take a good look at your knight in shining armor, Kate. You see that? He's a junkie. A pathetic junkie. Some hero you got there. Pay attention, Kate."

She was still screaming, a constant wail. Schulman loomed over her. "Shut up." He slapped her, hard, backhanded, and her head hit the porthole. He wiped his hand on his pants. Her nose was bleeding. She stopped screaming.

"Look at him. Did you think this miserable wreck could help you? The cheap whore who serviced him watched him crash. She told me, one measly little pill and he was good and ready to go at her again. All night long. Pharmaceuticals are wonderful. You pegged your hopes on a piece of trash, Kate. I think I'll hook him on one of your fishing lines, cut him a little to make him more appetizing. Do you think he'll make good bait? You're the expert, you know all about fishing in these waters. What do you think, on the line or in the net, trawling? Or maybe him on the line and you in the net, like a mermaid."

Her head hung low, down on her chest.

All of a sudden, Declan's shakes subsided. He turned on his side and bent to reach for the hunting knife. His heart was beating a frantic drum solo. He prayed for a little time.

Schulman opened the galley door and called Craig Blaisdell. "Get in here with a rope." He went out, back to the helm.

By the time the rogue cop came in with a greasy rope, the hunting knife was in Declan's hand.

Craig pulled out his service gun and held it by the barrel. He swung the gun and couldn't complete the move. Declan launched himself at him. He buried the hunting knife in Craig's leg and headbutted him. The force of the assault drove the cop backward and down. The nape of his neck connected with the edge of the metal sink with a resounding bang. The handgun slid on the wet floor toward the galley door. Declan didn't waste time checking the cop's condition. He scrambled toward the corner where the flare gun beckoned like a red flag.

Schulman must have heard the crash over the sound of the

sea. He appeared at the door, gun in hand. He fired. The shot shattered the wood panel behind Declan and showered him with splinters. He fell on his side, the bad one, and aimed the flare gun at the galley door. The flare hit the doorjamb and lit the night with bright red sparks. Schulman's silhouette was outlined in the door opening.

Declan dropped the flare gun, and lunged for Craig's pistol. He shot the ceiling lantern, and threw himself at the galley door before the crimson glare faded. He slipped on the wet floor and fell face first on the rear deck. Shots rang above him. There was a sound of broken glass and Kate screamed. The boat rolled side to side and threw Declan against the railing. His injured arm took the hit. He crashed into a stack of lobster traps; bullets nicked the deck inches from his legs. The sea was neutral in the duel, as contrary to his intentions as to Schulman's. He released two shots in the man's general direction. The boat swayed. Schulman cried out and swore. In the sudden blackness after the flare explosion, they were both blind. The rear deck wasn't much larger than the galley and there was nowhere to hide. Declan's hand closed on a metal can, he threw it toward the back, and slid to the galley door. Schulman sprayed his shots and emptied the gun. The moon chose that moment to peek through a rip in the clouds. Schulman was fast and unimpaired. The bullet must have grazed him. He jumped at Declan and hit him full in the chest head first, making him drop the gun. He slammed Declan's back against the rail. One hand went to Declan's throat, fingers like steel, digging, the other punched the injured arm. The fight was uneven. Declan's kicks were ineffective at close quarters. Schulman pushed him against the rail with his entire body. The railing dug into Declan's waist, bent him in a back breaking position. The rolling of the boat didn't help. Schulman pushed down and the waves came over the side, soaked Declan's back, and weakened his already slippery foothold on the deck.

The blast of the flare gun froze them both for an instant. The brightness etched Schulman's gargoyle face with black and red streaks. The demonic vision imprinted itself on Declan's retina. Then the strangling hand released its grip and the man's body crumpled. The smoking burning flare protruded from the middle of his back like a ghoulish fourth of July celebration. The boat swayed and Declan tumbled forward. The stench of burning flesh made him gag and he vomited. The waves cleaned the puke. They also extinguished the fire.

The moon was clear of the clouds and silvered the crest of the waves. It illuminated the nightmare on the deck. Kate stood by the galley door, red flare gun held in both hands like a trainee at the gun range. She was barefoot, wrapped in a bedsheet with Declan's leather jacket thrown over it. A punk Athena.

"You're beautiful," Declan muttered, on his knees at the feet of the goddess.

"Did I ..."

Declan reached for Schulman's wrist. No pulse. He put a hand in front of the man's mouth. Breathing had stopped. "He's gone."

"I was so afraid I'd hit you."

It was a gutsy shot. Another brutal sway and they embarked more water. Declan's teeth clacked. With adrenaline in retreat, he was freezing. Kate couldn't be much warmer in her improvised toga.

"Shouldn't we get out of here?" he said.

Kate gave him the flare gun and went to take the helm. "Go inside. I have this."

Getting up was an ordeal. Declan was bent like a frail octogenarian. The galley was as dark and wet as the rear deck. He skirted the body of Craig Blaisdell and sat on the padded bench.

The boat steadied after a while. When the sway wasn't more than a slow roll, the engine stopped and a clanging sound came from the front. The drop of the anchor. Kate came in with a Coleman lantern.

"We have to get the body out of here," Declan said. "Can you help me drag it?"

They left Craig Blaisdell outside the galley door.

"Let me look at you." She sat next to him on the bench. His shirt was soaked with blood and sea water. "Does it hurt?"

"It's numb." He shivered.

She got blankets from a cupboard and retrieved a first aid box from a drawer. She cut off his shirt and cleaned the wound the best she could. Two kitchen towels covered the damage.

"The bench opens as a bed," she said. "It's more comfortable than the berths and we can keep each other warm."

"We should go back to port." His teeth were clacking.

"They've destroyed the console and the radio. I have no idea where we are. That's why I dropped the anchor. I can't think straight right now."

She helped him out of the boots and soaked jeans. She dropped her wet bedsheet and slipped under the blankets with him. They were both freezing cold and his injury didn't permit a comfortable spoon. He lay flat on his back with Kate's arms and legs wrapped around him. It took some time but they started generating heat. She fell asleep before he did.

TWENTY-NINE

"KATE?" DECLAN WHISPERED. "There's somebody on the boat."

Pale light came through the portholes. Early morning.

Whoever it was tried to be quiet. There was an occasional soft bump from a boat tied alongside, and shuffles on the rear deck. The footsteps on the roof of the galley were less discreet. Declan found his jeans, still damp, and struggled to pull them on. The flare gun and the last cartridge were in the kitchen sink. Kate loaded the gun. If the visitors were hostile, this battle would be lost fast.

Sounds outside stopped. The troops were in position. A gull shrieked above head, the water lapped at the hull.

A bull horn. "Police. You are surrounded. Come out. Show your hands."

Declan moved to the door. "Who's out there? Chief Halston?"

The cops must be trigger tense. The body of one of theirs lay on the deck.

"Declan? Who's with you?"

It was Barnstable. The FBI. Better late than never. "Kate Redmont is with me. I'm opening the door."

Orders were shouted. "Stand down. I say everybody stand down, God damn it! Do you have a gun, Dek?"

"No." Then he remembered the flare gun. "Wait. I'll throw something out." He pushed the flare gun through the narrow door opening. "That's it. I'm coming out now, okay?"

"Everybody step back," Barnstable yelled.

The shuffle of feet indicated he was being obeyed. How many people were out there? It must be crowded, with the two corpses.

"Come out now."

His apparition, one hand in the air, bent in two, black and blue from the beating, with bloody kitchen towels tied around his neck and arm, made an impression.

Tendrils of mist floated over sea and land, seagulls shrieked, terns dive bombed, and cops stared. It was chilly. The boat rocked gently.

Barnstable took off his FBI windbreaker and wrapped it on Declan's shoulders. "What did you run into, a baseball bat tied to a cannon?"

"It was a spirited fight."

"What the fuck's Craig doing here?" Halston said.

"He worked for Schulman. It's a long story. Kate needs help."

A female officer came forward.

Declan grabbed her arm. "Take it slow, okay?"

The agent patted his hand. "Understood. Ms. Redmont? I'm Abby DeSouza, FBI. I'm coming in." She closed the door behind her.

A uniformed cop called. "Do you want me to call the coroner, Chief, or should we, uh, offload the bodies?"

"Just a minute," Barnstable said. "Everybody off this boat. Not you, Chief." He waited till they were alone. "Now, who killed who? Succinctly, if possible."

"Craig Blaisdell died first." Declan pointed at the galley. "In there. I stabbed him in the leg and pushed him back. He broke his neck falling on the sink. Schulman died out here."

"You shot him?" Halston said.

"He was strangling me. Kate shot him in the back with the flare gun."

Barnstable turned to Halston. "We can't process the scene here. Your craft can tow us in?"

Halston looked around. "No instruments worth a shit. Damn mess. Who touched the helm?"

"Everybody but me," Declan said. "It happened in rough waters. Kate dropped the anchor. She couldn't figure where we were in the dark."

"I'll take us in," Halston said. "You can tell the story underway."

"All right, but let's get Ms. Redmont off and to the hospital. There will be a crowd in port. Let's keep her away from it." Barnstable knocked on the galley door. "Agent DeSouza, may I come in?"

A moment later, Kate appeared wrapped in a blanket with DeSouza's jacket over it. Her eyes were red from the tears and she leaned on the much shorter FBI agent. She turned to Declan. "Thank you."

"I'll be with you as soon as I can," he said.

DeSouza and Barnstable helped Kate onto the police boat and Chief Halston fetched two tarps to cover the bodies. The sun melted the last remnants of the mist. The day promised to be perfect for fall foliage photography.

• • •

Declan spent quality time with Nurse Clodagh. This time he was the patient. She hauled him off to radiography. He could have told her that nothing was broken. Nobody walks with a cracked back. He was compliant. It would get him out faster. There was a short tussle with the doctor who wanted him to take painkillers before he examined the bullet wound. This was a slope Declan didn't want to go sliding down again and he made his position clear. They compromised on local anesthesia. The wound was cleaned and patched, antibiotics were prescribed.

Nurse Clodagh had finished taping the dressing when Kate walked in with Jean Heyzer. The uncertainty in Kate's eyes was still there, fainter. Declan hoped that firing the flare gun at Schulman and watching him burn gave her a measure of closure. He would never recommend revenge as therapy, but there was satisfying primitive justice in slaying a monster with crimson fire.

"I called Jean," Kate said. "I needed clothes and she brought you some too."

"You're a godsend. How's Bernadette?"

Kate smiled. Yeah, there was healing at work there.

"You should have seen her face when Kate called," Jean said. "She was so relieved. She wanted to come but I didn't think it was a good idea. I didn't know in what condition you two were." Jean sat in the visitor chair with a sigh of relief. "The most horrible rumors circulate in town."

"Didn't you say you never believed any of them?"

"I don't but the police are mute and that doesn't help any." Jean extracted clothes from the bag. "Is that arm useless?"

"The doctor wants to see you again in a couple of days, Mr. Shaw," the nurse said. "Keep the dressing dry. A plastic bag will do the job. And take the antibiotics. No skipping a dose, you hear?"

"I won't. Thanks, nurse."

His meek tone made Jean smile. She watched the nurse exit. "You're on a course of chill pills?"

"I'm not giving them an excuse to keep me." Declan looked forward to a blistering hot shower at the lodge. And he was starving.

Jean must have sensed it. "I made a big pot of onion soup. I believe in the healing power of the potage. Let's go, kids, before these doctors change their mind."

Or before the cops decided they needed to talk to them again. Declan could have slapped himself for having that thought because, sure enough, it summoned Barnstable.

The FBI agent intercepted them in the hallway. "Where are you going?"

Jean raised to her full diminutive height. "I'm taking them home, sir, for a decent meal and a quiet night afterwards. Or do you intend to drag them to jail in shackles?"

Barnstable was taken aback. He wasn't used to being assaulted by small gray-haired ladies. "I just wanted to have a word with Declan." He sounded apologetic.

"This is Keith Barnstable, from the FBI, Jean. He's a friend."

"Well, he can come to dinner. At six. On the dot." She walked to the elevator, holding Kate's arm with a firm hand. Declan and Barnstable followed.

"I tried to call you last night," the FBI agent said, "as soon as I got your message. Halston tried too."

"My phone is ringing for the fishes. Did you get the pictures I sent to Moira?"

"They're at the lab. What do you think these records are?"

"Schulman had money. It didn't come from the art galleries. Maybe the real estate cover is genuine, but the transactions in the ledger look too small. If they are legit, why did he bother to encode them?"

"Our guys are good, they'll crack it. I'll see you at the Heyzer lodge."

THIRTY

Barnstable waited until after dessert when Declan went out for a smoke. His boots and cigar case had been returned to him. Barns didn't smoke, of course. The Bureau didn't condone bad habits.

"The spooks want a meeting," Barnstable said. "They arrived in town this afternoon. I held them off. Told them you were in the hospital. They expect us at city hall tomorrow at ten."

"What do they want?" The cigar tasted better than a cheap cheroot had any right to taste. "They should give us a medal."

"They want to deep-six the entire thing," Barnstable said.

"It's negotiable." Declan lowered himself into a deck chair. Slow and careful. His back was killing him.

"They don't negotiate, Dek, they push and shove and threaten, and they don't care what and who they break."

"What's the Bureau's position?"

"You think I'm qualified to state the FBI's position? I'm little better than a cog. My boss doesn't plan to start an inter-agency war, if that's what you're after."

"There has to be a way to handle this. Sit down. Let's talk strategy."

• • •

They walked into the meeting together. Declan, Barnstable, DeSouza and Chief Halston. Jennie Watts was five minutes late. She drove in from New York. The spooks didn't expect a *civilian* lawyer. When she walked into the room they found themselves outnumbered and it irked them. Halston solved the problem by sitting at the head of the table. He had the right. The strangers were on his turf and he was everybody's senior. It made him look like a referee and he relished it.

Declan sat between Jennie and Abby DeSouza. They were the only women in the room. Barnstable was the only Black man. The other side of the table was white, male, clean-shaven and suited. The symbolism wasn't lost on anybody.

There were no introductions. No agenda was distributed. It was individuals against a block of uniformity. Declan found it irksome before any exchange had taken place. He tried to rein in his irritation, and failed.

"You wanted a meeting," he said.

"Where is Ms. Redmont, Mr. Shaw?" The man with the best suit and the most expensive watch said.

"Recovering. She gave a complete statement to both the local police and the FBI." He implied there were people in the room who could answer all questions. In case these guys hadn't seen Kate's and his statements, which they certainly did.

"What do you know about Gabriel Schulman, Mr. Shaw?" Big watch guy spoke for The Man. The others were supporting players, a potential Greek chorus, if their counterpointed wails were needed for emphasis at some juncture.

"I know he's a murderer, multiple times over. He raped and decapitated a little girl, he shot my friend, Carlton Marsh, he burned a woman alive in North Carolina, he's responsible for the death of a fifteen-year-old boy, he tortured and killed an Old Mapleton fisherman. And he came close to adding Kate Redmont and myself to his tally."

"There are three reasons why this is in the FBI's purview," Barnstable said. "Interstate crime and two counts of kidnapping."

Big watch looked at the ceiling. "It's more complicated."

Declan pulled out his cigar case and lit up. The ripple of disapproval on the other side of the table pleased him enormously. "It is not complicated. In older times, Schulman would have been dragged in front of a judge, found guilty, and executed by whatever means were customary. As it turned out, one of his victims buried a rocket in his back and sent him *ad patres*. I call that a happy ending."

"There are implications well beyond a criminal case."

"Like what?" Declan blew some smoke. These guys were so mired in their circuitous ways that they were unable to come to the point without going around the building fifty times.

"You know what I'm talking about, Mr. Shaw."

"You lost Gael Balaguer in Florida," Jennie Watts said. The men in suits did a collective double take. They didn't expect a woman to talk, and not in that cutting tone. "You are responsible. The people you report to are responsible. If you had left Balaguer to rot in El Salvador, he wouldn't be a problem on these shores. I might add that if you had opened your wallets and given him a more generous package instead of nickel and diming him and washing your hands off him, he wouldn't have gone to his half-sister for money, the little girl might still be alive, and we wouldn't be counting the corpses. Maybe."

"That is ludic…"

"She said *maybe*," Declan interrupted. He stubbed his cigarillo on the sole of his boot. "Balaguer should have been eliminated or locked up a long time ago. You gave him a pass. Jennie is right. You are responsible. Why you decided he should be given citizenship instead of a bullet in the back of the head is beyond me."

The spook leader was deep in thought. "Do you have a suggestion?"

"An imperfect solution. Most solutions to thorny problems are imperfect. In summary, nobody gets what they want. The victims in El Salvador don't get public justice and the master manipulators in D.C. avoid scrutiny. There's no big victory lap, no fat headlines, just the satisfaction of writing *Closed* on a handful of criminal cases. The FBI and local law enforcement get the credit."

"The people in this room know the truth."

Ah, the obsession with silencing the dissenters. "We have no proof," Declan said. "We have nothing that connects that body in the morgue with mass graves in Central America. Maybe you do. My guess is that you purged your files a long time ago. If you hadn't, you would have found him before I did and we wouldn't be haggling here."

The man returned his pristine notepad to his briefcase and the silent Greek chorus imitated him. No notes had been taken. How much did it cost the taxpayer to transport this gaggle of robots from D.C. to Old Mapleton?

"I hope I never hear of you again, Mr. Shaw," the man with the expensive watch said.

The spooks filed out.

"Was that a threat?" Jennie said. "It sounded like a threat."

"Some guys need to have the last word. He can have it. I don't give a shit. What's next on the program?" Declan said.

"Autopsy, crime scene investigation, reports in triplicate," Chief Halston said. "Real police work, thank God, not this rigmarole."

"Press briefing in an hour," Abby DeSouza said.

The Chief looked hurt. "You handle that, kid. I don't have a face for prime-time TV." He turned to Jennie. "I'm reopening the investigation on Carlton Marsh, not that it's ever been closed, mind you. Let's have a little chat about it. How we're going to bring this all together without upsetting the powers that be."

They left. Declan and Barnstable were alone in the large meeting room.

"Are you attending the press conference?" Declan said.

"We keep it local. DeSouza is in charge. I'll dig in Schulman's ledgers. What do you think he did between the Ella Cavendish murder and going after Marsh? Nutcases like that don't take a thirty-year sabbatical." He sighed. "It'll keep me busy for a while."

"Schulman paid his informants—Daryl Markus, Craig Blaisdell. Their names might be in the ledger, on the debit side. Jack Corvill too, maybe, even if he got a monthly retainer from that bank account. Any luck on that?"

"We traced the account to a company with ties to the Caribbean," Barnstable said. "If Schulman was one of the principals, he used an alias. We haven't brought Corvill in. He's under surveillance. We'll shake him, see what he's got."

"He was Schulman's mole."

"He was more. The fingerprints on that champagne glass were Schulman's."

It made Declan sick. After torturing Mike Hannigan, the freak boogied between the sheets with Corvill.

"Have you searched Schulman's lodge at the art colony yet?" he said.

The FBI had a team combing through it. The golf course villa and the gallery were also being searched, top to bottom.

"We'd like to talk to the gallery girl," Barnstable said. "Where is she?"

"I don't know. She's out of town." Declan shrugged. "I put her in a cab."

Barnstable's eyes opened wide. "She's loose?"

"I have her phone number. What should I have done? I thought Schulman would come for her."

Barnstable chuckled. "You're such a sucker. Do you always pick the wrong girl?"

"I had my reasons."

"I can think of a few."

Declan sighed. "I'll call her, okay? She hasn't done anything wrong." He felt a need to defend Isabel. "She hates Schulman. He used her to get close to people he was interested in."

Barnstable was quick to see the connection. "He pimped her out. There are names on the credit side of that ledger, Dek. She knows these names."

"I don't think it's that crude."

Barnstable squeezed Declan's good arm. "Of course not, buddy. I'll buy you lunch. What's good around here?"

"The marina café, they know me."

"Wait, don't tell me, the hostess is cute?"

· · ·

Declan watched the police operations from a distance. Chief Halston and the FBI handled the surge of media interest with commendable competence. The fidgety operators in D.C. could breathe easy. The entire story revolved around the mysterious Gabriel Schulman, art aficionado and child murderer, who went on an atrocious killing spree when investigative reporter Carlton Marsh, an old friend of the Cavendish family, threatened to expose him. The cops implied that a lot more was expected to come to light about Mr. Schulman's nefarious activities. The town of Old Mapleton breathed a protracted sigh of relief. The stigma of the Ella Cavendish unsolved murder was lifted at last, and the girl's sister, Kate Redmont, risked her life to uncover the truth.

"They're all bending backwards to clear the town's reputation," Kate said. "After what they did to my parents, it's disgusting."

"Collective memory is even more selective than individual memory."

Declan felt mellow. Halston, Barnstable, and DeSouza had come for dinner at the lodge. They were gone now and the Heyzers had gone to bed. Bernadette Hannigan was asleep upstairs, tucked in by Jean. Kate was wrapped in a blanket in front of the fire. The weather forecast announced the first cold snap of the season. Bill Heyzer had brought in the logs and ceremoniously lit the pile. He called it the official start of fall.

"I talked to Dad," Kate said. "He's excited."

"Bernadette is too. I didn't know you could say kangaroo so many times in one evening. Are you ready to make the move, Kate?"

"It's an exploratory trip. And I want to adopt Bernadette." She looked at Declan with a question in the raised eyebrows. "I'm surprised you're not on a plane back to Houston yet."

"I like to see the end of a case. Carlton's memorial is next week. Jennie Watts wants me to speak. I'm not sure what to say."

She got off the floor and sat on the sofa next to him. "Don't you have memories to share?"

"From my student days? When he made a pass at me?"

"I sympathize. With him." She was on Declan's good side for a snuggle. She inched closer.

"This might not be such a good idea, Kate."

"You don't have these freak fits anymore, do you?"

The imaginary pain had retreated when it had to compete with the real thing. "You know what I mean."

"I'm not asking you to marry me, Declan. I want to see where that conversation on the dock could lead. When I was cleaning fish. You hit on me."

"You held a very sharp knife. I was intimidated."

"I didn't bring the hardware tonight. Did you?"

"Search me."

Declan wiggled his bare toes in front of the fire. The hunting knife was in the evidence locker in Halston's temporary police station. He doubted he would get it back. Jean Heyzer said she could restore the cowboy boots to their former glory, and she knew somebody who could patch the leather jacket. Declan had full confidence in her.

ACKNOWLEDGMENTS

A FRIEND WHO READ the manuscript of *Catch Me on a Blue Day* asked me where Old Mapleton was located. The question made me happy. It meant I managed to make the place feel real. This isn't a spoiler. The small Connecticut town where the book takes place is entirely fictional. There is no Grandin, the bakery-chocolatier, although I know yummy shops like that, there is no Isthmus art gallery, and no Tudor-style police station. In Love You Till Tuesday, the first Declan Shaw book, I had no qualms about using real locations in Houston. In a metro area where seven million people live, things good and bad happen all the time. Quaint little towns are a different matter, and when the plot revolves around a gruesome murder, collective hysteria, and a media frenzy … the setting has to be fictional.

The violence that threw El Salvador into chaos in the 1980s is only too real, and documented. A few actual places, people, and events are mentioned in the course of the narrative. I hope I was true to the facts. What unravels in the plot, however, is entirely imagined.

I want to thank my early readers who have been wonderfully

helpful in catching slips and slides. Special mention to Craig Terlson who let me know that art galleries often take 50% of an artist's haul, yes that's a lot! Big thanks also to the writers and editors who gave me quotes and reviews. Your support and friendship are invaluable. You make this writing journey a pleasure.

Thank you, Ron Earl Phillips, for inviting Declan Shaw and me for a repeat visit. When I started writing crime fiction, I dreamed of being published by Shotgun Honey. Seeing my books among so many I had so much joy reading will never stop to amaze me.

In closing, thank you Jim for being so patient with me when all I can talk and think about is the book, its characters and mishaps. You're the first to read all of it, often more than once, and your comments are most precious. When you like the yarn, I breathe a little easier!

M.E. PROCTOR was born in Brussels and lives in Texas. She's the author of the Declan Shaw detective mysteries. The first book, *Love You Till Tuesday* (2024), came out from Shotgun Honey. *Catch Me on a Blue Day* is the next installment in the series. She's the author of a short story collection, *Family and Other Ailments*, and the co-author of a retro-noir novella, *Bop City Swing*. Her fiction has appeared in *Vautrin*, *Tough*, *Rock and a Hard Place*, *Bristol Noir*, *Mystery Tribune*, *Shotgun Honey*, *Reckon Review*, and *Black Cat Weekly* among others. She's a Shamus and Derringer short story nominee. Website: www.shawmystery.com.

ABOUT
SHOTGUN HONEY BOOKS

THANK YOU for reading this Declan Shaw Mystery, *Catch Me on a Blue Day* by M.E. Proctor.

Shotgun Honey began as a crime genre flash fiction webzine in 2011 created as a venue for new and established writers to experiment in the confines of a mere 700 words. More than a decade later, Shotgun Honey still challenges writers with that storytelling task, but also provides opportunities to expand beyond through our book imprint and has since published anthologies, collections, novellas and novels by new and emerging authors.

We hope you have enjoyed this book. That you will share your experience, review and rate this title positively on your favorite book review sites and with your social media family and friends.

Visit ShotgunHoneyBooks.com

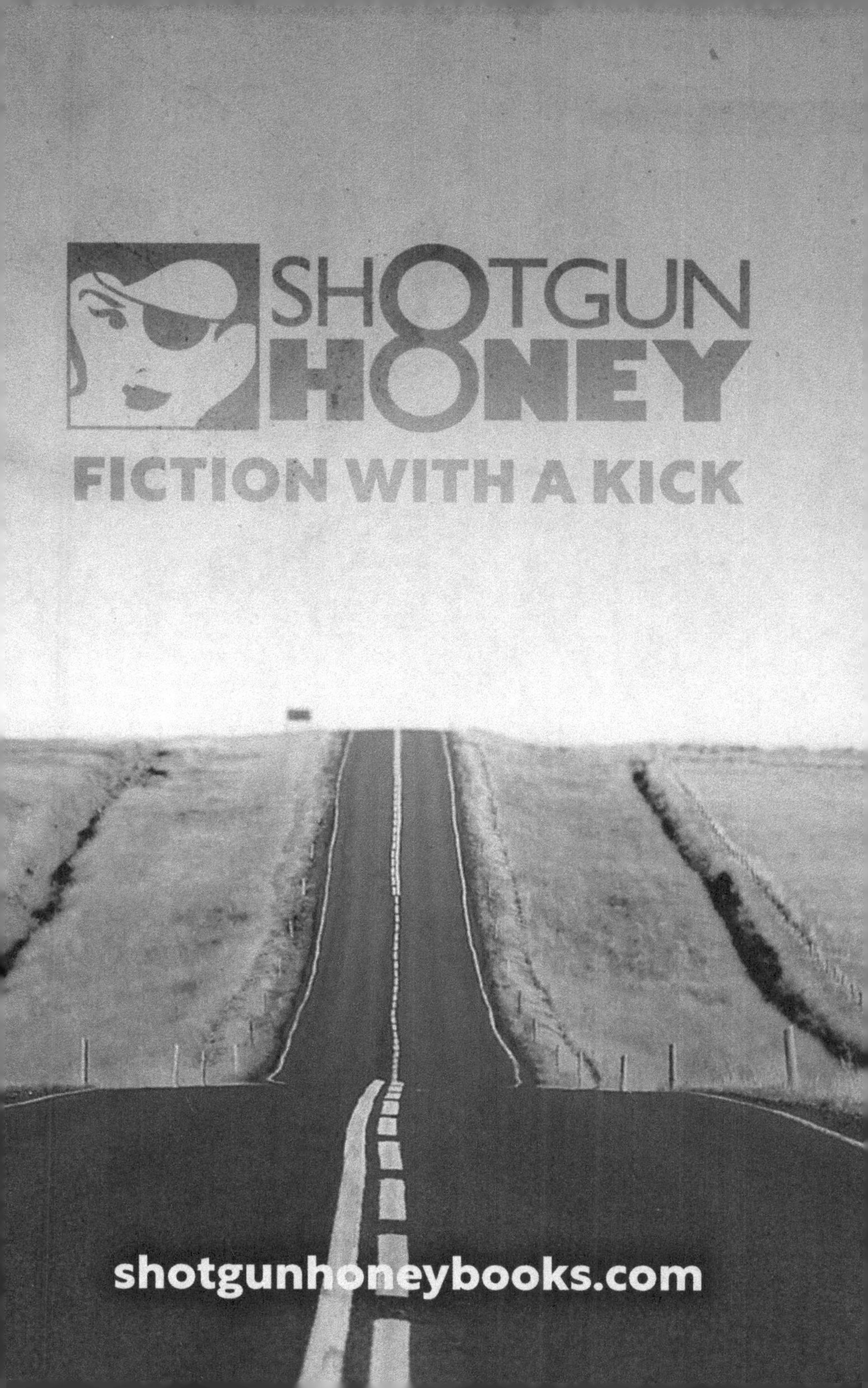
SHOTGUN HONEY
FICTION WITH A KICK
shotgunhoneybooks.com

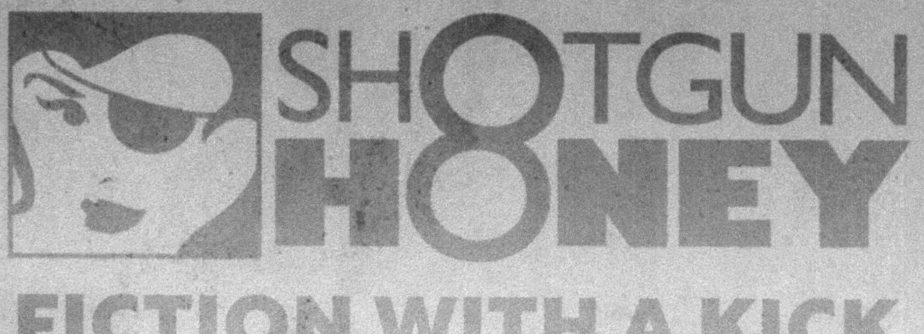